To Mary,

Babs

H.

search for a cu... or a killer?

by Babs Carryer

First edition

ISBN-13: 978-1518766206
ISBN-10:151876620X

Cover art: Justine Carryer

Preface

Startups rise and fall like empires – some wildly successful, some quiet dreams. With 20 years' experience in building and launching startup companies, I have participated in the dynamics of these macroscopic worlds. I realize that most people never have the opportunity to see biomedical entrepreneurship in action. The brilliance and tenacity behind successful startups flutter in a mirage of stunning, invisible creativity. I wrote *HD66* to tell the story of a biomedical startup through the lens of my experience. I chose the genre of mystery because the intrigue of solving the crime maps perfectly onto the ups and downs of an early stage venture.

The character of Brie is your guide to this world. Women are underrepresented in startup culture, and it was more effective for a non-scientist to walk the reader through the story. A few years ago I co-founded a group called "Women In Bio-Pittsburgh" to accelerate the inclusion of women in the life sciences, and the group has blossomed. I hope that my readers – especially women and STEM-oriented girls – see in *HD66* the excitement (and pressures) of a dynamic and compelling world that needs them.

Startup culture matters. It matters to researchers and investors, but most of all it matters to all of us. Research leads to breakthroughs. The more we understand the complexity of biomedical entrepreneurship, the better we can foster growth and discovery of new cures.

Unweaving fact and fiction is a critical part of research, so to properly introduce the world of startups, I wanted to provide certain scientific realities and background for book group discussion and individual reader consideration. Huntington's Disease is a devastating genetic ailment, of the family of neurological impairments including ALS (amyotrophic lateral sclerosis) and Parkinson's. Huntington's has no cure. In a society where illness is the root of so much suffering, healing is the root of justice. If you accept that premise, then you will understand that startups are more important than ever.

In this spirit – please enjoy the story.

Disclaimer

Chapter 1
March 4

Buzz! I shoot out of bed, afraid that the bees will get me. Shadows surround me. Buzz! Where are the bees? I look around. It's my phone buzzing. I glance at the clock, 4:06 a.m. The caller ID tells me that it's Matt House, Quixotic Pharmaceutical's chief executive officer.

I work for a startup. We work all kind of hours. Matt's on the edge; as CEO he has to be. But I've never received a call from him in the middle of the night, early morning actually. Of course, Errol called me at all hours. "Matt, what's up?"

"Errol's dead," Matt barks.

He can't be serious. "What? But..."

"This will fuck Quixotic," Matt says gruffly. "I'm calling an emergency meeting. Now."

"But, what?" The line is dead. "Of course. On my way," I say to nobody. *What has just happened?*

Rain spatters on my window. My room is still dark, but my eyes have adjusted. I sense that it's cold and gray outside. It's almost spring, but winter has curled its fingers around the City of Pittsburgh and won't let go. I know that the floor is cold. But I don't feel my feet. I don't feel.

Pushing the thoughts away, I hurry to get dressed. "Shysta!" I stubbed my toe on the door jam. Limping, I race down the stairs of my Shadyside apartment.

. . . .

4:39 a.m.

"Errol drowned. His boat went over the falls at the bridge. The lock falls." Matt addresses us from the head of the conference room table. Our chief financial officer, Gigi Loft, stifles a scream. She's standing, holding herself tightly around her tiny waist. She's dressed in black jeans and a black sweater – *cashmere I guess?* No makeup, no jewelry. Her pale face is as naked as a face can be.

Our board chairman, Jim Reichert, dressed in a suit, steps away from the wall with a grunt. He's holding a tray with donuts and coffee, which he sets down gently. *Where did he find donuts at this hour?*

The heating system of the former warehouse that is now our office creaks to life. No one moves; no one speaks.

Errol is an experienced boater. He keeps his boat, the "Random Scoot," on the river near the Highland Park Bridge. I've been on the "Scoot." We've all been on her. Errol must have piloted her a hundred times through the lock. *How could he have possibly gone over the falls?*

"What do we do?" I didn't think I spoke aloud.

Matt slumps into a chair and runs his fingers through his salt and pepper hair. "I don't know. This is fucked, totally fucked."

Jim pushes the donuts to the center of the table and busies himself setting out cups. He opens a small bottle of Johnny Walker Black. I see shot glasses on the coffee tray. The golden liquid hitting the glass is the only sound in the room. Jim nods at Matt and hands him a cup of black coffee. Stirring sugar into a second cup, he hands it to Gigi who takes it without noticing. He pours cream into a third cup and walks over to me. *How does he remember how we each take our coffee?* He hands each one of us a full shot glass.

I take my cup with a shaky hand. "Thanks," I hear a high, frightened voice and realize it's mine. Jim smiles sadly at me.

Quixotic is our baby. For me, it's more than a job. It's personal. The clinical drug we are commercializing is my only hope. *I need Errol.*

I glance around the room at the company's leaders. We were one of the first to rent space in the formerly run-down neighborhood of East Liberty. The startup accelerator, UpWind, helped us secure the space. Errol was friends with the founder. UpWind is next door. Now, there are other startups. Coffee shops, bars, and restaurants have been popping up everywhere. We've thrived in the burgeoning startup environment in Pittsburgh. But this is too much. *Can we survive?*

Sadness hangs in the silence like Spanish moss on an old tree. Gigi takes a deep, uneven breath and looks at Jim. She sits down at her laptop. "The ambulance chasers know already." She starts to read:

> Renowned scientist is found dead on a boat floating in the Allegheny River. The boat and its passenger apparently went over the lock falls just west of the Highland Park Bridge. Errol Leopold Pyrovolakis, MD, PhD, was a physician and scientist at Centre-Pittsburgh University's Institute for New Diagnostics. Centre-Pittsburgh was founded in 1989 as a collaboration between the two research universities, Carnegie Mellon University and University of Pittsburgh, to focus on research and development in healthcare and information technology. Dr. Pyrovolakis also was chief science officer of local startup company, Quixotic. The scientist was pronounced dead upon

arrival at St. Anne's Hospital at 2 a.m. The boat, "Random Scoot," is registered to Dr. Pyrovolakis. Fellow boaters from nearby marinas say that the "Scoot" was often seen out on the river. Dr. Pyrovolakis was "an avid fisherman and loved to spend time on his boat," his wife, Amy, stated. Mrs. Pyrovolakis further said, "It was not unusual for my husband to go out alone at any time of day or night on the "Scoot." In fact, Errol often came up with his best ideas on his boat.

Gigi looks up from her laptop. "Errol was born on a boat. Now he dies on one."

No one speaks. This is terrible for her. Not only did she work with Errol at Quixotic but I recall that their relationship goes way back.

The rain pounds against the windows. *Not exactly boating weather.* Jim munches on a donut. His broad face is furrowed with concentration. He swallows, clears his throat and says, "We have no idea what happened. We need to not panic or jump to conclusions. I know that we all are shocked by the suddenness of this tragedy. We share a deep sadness for which words do not do justice." He asks us to pass a moment in silence "in honor and reverence to the great man." In the harsh neon lights of the conference room, the loss is unbearable.

Errol was the brains behind our company. His invention of a new drug to cure an incurable disease was at the core.

Matt interrupts our thoughts, "We all loved Errol as a friend. We must not forget that. But right now we have to think about Quixotic. Brie, we need you to write a press release that minimizes the damage." He looks like he might split open. He's sweating and breathing very fast. Startups are stressful all the time. But this is past stress.

Jim takes over, "Brie, remember that resource I sent to you on crisis management?"

I remember the lunch where he lectured me on the topic of public relations in negative situations. It was one of our first monthly lunch and learns. They were fun. Jim taught me about entrepreneurship using examples from his own experience. Plus, the lunches were free. Jim always picked up the check with a laugh: "We lunch; I teach, but really it's me that learns."

A few days later I saw a post in his "NewVenturist" blog related to our "learning." I can only imagine the next one. *My life in a startup.*

I know what I need to do. As manager of marketing and media for Quixotic, I've never been in an emergency like this, but Jim knows his stuff. He was an investigative journalist for over 20 years with *The New York Times.* He understands how bad press could hurt Quixotic. We have investors and corporate partners. Negative media coverage about Errol could hurt us. *It could kill us.* I wince at my thought.

"On it." I get up to go.

"Wait," Jim commands gently. "Before you start, let's think through what might have happened." He glances around at each one of us. "We have to consider all the possibilities. We don't know the circumstances. We need to look at different scenarios. Just in case..." he trails off.

"Good idea," I say. "I'll take notes." Gigi frowns at me. I put down my pen. *Or not.*

"This looks like an accident," Jim says sadly. "I suspect a heart attack. He's male, the right age..."

"Bullshit," Matt butts in forcefully. "Look, it's possible. But, Errol's in super shape. He's so easygoing; he doesn't feel stress like I do. A heart attack doesn't make sense."

"No it doesn't," Gigi says quietly. She looks like she's seen a ghost.

"What does Amy think?" I ask, referring to Errol's wife.

"Amy told me that Errol had been acting 'secretively.' That's the word she used," Matt pauses awkwardly. "She's not sure what was bothering him, but she thinks it has something to do with the lab. You know how he is. He obsesses over his inventions." *Of course he does. That's what it takes.*

Jim grunts, "You know, Errol was up for tenure at the university. That's a lot of pressure." There is a long pause. *Yes, but Errol thrived under pressure.*

Matt continues, "Plus, the NGX deal going sour and the clinical trial being pulled for our – sorry, for his – drug. That could shake anyone to their roots." He was referring to NeuroGenex, which had licensed the drug to take it to the final stages of clinical trials and to the market. Recently, and unexpectedly, NGX had cancelled the deal. We had other options, but it was going to be difficult; we all knew that. *Are they kidding? Do they think Errol would give up?*

"There might have been something else," Jim states softly. "Maybe something happened between Amy and him?" He looks at Gigi.

"Errol loved Amy," I chime in, defensively. "And he was perfectly happy when I saw him yesterday. "Why, it's absurd that he would pilot his boat over the falls. No matter what, Errol would have stopped that from happening. Look, if it's not an accident, and it's not suicide, then what happened?" All eyes turned to me. Gigi downs her glass of scotch in one noisy gulp.

"Ah-hem," Jim continues, ignoring me. "It's got to have been an accident. He must have gotten distracted and then…"

Matt says darkly, "I don't think so. He hated the NGX guy. He hated that we had to take institutional money. You all know how he felt about our 'so-called' venture capital friends. Assholes," he says bitterly.

"He was particularly negative about the Russians," I add, trying to be helpful.

"The feeling was mutual," Matt admits. "I don't know who hated each other the most."

"Something might have been up in his lab, you said?" Jim asks, deep in thought. "What about his students, his colleagues? Maybe he was disturbed about something?"

"Yea, who of us really knew Errol?" Matt asks miserably.

"The hard things in life could get to anyone," Jim announces.

Gigi gulps for air. I hold my breath. *They've got to be wrong. Errol would never do this.*

Stunned silence surrounds us, envelopes us, oozes into the room. I feel sick and grab the edge of the conference table. Jim takes a deep breath and reaches for another donut. "We don't know what happened. Just imagine how amused Errol would be if he were here and heard us guessing…" I can't believe my ears, but Jim just let out a low chuckle.

. . . .
5:30 a.m.

We agree to split up. We're to meet at the Highland Park Bridge. I stay in the office to draft the press release. Gigi, too. She urges me to hurry. We may be devastated, but, to the world, we have to pretend that his death will not adversely affect the company. I feel disloyal. "Don't think about it too much," Gigi warns me. "Get it done." Her dark eyes bore into me.

It is eerily quiet as I make my way down the hall to my office. The lab doors are dark. The street lights outside glare through the windows as I enter my office, leaving the door open. As I sit down at my desk and start to write, I hear a strange sound coming from the common room at the far end of the building.

Buzz! I jump, thinking *bees*! I'm deathly afraid of them. I'm allergic. *Brie, get a grip*! It's just Gigi calling me on my cellphone with a few additional pointers for the release. I focus and continue typing on my computer. I still hear the odd sound in the background. Steady, rhythmic. I save my draft, email it to Gigi and walk softly down the hall. I think of home, of my dad. The back of the office is like a den, with couches, television, old game consoles, and a ping pong table. I remember Errol thwacking the ball, acing us all in the last tournament. The sound is louder. Through the blackness, I see a figure on one of the couches. The sound is snoring. "Hello? Who's there?" I ask.

The form on the couch stirs and says in a heavy accent, "What, who? Oh, Brie. Yes, hello."

It's Boris Zokshin. He's one of our scientists who works for Errol. He's Russian, I recall, although I can't remember much else about him. Except that he introduced us to the Russian venture capitalists that Errol hated.

"Hi Boris," I say awkwardly. *What's he doing here?*

"Sorry, I here," he responds in his thick accent, the vowels and consonants leaning together. "I no place to staying tonight."

"No worries, Boris," I say brightly, pretending that it's normal. "Quixotic had an early start today. Lots to do.

See you later." I leave him and return to my office wondering: *Did he hear us? Does he know about Errol?*

I jump at the sound of my door opening. "Hey," Gigi says. "I made a few corrections to your draft. Here it is," and she hands me a sheet of paper with red marks. "Make the changes and then let's go. I'll get my coat and be back in a minute."

I revise the release and email it to my media contacts. It's official now. It's public. I listen. No snoring. Creeping to the back, Boris is gone. I approach the sofa. It's empty. I see something on the floor. Prodding it with my foot, I feel a small puddle of wetness. Water. *Why?*

"Brie!" Gigi is calling me from her office. "Is it done? We have to go!"

I duck back into my office for my coat. I can't resist checking my voice mail. One message. It's too soon for it to be a media contact. I punch the required password. My vision blurs for a moment as I recognize the voice. My heart pounds. It's Errol. He sounds far away, there is background noise like a truck. I sit down and breathe for a minute before listening again. I repeat and hear the date and time. Last night 11:01 p.m. Oh my gosh, he called me just before...

> Brie, I have something for you. Something important, relating to what we talked about. Too important for email. I can't wait to tell you. No one else knows. I will leave it for safe keeping in...

The voicemail stops abruptly. The background noise cuts out. It was his engine, I realize. He called me from the "Scoot." *What did he have for me? He said it was important. He's the only one who knows about my father. About me. He left it somewhere for safe keeping. Where? I have to find it!*

"Hurry up!" Gigi commands as she sweeps past my door. "Let's go!"

Chapter 2
6:14 a.m.

We're in Gigi's black Mercedes speeding up Highland Avenue. It's still dark, but glimmers of dawn peek at us as we top the crest by the park entrance. The statues beckon like dark shadows. Below us snakes the Allegheny River like a sinister black ribbon. I remember that the "Allegheny" comes from "oolikhanna," which means "best flowing river of the hills." There is an Indian legend of a tribe called "Allegewi," who used to live along the river. I had googled all of this when I first arrived in Pittsburgh to get an MBA at Carnegie Mellon University.

Gigi's tires squeal as she runs the stop sign and races down the curves of One Wild Place past the zoo. I hear a roar. "Hey, Gigi, Errol always told me that he could hear the lions roar from his house. Did you just hear that? It sounds like..."

She looks at me, and I stop talking. I hear a woman scream, but, before I can react, Gigi quells me sharply, "It's a peacock, Brie." *Errol told me about those too.*

At Butler Street, Gigi turns left, heading away from the bridge. "It's quicker," she states as she swerves into the Bailey Creamery, screeching to a stop. "We can walk down to the river from the ice cream place, right here," and she quickly exits the car.

I was in this very spot last summer, licking a dripping ice cream cone while gazing out over the river. I ruined a nice blouse from chocolate stains. I can see the bridge to our right. I see flashing lights and barricades. They've closed the inbound lanes of the bridge, and there are three police cars, a fire engine, and a few other cars parked with flashing lights. One of them is Jim's BMW; I see its silver sheen reflecting from a street light on the bridge. Something is swirling in the river below.

Gigi starts down a set of steep stairs that plummet down to the river bank. This will put us just downriver from the lock. As we navigate down, I see that she has completed her black outfit with black leather tennis shoes, not her usual six-inch heels.

I remember being on Errol's boat, going through the lock and glancing back at the falls. The drop is not that far, maybe 10 feet, but it goes all the way across the river. When you are on a boat, above the lock, the river looks like a continuous level. It's deceiving. You can't see the drop. Once you get out of the lock and look back, you see the giant wall of water falling from one height to the other. I shudder and trip, falling to my knee. Getting up quickly before Gigi turns around, I continue down the stairs, rubbing my knee.

As we arrive at the bottom of the path and make our way towards the river, I see a cluster of people on the shore. Matt and Jim are there. They probably came by way of the path from the bridge. As we walk towards the group, I hear the sound of the water crashing over the weir. The high-powered flashlights are trained on something in the middle of the whorl. It's the "Random Scoot." I recognize Errol's boat even though it is half submerged.

Jim greets us, "They can't get the boat until it's light. Soon I guess," he says glancing towards the dawn trying to break through the clouds behind us. There's a dog barking somewhere on the opposite shore of the river. Gigi frowns in its direction.

Two uniformed policemen approach us. I've had no dealings with the police in Pittsburgh in the four years I've lived here. I haven't even gotten a traffic ticket. I hear snatches of conversation as they approach. Something about a bob. Capturing the bob. Maybe they're referring to the boat bobbing in the water? I wouldn't describe it like that. I look at Errol's boat. The engine is down and the boat is twirling in a sad, slow motion dance.

The beefy policemen are pure Pittsburgh, I hear by their accents as they introduce themselves: "Officers Bill Ramping, Ramone Shyler."

A third form approaches, a woman police officer. She is short and slim. She introduces herself. "Hello; I am Officer Tania Aguiar." Officer Aguiar rolls her r's, but she's easy to understand. We introduce ourselves.

"Youse're friends of the guy on the boat?" asks Officer Ramping. He waits expectantly.

Jim responds, "Errol was our chief scientific officer. We're all involved in a startup company together. Errol invented the technology that we're bringing to market."

I see a wide smile on Officer Shyler's face. "Oh yinz'r entreeeepreneurs!" he says drawing out the "e's in the word. "My nephew'z at Car-Neggy Mellon," he continues in a broad Pittsburghese dialect. "Yup, CMU 'z where he'z studying entreeepreneurship!"

Jim responds for all of us, "That's great. We have quite a few alums." The officers look at him. "Who went to CMU, Carnegie Mellon," he explains. "Gigi here, and Brie," he nods towards us. "I do some teaching," he adds. "Of entrepreneurship." Jim smiles at Officer Shyler. "Errol..." he starts, "the deceased, was at Centre, you know, Centre-Pittsburgh University, not CMU," he trails off lamely.

"Yes, that's what we understand," says Officer Aguiar, her r's flowing like the current of a river. She frowns at Officer Shyler. "We talked with the wife, one Amy Prrrya..." she begins stumbling over the last name.

Jim immediately interjects, "No one can pronounce that name."

The three officers chuckle among themselves. "Sir," Officer Aguiar starts, "We see this all of the time. Someone is careless; they don't see the warning signs, and they tumble over the falls. It is almost impossible to survive that. The whirlpool, as you see, is very powerful," she says, the letter r swirling above our heads.

"And usually dere's al-co-hol involved," Officer Ramping adds. "Why last summer we lost three fishermen out real early…"

Officer Shyler interrupts, "Actually, I think they were out reeeel late."

Gigi inhales sharply. Matt lets out a choking sound. Jim clears his throat and says, "Officers, Errol was a very experienced boater and…"

"Yes, Mrs., um Mrs. Errol, she told us that," Officer Aguiar responds.

Gigi says, "Errol was raised on a boat. He sailed all over the world. He has his Captain's license, which is very demanding, and there is little likelihood…"

"So, you knew him pretty well?" Officer Ramping asks, staring at Gigi. She looks at him like she might bite.

"Yes, she knew him well," Matt snaps. "We all knew him very well."

"I see," Officer Shyler says. "This looks like either an accident or a natural cause. We gotta classify somepin like this as an **N, A, S, H,** or **U.** That'z **N**atural, **A**ccident, **S**uicide, **H**omicide, or **U**ndetermined," he says, emphasizing the first letter of each word. "Thoze'er the letters, **NASHU.** Right now, we think that this here'z an **N** or **A.** If youse thinkin' this is an **S**, we could consider that too."

"How would we know?" Matt snarls.

"But he was under pressure; we know that." Jim adds quietly.

"OK, da **S** is in. We'll add it." Officer Ramping turns towards Shyler.

Officer Aguiar dismisses her colleagues with an impatient wave. She turns to us, "I am very sorry, but these letters, the **NASHU**, they are classification categories. We have to classify the incident and to file a report. Of course, it does not mean that we know for sure. That comes later."

Jim says, "We don't want to jump to conclusions."

"Riiight," drawls Officer Ramping. "Look, we gonna put in the **S**, and we gonna keep da **N** and da **A**. Sometimes it's both **N** and **A**. Know what I mean? But it can't be **N** and **A** and **S**. See? **N** can include **A**, and **A** can include **N**, but **S** means it can't be **N** or **A**. Sometimes it's just **U**." He shrugs his shoulders.

Are they kidding? This is like "Who's on First?" "What if it's **H**?" I ask. I could feel six pairs of eyes on me. "Of course, I don't really know…"

It's daylight now. A few rays of a cold March sun pierce through the wintery clouds. The dog is still barking like crazy across the river. The officers shift their feet.

"The wife, Mrs. Errol, she can order an autopsy," Officer Aguiar says. "She'll have to talk to her husband's physician first. To rule out, you know, any obvious conclusions."

"Like 'he was a ticking time bomb, ready to go at any time,' that kind of thing," Officer Ramping offers helpfully. Gigi chokes back a snarl.

Officer Aguiar rolls her eyes at us and continues. "If the physician gives the OK, that there is nothing that would cause a natural death – **N** – we can get the medical death investigator, the MDI, involved. She, because she's a she in Pittsburgh, has to accept jurisdiction. That gets the medical examiner, the ME – and he's a he – involved. If the ME accepts the case, then he does the autopsy." She pauses and gives me a smile. "We are still thinking it's **A** or **N**, OK? Maybe **S**. But, if something turns up in the autopsy, then who knows? Let's start with the physician. That's what we told…" She looks at me, "the wife. We didn't tell her about the letters." Her consonants are lovely, the lithe r's a distraction in the surreal dawn.

"Spare her the acronym soup," Gigi hisses through her teeth.

Officer Shyler leans towards us. "Look it'z 7:30 and we gotta open up the bridge." Officers Ramping and Shyler nod at us and start walking away. Officer Agiar hands us each a card and quietly says, "Call me if you need us." She grins, and hurries to follow them.

"Thanks so much, officers," Jim calls out to the trio.

"Jus' doin' our jobs iz all. Yinz'r welcome too," Ramping tosses over his back.

We're left alone. I stare at the river. We see a tug. It's an orange Coast Guard craft. The tug has lines to the "Scoot." It takes a long time to get control of the boat, like she doesn't want to go. But they have finally lassoed her. The tug drags her out of the vortex and downriver where the water is calmer. The convoy veers to the right and approaches Silky's Marina on the other side of the river. The "Scoot" is riding low in the water, but her railing is just visible above the water line. She looks burdened and sad. I see one glimpse of her bright red hull in a ray of sunlight.

Errol was proud of the "Random Scoot." I remember the first time he took me out to explain the science behind Quixotic's lead drug that he had invented.

"Scoot's my powerful lady, with 225 horses on the transom," he told me as he patted her like a dog.

"She's lovely," I had replied, admiring the shiny red hull. We went through the lock and motored downriver. By the time we returned, I understood exactly how the mechanism of our drug worked. I created a PowerPoint slide image shortly afterwards that captured the essence of what an investor would need to know about why the drug would work on patients who suffered from Huntington's Disease.

The "Scoot" has her stern to me as she is dragged away ignominiously. The barking dog is running up and down the bank on the other side of the river. The dog is jumping and barking at the boat. I am struck by a bolt of realization. "My gosh," I shout. "It's Luna. Errol's beagle. Look!"

"What the fuuuu…" Matt starts.

"She's right!" Gigi says excitedly. "That's Luna!"

"Luna must have been on board," Jim reasons. "Well if the dog swam across the river then why the heck didn't…" Jim doesn't finish his thought, but we all have the identical insight.

"Oh my God," Gigi cries. I see tears running down her face.

My mouth is open but nothing comes out. *If Luna could swim out of the whorl, why couldn't he?* The water winks at me as the sun peeks through the clouds and then disappears. On the far bank, Luna starts to howl.

Chapter 3

June 11, six years before the incident

Errol awoke with a start, the Voice still inside his head. He was in a cold sweat, but he could see the glimmer of sunrise out his bedroom window. Amy was peacefully asleep beside him. He heard Luna's gentle snore at the end of the bed. He crept out of bed and stretched his long limbs.

Standing by the window a few minutes later he heard the familiar roar – feeding time at the zoo. He chuckled at the sound. From his Highland Park house, Errol could hear the lions roar every morning. The Pittsburgh Zoo meanders its 77 acres up the hill towards the park, one end of which stretches to the end of his street, Sheridan Avenue. He heard a woman scream and smiled, recognizing the sound belonged to a zoo peacock.

Errol glanced at the clock on his bedside table, but he knew exactly what time it was: 6 a.m. He woke every day at the same time for as long as he could remember, with the recurring nightmare on his mind. The Voice. He tried to be quiet as he was leaving the bedroom. "Shit," he blurted as he stubbed his toe on the door jam.

Amy stirred as she changed sides and pulled the covers closer over her. "Errol?" she pleaded sleepily.

"I'm sorry, honey." He tiptoed out the door. Luna jumped down from the bed, jangling her tags, and noisily bumped into Errol as she raced down the stairs.

"Please!" Amy groaned, pulling the covers over her head.

Bumped off balance, Errol nearly fell but caught himself on the railing, yanking a bracket from the wall with a loud squeak. He looked in dismay at the hole in the plaster and dust on the stairs. "Shit!"

"Errol!" she cried.

"It's nothing, honey. Sorry." He heard her snort with frustration and lapse back into silence.

The sun's first rays streamed into the kitchen as Errol brewed espresso, popped a piece of bread in the toaster, and walked out onto the deck. He fed the fish in the pond. "Hello Tom, Dick, and Harry," he said fondly to the three goldfish who gulped the pellets floating on the surface. The cloudless sky was reflected in the water, broken only by the orange flecks of the fish as they darted around the pond that he had built. He thought of how perfect it was, their enclosed world. No stresses, no worries, just nibble the algae. "Shit." He had fed them too much.

He settled on a deck chair with his lab book and read over his notes. He was deep in the book when Amy walked out with a tray.

"Good morning," she said as she placed the tray down. "I couldn't get back to sleep. You burned the toast, and your coffee is cold," she said with a sigh. "I made a fresh cup." She handed him the small white cup and planted a kiss on his forehead. She sipped from her cup.

"Mmm, thanks," he said, not listening and tipping his cup. "Oh piss," he said as the coffee spilled.

"I'll get it," she chuckled and went back inside for a sponge to mop up the spill. When she got back, he was sipping her coffee. "Honey, I have news."

She took her cup back. "What?"

"I'm starting a company today," he announced and reached back for her cup.

She slammed the cup down on the table. "A company? Really? On top of everything else? Oh Errol."

As he mopped up her spilled coffee with the sponge, he pleaded with her. "I have to Amy. If I don't form a startup and license my technology into it, all my work will be wasted. Look, you know that two years ago I discovered a drug that cures Huntington's Disease. You know that it's a condition for which there is no cure, no hope. I have to bring it to market, or it will never save a soul. My discovery will be meaningless."

"Couldn't you just license it, Errol? You know, to a big..." she fumbled with her hands.

"You mean pharmaceutical company?" he responded.

"Yes, exactly."

Errol snorted through his long nose. "Pharma's not interested until it's less risky. I have to get it to the next level before they'll take me – it – seriously. I have to de-risk it for them."

"That seems so petty. Can't they take the risk? Don't they have gobs of money?"

"You're right, of course," he said stroking her cheek. "But they don't take risks, not really. Later, when we're further along, when we've done more testing and have results, they'll pay a premium because we'll have lowered the risk."

She raised her now empty cup with a frown. "There's no stopping you, is there? You'll do this no matter what?"

Errol looked in her eyes, hoping that she would understand. "I have to."

"Why now?" She glanced upwards.

He winced, thinking about the tousled teens upstairs: Sam, their son, and Ariel, their daughter. School was out. Amy had wanted to take a longer vacation this summer. Sailing. She knew that he longed for the sea. For years he had refused to take her to Greece, where he spent so much time as a boy. But he had promised her that they would go this summer.

Errol shook his head. "It has to be now. It can't wait." They sat in silence, the sound of the pond's waterfall in the background. Amy looked at her husband and sighed. "OK, Errol, I get it." She smiled. "So, give me your pitch."

"I thought you'd never ask!" Errol launched into a rapid fire sequence, peering at her over his glasses like she was one of his students. "Huntington's is a devastating, progressive, neuro-degenerative disease. HD, as it is known, is one of the most tragic of all nervous system disorders. The symptoms may start out as mild and unnoticeable, but inevitably they progress to complete nervous system failure. The end result of Huntington's is always death. There is no cure. Until today. My drug, HD66, offers HD patients – and their families – hope."

She picked up the tray. "It's good. Who's the team?"

"Oh, Jim of course, and this great guy as CEO, Matt House. Gigi thinks we can raise money."

Amy frowned. "Gigi's a part of this?"

"Yup, the four of us as co-founders. We're ready. It's the perfect storm of opportunity. I have to jump. It's now – or never."

Amy studied her husband. She stepped close to him. "I don't mean to be selfish. The world needs this, right?"

Errol clasped her to his chest tightly, and breathed in her smell, looking over her head at the sunlight piercing through the greenery that they had planted when they moved here 12 years ago. "I need you to understand."

"We can go sailing next year. For now, you go ahead and save the world," Amy whispered as she reached up on her tiptoes to kiss his cheek.

"It's timing, you know," he continued, oblivious to the caress. "That's why it has to be now. The federal government sponsors research up to a point. But it doesn't really support translational research."

"Yea, I know – getting from the benchtop to the bedside," Amy said. "You've told me."

"Exactly. The White House – and Congress – figure that the private sector is responsible for that. So, I have to do this. If I don't, the drug stays in the university lab. Great patent, great potential, but no product. You know how long it's taken to get to this point?"

"Years," she admitted with a roll of her eyes. "I've been here the whole time you know."

Ignoring her quip, Errol was on a roll. "First I had to develop a mouse model. Because Huntington's is a genetic defect, I had to create a knockout mouse where I removed some of the mouse's genome and replaced it with the human defective gene that causes Huntington's. To create the same effect as HD in humans."

"The repetition on chromosome four?" She smiled at his surprised look. "I do listen, you know."

"Ha. Imagine being able to offer my patients a cure." He held up his hands, helpless.

"Yes, Errol, I can imagine," Amy responded softly.

"Think about their faces, their bent and twisted bodies."

"I think about their families." She carried the tray back into the kitchen and began to load the dishwasher.

Errol closed the dishwasher and pushed her up against it. "I have another idea."

"Oh… that." She laughed as he led her by the hand upstairs.

Later, in the shower, Errol pondered the steps of his journey. His positive results from the lab had propelled him to Centre-University's technology transfer office. The university applied for patent protection for the HD66 drug and then helped Errol submit the paperwork to conduct his own investigator-initiated Phase I clinical trial in humans. The small study proved that the drug was tolerated and had no discernible side effects. He was accepted into the faculty incubator, Startups@Centre, which provided him with seed money, mentorship, and basic entrepreneurship training. He got help in recruiting a startup team. One of the best lessons drilled into him was the Jim Collins admonition to get the right people on the bus, even if you don't know exactly where the bus is headed. *I'm on the bus*, Errol told the Voice, and stepped out of the shower with renewed determination.

"What's the name of the company?" Amy asked from the bedroom.

"Her name is Quixotic."

"Funny you should name her like a boat," she remarked as Errol loped downstairs to his home office. He peered at his lab book scratches once again. He had to hurry, knowing that he needed to stop by the university lab to talk to his students, then make his way to his clinic to see his patients. He would end the day back at the university – for Quixotic.

"Remember, I have the day off." Amy called down the stairs. "I have plans for the kids. Starting with Sam's doctor appointment at 10." She waited, her foot on the top stair. "Oh, and Ariel has a gymnastics tournament at five." She paused, "You coming?"

"Oh, wow," he started.

"Oh never mind," Amy stopped him. "I didn't know how big a day this was for you, but I figured you'd be busy. I promised Ariel a night out with her friends. Sam will be at Brett's, and I have a report to write tonight. We'll be fine. Get going, Errol. Oh, and rock 'em babe," she said as the bathroom door closed with a click.

He patted Luna goodbye and went out to his bike on the porch. *I have it all: my research at the university, my neurology practice and now my startup – my life.* He jumped on his bike and pedaled down Grafton Street, thinking about his afternoon meeting with co-founders, Matt, Jim, and, of course, Gigi. He couldn't wait. They legally formed the company some time ago, but today they would sign the license for HD66 with the university. They would receive "exclusive, global, and in-perpetuity rights," the document said. Why it takes 80 pages to say that, he didn't get. As co-founders, they planned the signing as a group event, even though they had agreed that the sole signature would be his. *I hope someone remembers champagne,* he smiled as he turned south onto Highland Avenue.

Errol thought about his patients. He has no good news for his HD patients – their unmendable brains, the inevitable athetosis of the fingers and toes, the uncontrollable chorea. He knew that he word came from the Greek "χορεία," which means dance. But chorea is far from a dance. There was nothing that he could offer his patients, beyond managing the inevitable descent. No good news – yet. *But soon.*

Errol swerved to avoid a car door opening. "Jerk," he shouted and pushed his bike faster along Ellsworth Avenue, cutting back to the right as he neared the university. As he turned onto Centre Avenue, Errol recalled the thrill of discovery. He had focused on HD and other neurological diseases for his whole adult life. It's why he became a university researcher. For years, he experimented with different drugs to counteract the CAG repeats on chromosome four – the *huntingtin* gene, or HTT, spelled differently from the disease, codes for the huntingtin protein. Eventually, he discovered that small interfering RNA, abbreviated as siRNA, would interfere with the expression of specific genes – in this case with HTT. siRNAs and their role in gene silencing was only found in 1999, and Errol had been experimenting since the article came out in *Science*. It took him almost three years to make it work.

Every scientist lives for that moment, that "Eureka-I-found-it" moment of discovery. Many never get there. It's just too elusive. He was lucky. But the Voice would not call it luck. "The fish do not come to you; you have to find them," the Voice had reprimanded him.

"I got the big fish," he whispered.

A few hours later, he was smiling as he walked into Centre-Pitt's tech transfer office, on the 40th floor of University Tower. As he stepped off the high-speed elevator, Jim and Matt greeted him with broad smiles. Gigi reached up to hug him. He spotted a bottle of champagne bulging out of her designer purse. She giggled as they strode into the conference room.

"Let's rock!" Errol shouted. Quixotic was born.

Chapter 4

June 1, five years before the incident

Shala was the first one to arrive this morning. She unlocked the laboratory door and stepped inside. It was her first day back. It was also the first day that she entered the lab, not as a PhD student, but as a post-doctoral researcher. She was proud and happy. Sure that she was alone, she sang a song from her childhood. As she sang, she twirled around the room, enjoying being completely free.

Thinking that she heard something she stopped mid-twirl. She stepped over to the lab bench to appear busy. But it was only someone outside. She could hear them talking even though the windows were closed. She began to hurry as she knew the others would be here soon.

Pushing aside papers from the lab bench, she turned on the computer. It was brand new. Dr. Errol had bought it for her. She'd never had a computer of her own. As a PhD student she had access to a computer, but she had to share it with other students. She would have been able to have a laptop like the other graduate students if she hadn't sent money back home.

The computer screen lit up. She entered her username and password. She had only a few minutes before Dr. Errol and the others arrived. She hoped that the new students would not come in until Dr. Errol was here. She wasn't sure what to do with them if he was not there. She was afraid they would laugh at her if she said she was the boss now. She wished that they were not all men. She looked at the clock on the wall and started to type.

Dear Pliya,

My dear sister, you cannot imagine the joy with which I write and am now sharing with you. I am so glad to have seen you. It was a long flight back to the United States, and then I slept for a whole day from the jet lag, you know? But I awoke to very good news.

I have been chosen for my post-doctoral work at Centre with Dr. Errol in his lab! This is very important university near other important universities. Also it is nearby the hospitals. Important because we are working in the health studies. During the defense of my thesis Dr. Errol and others they asked me very difficult questions. It made me so nervous. But Dr. Errol told me yesterday that it will be an honor to have me stay on in his lab. An honor for him! Think of what an honor this is for our family. I am a real scientist now with letters after my name and a job in the United States!

I told you that I am very happy here. Pittsburgh is a nice place with many things to see and favorite places that I go. Because I have been offered a post-doctoral position, I am hoping that this will be my home forever. Here, women have much freedom. I am trying very hard to be like an American girl here. I am just doing as others do. Ha ha!

I hope that you like that I am writing you in English. It is good practice. Not only for me, but for you! One day, you will thank me because your English will be so good.

I am nervous on this first day of my new job. As I told you, we are making important discoveries in the lab. We are finding cures to bad diseases. Dr. Errol says that we will help people everywhere. Not everywhere, I think, but I do not tell him. He does not know, Pliya. I will not tell him.

Dr. Errol is such a jokester. I used to be afraid of this. But now I am determined to join in the fun, and I will try to play little jokester games to make Dr. Errol smile and laugh. It is so freeing to not have to watch what I say, what I do, where I go. I remember. I am still sad for you. My heart reaches out to you with my love. This morning I read in the newspaper that there have been more rapes. I read that police not arresting any people. I am sad to read these terrible stories.

I have a surprise for you. You will be receiving a wheelchair very soon. My gift to you! Guess what? It have buttons to help you do things! Someday I hope to push you on an American street. I would like for you to see what I see here in this different and freedom land.

I will write you again and I hope that you will find a way write to me. I miss you so very much. I am thinking of you, my dear sister.

All my love, from your doctor PHD sister with letters after her name,

Shala

Chapter 5
March 8

We're a mess since Errol's death. It's been only a few days since we found out. Almost two weeks since NGX stopped the trial. Everything is a blur. I have lost all sense of time. We come into the office; I'm not sure that we are working. I know that I'm physically present, but I'm really not – present or working. Glancing at my phone, I see that it's 11 p.m. The office lights are still on. I don't know who's here, who's not. I don't care. I don't want to go home. I can't face it.

Buzz. It's Errol! No, it can't be. It's Neal. I tell him that I have a few more things to do, to wrap up. He's understanding. We haven't talked about it much – about Errol, about what happened.

To top it off, I sprained my ankle walking up the path from the falls that day. It's not a bad sprain, but I've been obeying RICE: rest, ice, compression, exercise. I'm elevating my injury by keeping my ankle on top of my desk, but that makes it difficult to work. Which doesn't matter because there's no work to be done. No one tells me what to do. Not even Gigi. We're lost.

As I re-wrap the ace bandage around my ankle, dutifully applying compression, I can't stop thinking about the timing of NeuroGenex cancelling our deal and Errol's death. I know what the others think: something big like that could have caused a heart attack. They're right. To know that his cure would never make it to market – that could kill anyone. But so could something else or someone else.

I stare through my glass door at the DNA sculpture that hangs in our hallway. Errol made the 20-foot aluminum wire sculpture in his basement. In his spare time,

I muse, thinking about Errol the scientist, Errol the doctor, Errol the university professor, and Errol the artist. The sculpture is visible from the outside too, and at night, like now, it's beautifully lit. I was so impressed by it when I first saw the office. I remember that first time like it was yesterday.

. . . .

Three and a half years earlier

Although I interned at the company the summer before, while getting my MBA, Gigi insisted on a full orientation on my first day. Which was kind of a joke, since Quixotic was still a startup, and they didn't have any processes or procedures in place. I began by reading the business plan that the team wrote in 2007 when they founded the company.

I realized before I joined Quixotic that we had something unique – our drug. It's a great story. It's why I took the job. I get to help tell the story about treating a previously untreatable disease. *Ha! F you, fellow MBA students working on Wall Street. What the heck difference can you make in your job? Me, I get to CURE PEOPLE!*

I was so glad to get this job. In my masters' program, everyone knew EXACTLY what they wanted to do post-graduation. Me, I had no clue. I wanted to do something real, something that would "make meaning," as Guy Kawasaki would put it. I loved my internship at Quixotic. But I never thought that they would offer me a job. They were so experienced. I was so – not.

But I wanted to stay in Pittsburgh. I'd met Neal. Cute, square-jawed Neal Raja, whose white teeth against his dark skin made me swoon when he smiled. At Quixotic, I am geographically proximate to him. His office is also in East Liberty, although in a different building than ours. We're in an old warehouse; he's in a remodeled factory where they used to make aluminum parts. *He has a driveway INSIDE the building! How cool is that?*

"Join us, Brie," Jim had said after the lunch that was an interview. I felt drunk. I was wanted. Working for a startup is exciting and dynamic. But it's also scary. They're not kidding when they say it's like a roller coaster. I hoped that I was up to the challenge.

I barely made it through that first day. I remember Gigi interrupted my business plan reading because she wanted me to create an investor presentation. I didn't know that she would do this over and over since then – no sooner am I in the middle of some project than she demands something else, something impossibly difficult.

That first day she burst into my office, "Brie! I know it's your first day, but I need a PowerPoint presentation and I need it now!" She explained that they had been wooing a regional angel investment group for some time. The managing partner of the group, GreenBush Angels, had just called saying that they had a screening committee meeting the next morning. "If we want to present to them, now's the time!"

"OK." I felt incredibly dumb. "I got it."

"Take all the time you need. As long as it's less than two hours," she said, pointing her red nail at her diamond watch. As she whooshed out of my office she tossed an aside over her shoulder," You've got to be better at PowerPoint than we are!"

What exactly is she asking me to do? I don't know what goes into an investor presentation. I panicked. I was about to screw up and get fired before I had even finished the first day.

My parents were so proud of me when I got this job. I told them that the startup was commercializing a drug for a neurodegenerative disease. I didn't tell them which disease; that was irrelevant. What was relevant was that it was an important disease; that I had a position in the real world, outside of my cloistered upbringing in the Coho that we called home.

"Most scientists never get the chance to see their work in patients," Matt told me the morning of my orientation. "You can spend your whole fucking life at the bench working to solve a dreaded disease, but, at the end of the day, you are just one more drug program, and the chance that you will get to see the light at the end of the tunnel is almost nil. I saw my chance and jumped at it."

"We knew that it would take everything that we could muster and then some to build Quixotic," Jim had told me during his part of the orientation. "As we went through due diligence on the drug, HD66, we recognized that it had some exceptional properties. It was safe, and its properties were really promising. That is the pearl of great value. When you find something like that, you pursue it with everything you have."

Errol told me that he didn't need much convincing to start a company based on his technology. Peering down at me over his glasses, he told me, "One of science's dirty little secrets is that it tells you the puzzle, but it doesn't tell you the answer. You have to discover those pieces and how they fit together. When you do, it's beautiful. When you might save someone's life, it doesn't get any better."

Yep, startups are sexy. Few know how hard it really is, however. A lot has happened since my first day. It's after midnight. I have to go home. Errol's memorial service is tomorrow. Errol trusted me. I don't know why he picked me. But he did. He told me that I was the only one who would understand. Not his wife, not his students, not his Quixotic colleagues, not his university peers. Me. *What did you leave for me? Where is it?*

. . . .

There would be no funeral for Errol, Amy had informed us two days after he was gone. She would hold a memorial service in University Chapel on Centre's campus. She wanted his colleagues to say goodbye to him as well as to celebrate his life. "The service will be about his living and his accomplishments," she told us by email.

I choose a simple dark blue dress and put on my grandmother's pearls. I don't wear these often enough, I think as I gaze into the mirror, admiring their sheen.

By the time I walk through the arched, wooden doors facing the campus green, the back two thirds of the chapel is full of people standing in the aisles. I don't recognize most of those attending. I see Errol's colleague, Maya, standing with a group of other professor-looking folks in the right aisle. She looks like she is crying. On the other side, I see a lot of younger folk, Errol's students probably. Near them is a small group that I recognize: Shala, Yahya, and Patrick, Errol's lab students. I go over to them. Shala is crying, and the others look exhausted. Like us, they are in shock. I hug Shala lightly and am surprised when she hugs me hard back.

"Oh, Brie, I am so deeply sad. I cannot bear Dr. Errol to not be here. It is unimaginable." Her lovely brown face is streaked with tears.

Yes it is. I shake hands with Yahya and Patrick. Both are stiff and awkward in what look like new, ill-fitting suits.

The organ starts playing a mournful tune and those of us still standing move to find seats on the dark oak benches. I move away from the students to take a seat in the middle, next to people I don't know. Jim beckons me up front, and I slide into place beside him. The whole second row is taken up with my Quixotic colleagues. In front of us is Amy, the Pyrovolakis kids, and others who I assume are university leadership. The service begins. It's a typical non-denominational service. There is much music. I can hear sniffles from all around. The minister officiates, and people speak, extolling the virtues of he-who-is-gone. I can't bear to listen.

I gaze around at the lovely chapel. The building is a marvel of Pittsburgh gothic revival architecture. The light streams in through the floor to ceiling stained glass windows. The dominant color is blue – *how appropriate*. I was raised in cohousing, which I learned after I left was unusual. Our development was a cross between condominiums and a commune. Growing up, I never went to church. Maybe that's why I'm fascinated now. The smell, the dark paneling, the lights – inside, it feels timeless and endless. Unlike why we are here. *Errol, what happened to you?*

Jim gets up to deliver the eulogy. He's a wonderful speaker. But he looks thin and strained. He looks older too. *I guess we all do.* I think about how I first got to know Jim.

. . . .

Quixotic started with Jim Reichert. He had formed a life sciences incubator called Cyteoff to create startups that would advance human health. I knew from my science undergraduate days that "cyte" meant cytology, the study of cells. He had explained, "Many of the most promising discoveries in the university lab never make it out to the patient. Oh, papers get published, but unless there is strong intellectual property and a desire to commercialize – by both the inventor AND the university – then the invention often sits there not helping anybody. I wanted to correct that and make money at the same time." That was his pitch to me to join Quixotic at the interview that was not an interview.

Jim's background was journalism; for years he had written a weekly column about entrepreneurship in *The New York Times* called "Voice from the trenches." He wrote a few books about entrepreneurship as well. They're good. Jim teaches an entrepreneurship class open to graduate students at Carnegie Mellon, Pitt and Centre. I regret that I didn't take it while getting my MBA. But I'm making up for that now.

Jim still writes. He publishes on his "NewVenturist" blog once a week. He aims his posts at first-time entrepreneurs, who need to hear the been-there-done-that voice. His posts have paralleled Quixotic's journey. Particularly the ones about funding. It's amazing that startups can attract funding when they are high-risk, pre-revenue. Statistically, most of us will fail. But, heck, if you don't try, you'll never get there. Jim had taught me that. "Aim high and don't give up." His latest series is called "Startup Briefs." He explained to me that it was supposed to be "everything I know about entrepreneurship in less than 50 pages."

Jim takes his seat, the eulogy over. I glance around the chapel at the myriad of faces. Errol could have had a heart attack. Or, he could have killed himself. *Or, any one of them could be the killer.*

Chapter 6
March 10

Buzz, buzz. My phone startles me as I drive. I glance at the caller ID. It's Errol. I lose control of the car and hit the curb. *What?* Fortunately, no other cars are around. "Hello?"

"Brie? I'm sorry to call so early. I hope that I didn't wake you," Errol's wife, Amy, says. *That's right. I have her listed along with Errol in my contacts.*

"Of course not, Amy. I'm on my way to the office actually." *Who sleeps now, anyway?* "Are you OK? I mean I know that you're not..." I shift into reverse, cringing at the thought of the dent in my Prius.

"I want to ask you something, actually. I need your help, Brie." *She needs MY help?*

"Amy, anything. What can I do?" I look around for a place to pull over before I crash the car again. I swerve into the Whole Foods parking lot, which is almost empty, given that it is 7 a.m. I slowly drive up one level to the parking area outside of the liquor store so that I can concentrate on the call. As I pull into a parking spot, I look out over the busway and Ellsworth Avenue. They had finished the walking bridge from the lot over to Ellsworth, and I notice a few bikers riding across. They remind me of Errol. He probably rode his bike over that bridge. I choke back tears as I brake to a stop. Oops, too far, I hit my bumper on the curb. These low bumpers and high curbs. Yikes! Another dent.

Amy is talking. "I know what everyone is saying. That it was a heart attack. I have my own suspicions. Errol was acting strange, erratic, I don't know, guilty. Something was up. I have no idea what it was." She pauses, and I hear ragged gasps.

"I'm sorry Amy, I don't know what to say." *I can't tell her about my own suspicions.*

"Look, everyone thinks this was a natural death." *Like a heart attack is natural.* "But Brie, Errol was very experienced with boats. He's not just a Pittsburgh river boater. He sailed in the Aegean for years growing up. He sailed across the Atlantic when he was 18, before college. Boating was in his blood. We got the "Scoot" so that he could, scoot around," she said and I heard a light laugh and then a gasp. *This is so hard for her.* She blows her nose.

I wait. When she comes back she sounds more definite. "Look, I'm sorry if I'm babbling but it's important that you understand that Errol would never, I mean never, allow his boat – any boat – to go over those falls. He could be dead drunk…ah." I think she realizes what she said. "No matter what, no matter who he was with, or what he was doing, Errol would guide that boat safely. He just couldn't go over those falls unless he was dead."

I am flabbergasted. *What am I supposed to say?*

Amy breaks into my thoughts, "In those first few moments when I was told, I had a funny feeling, I don't know, call it intuition or whatever, but Errol is not the type to have a heart attack. I mean his European upbringing, and we use a lot of olive oil – you know what they say about that. I just know, I really know, that he did not have a heart attack." She pauses. "Even if he did, you know, have a heart attack – which he did not, I am sure – no way would he die and then let his boat go over the falls. He's too experienced for that. He would know to sound the air horn, light a flare, radio the guys at the lock. Even with a heart attack, even in extreme pain, he would have had time to do something – not nothing."

"Amy, I believe you. How can I help?"

She ignores my questions and continues. "Then there is Luna. You know that beagle loved that man. She never wanted to be away from him. That damn dog." I could hear the gulp. "Luna got out and swam away. If Errol was alive..." *The beagle would not leave her master unless...*

"I know, Amy," I say softly. "But if Errol was dead before going over the falls, then..."

Amy's voice nearly jumps out of the phone, "I know that Brie. I am completely and 100% aware that something like that could have happened. But it didn't; I know in my soul that it didn't. There is something else going on here, something that I don't understand. And I need help." She trails off with an audible rasp, and my heart goes out to her. I can hear Luna barking in the background, the beagle bah-roo that I had heard at the river. *Help.*

"Amy, what if Errol was, if he..."

"Are you going to say killed himself? I know that's still on the table – it's one of those letters, right, the **S** in **SHNHU** or something? Listen, I know that it's possible to think that. I may have even put that thought in people's heads because I am the first to admit that something was wrong, something was really bothering my husband. But Errol, the man I loved, the man I married? NO MATTER WHAT HAPPENED, HE WOULD NEVER DO THAT." She stops and breathes loudly.

I let the silence linger. Something Jim had taught me. "Don't fill empty space," he had cautioned. "You learn more when you wait. And then listen with all you've got."

"Brie, you've got to believe me."

"I do, of course I do." *She must know. Isn't that what spouses do? Become soul mates? Know inside the soul of their mate? Can I do that with Neal?*

"Did you get the autopsy report?" I ask gently. I have no idea what an autopsy report consists of, but I know from what the cops told us that it might reveal how he died.

"Yes," she says simply. "It's very hard to tell what it really says. Thankfully, it's only a page…" she breaks off in a sob. "Brie, there's no sign that he bumped his head or that anything knocked him out. No evidence. I talked to his physician, Jerry, Dr. Jerry Bass, and he agrees that it's unlikely that Errol had a heart attack. In the autopsy they look for signs: enlarged heart, clot, aneurysm, anything. I gather that's routine. But, about Errol, they can't tell anything conclusive."

"Meaning what?"

"Meaning that he could have died of natural causes or not. They just don't know. His lungs were full of fluid… they had to be, of course. They found him face down in the…"

"Yes, I heard," I say gently.

"Look, I know the medical examiner here. I went to school with him."

This is such a typical Pittsburgh story. If you were raised here, you know everyone. The mayor is a friend of the lawyer who is a friend of the doctor – the golf courses are crowded with elementary school buddies who still do business with each other. As a native Pittsburgher, Amy knows a lot of people around town, so I am not surprised.

She continues, "Victor Williams, Vic, is our ME. He's a super guy. Friends with Errol too. And, you know, he's not just a coroner. In rural counties, the coroner is an elected official, so he or she might not actually know much about forensics or anything."

"Wait a minute, forensics? You mean forensics like in criminal investigation?"

"That's what I am saying, Brie. Look, Errol didn't kill himself. And he didn't die of a heart attack. Or any other natural cause. It just doesn't add up. So I think this is…"

Murder? I might have whispered the word. There is a moment of complete silence. I hold my breath. *I knew it!*

"Well, Vic is a superstar in criminal forensics," Amy states, ignoring my question. "See, he's an MD, a forensic pathologist; he went through college, medical school, did a few years of pathology, and then he had to complete a year of forensic fellowship training. To top it off, he had to pass his board certification examination." She pauses. "Like I said, he's a superstar. He's particularly revered in the African American community. He's from Homewood."

She draws another breath. "I used to date him – before Errol, of course."

Another Pittsburgh story. Somebody should draw a flow chart of the liquids that have flown from one body to another in this city. It would make a tangled web of sex intrigue. I vaguely remember seeing pictures of this guy in the newspaper. Handsome African American, local guy makes good kind of thing, education, a high-profile position. And friends with the Pyrovolakises.

"Vic agrees with me. It's not clear what the actual cause of death is. They did a toxicity screen to check for blood alcohol level or…" she pauses for a minute. "Or drugs. There was nothing. No definitive cause of death. No clear case. I don't have any proof. That's what they need, that's what Vic needs, to make this a criminal case. That's why I am calling. Look, Brie…" She pauses and clears her throat, clearly struggling to get something out.

"It doesn't look to me, or to Vic, or to Jerry, that it was a heart attack – or any other natural cause. Of course, we don't know for sure, but I know. I know that he didn't kill himself. So that leaves us with…" she trailed off.

I whisper into the phone, "You think that it's murder, don't you?"

"Exactly," Amy concurs.

I knew it had to be. But I don't know why. I don't remember the rest of the conversation or how we end it. I know that I sit for minutes gazing out my windshield but not seeing. I get out of my car and walk across the footbridge and up Ellsworth into the retail area, the stores dark and closed. I take the long way up to Shady Avenue, left on Penn, left on Highland, and right back into the parking lot. It was probably a 20-minute walk. I have been in a non-thinking state since Errol's death. If Amy agrees that it wasn't a heart attack or an accident – that confirms that it's not an **N** or an **A**. And it's not **S**. **U** is just a wimpy way out. I'm going with **H**. For sure. *What now?*

My mind syncs with my steps as I walk the circuit again. *Think, Brie. What happened? First there was Boris – his being in the office and the puddle. Then there is NeuroGenex. Errol hated some guy there. He hated the Russian venture capitalists too. What about his students? What about – us? No one is innocent.*

. . . .

Amy sends me an electronic copy of the autopsy report that afternoon. In addition to nothing definitive about the **N** – heart attack or whatever – there is also no sign of a struggle. "Unclear cause of death," I read, a "**U** – Undetermined." I read that officially they are ruling it as a drowning. I think that it's weird that he was still in the boat, even though it was full of water. There was water in his lungs, hence the verdict of drowning, but he hadn't fallen or drifted out of the boat. The boat was floundering, mostly full of water, but not sunk. There's no reason to suspect anything amiss; officially, no one seems to think it's anything but an **N** or **A**, or both. But Amy's insistence… I know that the cops can't investigate unless they have a case. *What constitutes a case?*

． ． ． ． ． ． ．

It's late. I have to finish the letter before I leave. Matt insisted on a letter to send to investors and partners about Errol. Something confidential but not revealing. I sit down to write. It's my job.

I remember how against venture capital funding Errol was. "I don't think they're all assholes," he'd smirked to me as an aside. "But they are VCs." He'd made it clear.

Errol isn't from Pittsburgh either. We both hail from Amherst, Massachusetts. Given our age difference, we didn't know each other back home. Errol left while I was still small, but we share some favorite places. "It's my fault that Amherst Coffee House morphed into an after-hours scotch bar," he told me once. "My friends and I from grad school would gather there late into the night. They finally gave in and served us what we really wanted – booze!"

I remember how Errol would come bounding in to the office, radiating a smile like a flashlight. "Hey beautiful," he would call to me. "You don't mind if I call you beautiful, do ya beautiful?" He'd laugh, delighted with his little joke. He'd then bounce his lanky frame towards the lab, shirttails and flip flops flapping, torn khakis trying to keep up with his legs. He'd boom "hallo" to the right and left, greeting everyone like it's been a long time since he saw them. Usually it was yesterday. His joie de vivre was genuine; you couldn't help but get sucked in. He wore delight too. He sported a Hawaiian shirt every day. Even in winter. "I have a whole closet full of them," he told me once, laughing. "Drives Amy around the bend! Oh, I'm a preferred customer of Tommy Bahama." He howled at the look on my face. Errol's beach foot gear disappeared only in the dead of winter, usually because of snow. I never, and I mean never, saw Errol in a suit.

Chapter 7
March 12

I'm dreaming of bees. I can't shake them. They're after me. Buzz! I wake with a start. It's Matt calling me. *Oh no, not again!* It's 6:30 a.m.

"Matt?"

"You talked to Amy, right? I'm calling another emergency meeting. I need you to come in right now. Fuck." *From Yale to the gutter.*

"Of course." Matt's already gone.

In the shower, the water runs off my arm in a waterfall and spirals down the drain. My cat, Arwen, tries to leap out of my way as I clamber out of the shower, stumble and catch myself on the sink, twisting my bad ankle, which aches.

"You're off early," Neal remarks.

I say nothing as I kiss him goodbye. I arrive 15 minutes early. No one else is there. I peer in at the empty offices.

Since the beginning, I've loved being in a startup. Who else gets to experience this rush? This thrill? All of my classmates wanted to be involved in startups. But most of them had no idea what that meant. It takes a whole lot more than dreams to get from idea to exit, where shareholders make their money. *Don't I know it.*

We'd come so far. It took a long time to get the company up and running. Bringing a new drug to market is a billion dollar effort and can take up to 10 years. Life in the early days of Quixotic had been constant fundraising. Bigfoot Capital, our first big investor, was the first West Coast venture firm to take a chance on Pittsburgh. Josh Matey, Bigfoot's founder, was born here. After graduating from Centre-Pittsburgh, he ended up in Seattle, with a stint at Microsoft, then Amazon, and two successful startups. When he decided to form his own fund, it was logical to base it in Seattle. Of course, he had an office in Silicon Valley too. But Bigfoot was aggressive about finding the best deals. The firm has portfolio companies in Ohio, Michigan, and now Pittsburgh. Josh comes back here pretty often. He has family here, including an aging mother. Huntington's is in there somewhere. I think that his mother's friend had it.

When I started at Quixotic, the team was raising a seed round that totaled $8 million from a bunch of doctor friends, individual angel investors, and GreenBush, the regional angel group, which pools investments from members. I love the story Jim told me about why angels are called that. Apparently, there was a rich man who had promised a young playwright that he would produce his play on Broadway. Before that happened, however, the rich man died. The playwright went to the widow to ask if she would still back him financially. She refused. But, a couple of weeks later she was going through her husband's desk and found a check written out to the playwright. Wanting to fulfill her husband's wishes, she gave it to the young man, who then declared that the man was an "angel" since the money came down from heaven.

Our second institutional funding round, our Series B, was excruciatingly drawn out. *Who knew that it would take so much time, that it would be SUCH a distraction?* Errol would do the funniest investor imitation: "What's my ROI, IRR, REQ, and can I get an REM and fries and a coke with that?" He didn't like the Russian VC firm at all. But we took their money anyway.

Then there was "the Deal." With the millions of dollars from NeuroGenex, we could conduct the final clinical trial for HD66. A Phase III clinical trial is

45

enormous in scope. Jim had patiently explained the clinical trial process to me. "Phase I trials are in humans. But healthy subjects. Big step: first in man." I had nodded dutifully. "Phase II is the first time the drug is used in patients."

"In those that suffer from HD," I added, thinking of my secret.

He looked sharply at me, "Yes, right. A Phase II trial continues to study safety with a higher volume of subjects over a longer period of time. It's also a chance to look at efficacy – does the drug work in humans? Phase II is often divided into A and B phases, like we did. Quixotic's Phase IIA trial was in 80 patients. Once we confirmed the hypothesis – that our drug appears to be safe AND to actually work – we moved to Phase IIB. That study was for approximately 180 subjects where we sought the optimum dose at which the drug shows efficacy with minimal side-effects."

"Meaning that we can reverse HD," I stated, trying not to sound hopeful. "That's why we need to raise capital, right?"

"Yep, clinical trials are expensive." Jim was patient with me. No question was too dumb for him.

With the NeuroGenex deal, the end was in sight. We'd get HD66 to market. *I needed it to happen.*

. . . .

I hear voices, and a few minutes later I step into the conference room. The team is there. Usually trim, immaculate, Matt looks like he hasn't showered or shaved in days. His hair is sticking up and more salt than pepper. Gigi is in black jeans, top and tennis shoes. Now that's all she wears. I had never seen her in anything casual until the morning of Errol's death. Where was the pound of jewelry?

The heavy makeup? She looks forlorn, standing in the corner. A new standard.

Stanley Gursky, our lawyer, is there. In spite of the hour, he looks crisp in ironed jeans and a button down shirt. He gives me a crooked smile and a nod. He takes his jacket off and hangs it carefully on the back of a chair, smoothing the coat with his long fingers. He sits and crosses his long legs. I remember cheering Stan on last year during the Pittsburgh Marathon at the corner of Bryant and Highland. Errol had hosted a bunch of us afterwards at his lovely house on North Sheridan. Amy and the kids were there. We drank retsina. I remember Matt gagging as Errol explained that the bitter tasting wine was made from pine resin.

"You mean like turpentine?" Matt choked.

I laughed and sipped. "I like it."

Errol complimented me, "You're all right, beautiful."

Amy laughed too. "You are, Brie," she told me as I left, a bit tipsy, later that afternoon. "Beautiful. I'm glad you're at Quixotic." She waved towards her husband, "He needs you. They need you," she added, nodding towards the drunk Quixoticers, lolling about in her living room.

I wonder if she knew how often Errol calls me. He told me I would understand, that I would carry on his work. *What was he talking about?* I was interested in the science, but I knew that it only mattered if it got to the market. *Is that the reason he picked me?* Because I know that the only way this works is if great inventions move from the benchtop to the bedside? *I won't let you down.*

"Sustenance, my friends," stalwart Jim announces as he enters the conference room. In a suit, he looks like business as usual. He sets down a tray of coffee and bagels.

I need the coffee for warmth on this cold March day. As I hold my cup, I hope that it gives me courage.

"Amy is going to the police," Matt begins. "She's talked to all of you. You've also seen the autopsy report? We have to take this seriously. And, as you suspect, there could be – excuse the Hollywood term – foul play potentially here. We can't dismiss that possibility. Fuck."

Jim takes over. "Of course there is no evidence, no clear anything. It's just Amy's conviction …" Jim looks down. The hush is deafening. "Of course Amy believes it's not suicide, but in this room, amongst ourselves, I don't think that it can be ruled out. We have to be open to anything, to all possibilities. This will be difficult for us, for Quixotic. To get through this unscathed." *What does he mean?*

Matt looks like he is having a heart attack. Gigi's head is on the table. Stan looks at me. Jim takes a bite of a bagel, chewing slowly and deliberately. When he has swallowed, he continues, "The police need our help and cooperation. We will all be questioned. As chairman of the board, I ask you to be completely transparent. I have assured them that we will cooperate – no matter what the outcome." *Does he suspect someone? One of us?*

There's a long pause. Jim sips his coffee. Gigi doesn't drink from her cup, but she holds it tightly against her chest. "Come on, say it," she pleads. Matt looks at her with steely eyes.

"OK. When the police start poking around, it could get weird around here. Be ready." Jim frowns at Matt who continues, "I think that officially we must adopt the attitude that none of us will be above suspicion." He looks at Gigi and Jim. "Even Errol. We don't know what happened, but the investigation may turn up surprises."

I'm on a merry-go-round, and I wish someone would turn it off. My head is spinning. My coffee slops on the table as I bang my cup down unsteadily.

Jim takes a slow breath. "Along with all of the stress of operating a startup and the usual challenges that we face, this will add a new and incredibly painful dimension. Plus the cancellation of our deal with NeuroGenex, our lead scientist dead, all of us under scrutiny, well, that's a tough one for any venture. We face losing the confidence of our investors, our partners – us." He picks up a half bagel and spreads blueberry-swirl cream cheese onto it. *Imagine the blog post Jim will write after this. A NewVenturist Startup Mystery?*

With a frown, Matt assumes command again, "I'm calling an all-company meeting for tomorrow. I'll let everyone know that there will be an investigation." He looks at me. The lights are harsh on his cold blue eyes. "Brie, make sure that everyone is there. I don't want this to get out, that there is an investigation, that anything is suspicious. Nothing gets out, OK. And, I mean nothing. Everyone will be questioned. There'll be spill-over to our investors. The press will be all over this. As if the NGX fiasco didn't already give them enough gossip. Fuck. We have to preserve what we can. Otherwise, we can just kiss this all goodbye."

I look at Matt. *What is he talking about?* He can't give up. None of us can. OK, we're all potential suspects. *Not me. I need to find out who. That will lead me to what Errol left for me.*

Matt brings me back to the moment. "Fuck. None of us knows what this means. None of us have been involved in a fucking murder before."

There, he said it. The word. The unlawful killing of a human being. I read in the "Post Gazette" that

Pittsburgh's murder rate last year was down to something like 44. Was Errol one of the statistics for this year? I imagine only a very few occur on any of the Pittsburgh rivers. Meaning Errol is a standout. *That's a terrible thing to think. It must be shock — our collective unconscious gone awry.*

Chapter 8
March 13

Sure enough, we get a visit the next morning from a detective. I notice the car parallel parking as I gaze out of my window on Broad Street. I see a guy in a suit, the detective, I guess, looking out of place and official. He has an unmarked car and pays at the parking station. *Do they have to do that, pay to park? Just like us? I guess he hasn't downloaded the parking app yet.* Matt is waiting for him when he steps off the elevator into our waiting area. He waves me over impatiently and introduces me.

"Pleased to meet you; I'm Brie Prince, marketing and media manager."

"Detective Straler Henrik."

Wow, that's a name I won't forget. Detective Henrik is tall, about 6'2" or thereabouts, thin, and he's young. Maybe just a few years older than me? And cute. He has a bright, wide smile as he looks at me. I detected a slight accent as he introduced himself. German?

He gets a serious look on his face, "I guess you know why I am here. My superior, Senior Detective Small, Jennifer Small, couldn't be here, but I am." He pauses. "Here, that is." He pauses again. "To investigate." Another long pause. He's definitely German now I hear the accent clearly. He looks it, with ash blond hair and piercing, cerulean blue eyes.

Matt can't contain himself. "Out with it, boy, I mean, detective." He gives his most charming CEO smile to the detective.

"I have been sent by headquarters;," the detective looks at me, "to investigate a possible non-natural death in the case of Dr. Errol Pyrosolakiss," he states, mispronouncing the name.

"Pyrovolakis," I correct gently, and the detective graces me with another big smile. I feel butterflies in my stomach. *He is too cute for this kind of work.* His ash blond hair is cut close with a cowlick at the front. I see Gigi, Jim, and Stan approach.

As the detective greets the others, Matt whispers, "They're not taking this seriously."

Detective Henrik glances back at us with a smile and one raised eyebrow. "Um," can we all meet somewhere?" He looks around anxiously.

Matt nods to me. "Right this way," I answer.

Once in the conference room, we sit down, but Detective Henrik stays standing, at the head of the table, awkwardly shifting from one foot to the other. I see that his boots are scuffed. He might not have a girlfriend. No ring either. *Shoot, stop that!*

Detective Henrik clears his throat. Jim pops a question, "Detective, would you like some coffee as we begin, or some snacks?"

He smiles my way, "I'd love coffee."

Jim nods, "OK, be right back." I can see that Detective Henrik is surprised that the senior guy gets up to get him coffee. *He probably has no idea what it's like in a startup. I don't fetch coffee. Here, everyone does anything and everything; there's no ego involved. That's how it is.*

Jim comes back in with coffee on a tray. The detective takes his and grants Jim a white-toothed smile. He gets the ball rolling, "Soooo, you all know why I am here. My superior, Detective Small, doesn't think this incident is anything but an accident, classification **A**, a health-related accident. We know that it's unlikely to have been a heart attack, but it's possible. There's nothing in the autopsy to say that this is anything but the body gone awry. There's no evidence one way or another." We all look at him. "But, as you must know, the wife, Mrs…" he glances my way and smiles. *Flutters again.* "Mrs. Pyrovolakis is convinced otherwise. It's a difficult situation, here, where you have no clear indication, no evidence, either way. My job is to investigate, to rule out the **S**, you know **S**uicide, or to solve the case assuming it's an **H**, **H**omicide." Matt taps his foot impatiently. Jim sips his coffee. Gigi glares at the detective like she is ready to snap.

"As you know, Amy went to the medical examiner, Dr. Victor Williams, who has agreed to take on the case. Which is why I am here. I'm here to investigate."

"Just to get things clear," Matt butts in, "Have you done anything like this before? A murder, suicide, you know this kind of case?"

The detective has pale skin, and I can see the rose blush rise from his collar and flood his face. "Well, actually, no. This is my first. Alone that is. I've been with my superior, Senior Detective Small, on some cases…"

"That's OK, detective," Jim interrupts. "We're here at your disposal. More than anything, we want to get to the bottom of this. We want to know. Errol was our friend." Gigi blows her nose.

"Thank you," the detective responds. "I appreciate your willingness to help." He turns to look at each one of us. "I need your cooperation. All of you. I would like to talk to each one of you, and to the rest of your crew, individually." He pauses. "I must ask that you not discuss these interviews with each other or anyone else." The detective looks older in his seriousness. "Your cooperation is vital. I am sure that you realize how important it is to discover how – and why – he died. And we will discover that, I promise." His clear blue eyes pan in a circle, penetrating all of us in turn. *He may be new at this, but he's good.*

"Yes," Jim says quietly. "We'll do whatever you ask. Why don't you start with Brie here, and then we'll figure out the order for the rest of us and others in the company?"

The detective gives a small smile and nods, "That would be great. Thank you very much." He turns to me.

Matt stands up. "There's one more thing. I know that you want us to keep all of this internal. But, we need to talk to our people. This is a business. We're vulnerable. Any whiff of panic will send our investors down a bad path for us. We have to manage this investigation with you. To make sure that the message is right. We need them to hear it from us, not from some leakage. You have a problem with that?"

The detective looks surprised, but he immediately nods assent. "I'd like to check on that. Just to make sure." He pauses. "If that's OK with you?"

"Of course," Jim replies smoothly. "Whatever you need to do."

They all leave the room. Detective Henrik sits down across from me. He looks embarrassed. "Would you like to use this paper and pen?" I ask, sliding over my yellow pad.

He gives me a thankful smile. *Uh oh, more flutters.*

"Ms. Prince," he begins.

"Let's start by first names," I say. "I'm Brie. Can I call you Straler?"

The detective smiles at me. "That would be great. Thanks, um, Brie." I find him reassuring in the chaotic aftermath of Errol's death, a baseline antidote to our cancer of fears and insecurities. Another smile.

He asks me the basics: "How long have you worked at Quixotic? Where are you from? What brought you to Pittsburgh?"

I respond crisply and to the point, Jim's lessons about the press in my head: there's no such thing as off-the-record; you only say what is necessary; you don't divulge what is not asked. This is not the press, I know, but I want to be careful.

"What kind of interactions did you have with, with the…"

I jump in, "You mean Errol?"

He looks at me, his blue eyes bright. "Yes."

"Errol was our scientist. He invented a cure for an incurable disease, Huntington's, if you know what that is."

He nods. "I read up some."

"He was a world-class MD. His HD patients and their families loved him. They didn't even know that Errol was trying to cure Huntington's. For them."

"Did you have any relationship with him outside of the office?" He pauses, pen raised.

"Of course I knew him inside the office and outside. We're a startup. We're like a family. We all know each other very, very well. We have to…"

"I remember when Gigi had warned me about his temper – the flip side of him that I never saw. "Errol is demanding as hell," she told me once when we found ourselves together in the ladies room. "Woe be to the recipient of his anger. Look out. He's like an exploding stew pot. I've seen him in action, believe me. You don't want to be there. It's terrifying." Then she'd added, "Don't get involved with him, Brie." She tore the paper towel off the roll with a vengeance and her eyes gleamed coal black at me.

"Ever been on his boat?" Straler asks.

"Yes, several times. We've all been on his boat. He loved taking us out."

I was a walking PowerPoint slide after those trips. He'd talk about the science, how I needed to help him articulate the complexity in a simple format that investors and eventually patients would understand.

"Do you know his wife?" Straler asks.

"Yes, Amy is lovely."

"What about the kids?"

"Yes, a bit."

"Any reason that you know of why Errol would commit suicide?"

"I don't think that's what happened. Amy is adamant that he would never have done that."

Straler pauses writing and looks at me. "How can you be sure?" *He has such piercing blue eyes. They disarm me.*

"That's ridiculous really. He had a perfect life. And he's – he was – a happy guy. Yes, he had some pressures at the university. I know that Amy says that he'd been acting secretive, but I don't think that he was capable of killing himself. Errol just didn't have that in him, you know? He was happy. All the time. I mean he wore these Hawaiian shirts, lots of bright colors, and he had these socks and flip flops and, I don't know, he just wasn't the type to do something like that to her, to his family, to us. *To me.* He used to call me beautiful – as a nickname, I mean." I grab a Kleenex and pretend I am not crying. "Look, he could be difficult, but he was a great scientist. He didn't solve just one incurable disease, he solved two. Or he was close on the second one. He wouldn't, he couldn't, just leave all that." Straler is looking down at his notes. His writing looks careful and neat. He's left handed. *A south paw, like me.*

"Anyone you know angry at Errol, angry enough to, you know…" He leans forward, his eyes unblinking.

"Kill him you mean? No, I don't know anyone who would want to kill Errol. He was a hero. To his patients.

Their families. They sent him letters." He looks at me, wide blue eyes staring into mine. "We loved him," I finish miserably. Straler gives me a moment to pull myself together. He has made a page of notes. "You can keep the pad," I tell him. "For the others."

He thanks me and picks up the pad to go. "Anything else you can add? Any details or thoughts that might be helpful."

"No. That's it. I don't have anything to add. At least not right now."

He hands me his card. "This has my number at the station. You can always call that. But here is my cellphone and email," and he scrawls on the card. "Don't hesitate," he says as he gets up. "These situations get solved because people help. I need help. If you have anything to add that you think could be remotely important, please contact me, OK?"

I stand up, "I will. Promise. And, Straler, you stay here in the conference room. I'll go get whoever they decided is next. We'll send everyone to you, OK? And depending on your timeline here, I'll make sure you get fed."

He gives me a wide, toothy smile. *Geesh!* As I walk back to my office I ponder what he said. What he asked. The detective asked for help. For MY help. Amy had pleaded with me too. *I have to help them.*

. . . .

Detective Henrik stays most of the day. By lunchtime he had talked to everyone on the executive team. At 1 p.m., he listens as Matt introduces him and explains to the Quixoticers what is going on and why they can't talk about any of this to the outside world. Matt informs them about the interviews and then reads the list of who goes when.

Several employees from the lab look like they are in shock. One of them, Chong, I think, actually drools out of his open mouth. I see Boris grow pale as Matt speaks, and his eyes widen as the detective looks through the crowd. He looks down as Straler's gaze crosses him. With a last name that starts with a Z, his name is towards the end of the list of interviewees. I remember the couch, the snoring, and the pool of water.

Straler stops by my office in the middle of the afternoon. He had run out of paper. I give him another pad. He looks at a messaging document that I created to use as a cheat sheet as we talk to outsiders, including investors. He asks me to send it to his boss at the East Liberty station. Buzz! He nods at me and gestures towards his phone. "Yes, Jennifer?" He steps out into the hallway. I can't hear what he says. He comes back into my office. "Sorry about that. I just needed to check that what you were saying about the investigation to the outside world was OK."

I nod, "I know, Straler. It's fine. None of us has done this before. Murders don't usually happen in the entrepreneurial world." He tilts his head to the side. He looks like a puppy. "We're a startup, Straler. Really early-stage. Pre-revenue. Like I told you, we're creating new drugs to cure terrible, incurable diseases."

He smiles. "Cool. And, it's alright, what you want to say. I just had to get some guidance. I'm sure you understand. But keeping it general is good. Nothing about murder is suspected or suicide or anything like that. Just stick to the story that the death is being investigated."

By the time Straler leaves, the office is shrouded in fog. There are people here, and I assume that they are working, but I am in an altered state of reality. I am not functioning well enough to know if anyone is actually doing their job. I see Boris duck out the back door right after Straler left. I never go out the back door. It leads to the stairs down to the garage, but there is no light in the stairwell. We never bothered to fix it because no one ever uses it. Boris must have used the stairwell before, I realize, remembering how he disappeared.

. . . .

That night, I sit on the small terrace outside of my building, bundled up against the cold, and nursing a glass of my precious The Balvenie single malt scotch that Neal gave me. Arwen is curled in my lap, purring. She hasn't a care in the world. Neal is working late. My thoughts are swirling. I stroke the cat. *I have to help. What should I do?*

A thought comes to me after my second scotch. If I were to go around asking a few questions, in the guise of my marketing role, no one will suspect anything. I'm just Brie, like the cheese. Harmless. I think of Amy and their kids, and how important this is for them. *I need to solve a murder. If I solve it, I will find what Errol left for me. For my father.* I'll never forget the weekend that I found out. I was home for Thanksgiving.

Chapter 9

November 20, three years before the incident

A doctor George Huntington....he gave it the name
and all these years later it's still the same
no cure but the patience of the ones you love
and the busy schedule of the Lord above
you can usually count on him....but's he's mighty slow
Woody Guthrie[1]

It was going to be just the three of us that Thanksgiving dinner. We lived in cooperative housing, the third such adult commune development in the U.S., started by my architect mother. As members of what was known locally as "the Coho," we had access to a large, communal garden. My mom did the gardening, but my father was the cook. The weekly community dinners at the Coho were orchestrated by my father since before I can remember. He approached cooking for 100 people like a conductor of an orchestra. He would direct individuals to do this, stir that, mix the other, and a meal would come together with camaraderie and song. I didn't know how sheltered I was in the Coho until I left it and discovered the real world.

My dad was the maestro of the community Thanksgiving dinner. Except for this year. How the rest of the Coho were going to pull off the cooking without my father I couldn't fathom, but I didn't question it. I was glad to be home and to be off the treadmill of a business that never rests. I had been with Quixotic for over a year, and I was tired. Still passionate about entrepreneurship and our

---

[1] Reference: Flannery, Tom. "Talkin' Woody Guthrie Huntington's Chorea Blues." *Songaweek*. 2004. Web. 10 Apr. 2010.
http://www.songaweek.com/woody/songs/huntington.html

mission, but I needed a break. I missed Neal, but I wasn't going to be the first to call. He was home in Michigan. We didn't discuss spending the holiday together. We're weren't there yet as a couple.

I sat at the kitchen table that Thursday morning, nursing a large mug of Peet's coffee and rubbing a bruise on my forehead from bumping the bedpost last night. My mom had fallen for Peet's brand coffee when she lived in Berkeley before I was born. I saw on the counter that we planned to celebrate Thanksgiving with a small, locally-grown, organic turkey. I had gotten in late the night before and had gone straight to bed. My dad must have been asleep.

As I sipped the rich brew, I watched my father prepare the turkey. He seemed to have trouble with the stuffing. There were breadcrumbs all over the floor. He seemed stiff and awkward as he made his way around the counter to the stove. I started to laugh, "Dad, no wonder I'm so clumsy. I see where I get it from!" I couldn't tell what he was doing, but I think that he was trying to open the oven. "Oh, do you need help?" He was talking to me, but it was hard to understand him. He was slurring his words. "Started early, huh, Dad?" I quipped. I was getting ready to pour myself a mimosa from a pitcher on the table.

I could see my mother outside on the porch chatting with a neighbor. She had a champagne glass in her hand too. I heard a noise and a scream that I couldn't place. I jumped out of my seat with alarm as I watched the turkey and pan clatter to the floor, the juices spreading across the tiles like an incoming tide. Then my father's arms started this weird set of jerky movements. His mouth started opening and closing like a fish. The whole thing was like a series of dance moves, except that it wasn't graceful.

"Dad, what's going on?" He started shaking his head, almost violently. I saw my mother through the screen start to turn to us. Her mouth was open. Was she saying something? I looked back at my father. This is not drunk, I thought. A seizure? I stared at him, but he couldn't look me in the eye. His eyes kept darting from one side to the other. "Mom?" I called to her through the door. "Something's going on with Dad. He's having some kind of seizure."

My mother opened the door and screamed sharply as the champagne glass slipped out of her hands. The glass shattered into a million shards of rainbow glass on the cement porch floor. She visibly composed herself as she marched in with a determined expression on her face.

"Mom, what's..."

"Not now, Brie," she said in her commanding I-am-taking-care-of-something voice. "We'll talk later. Right now I need you to get me some clean rags from the broom closet. And the broom and dustpan."

As I wiped the grease from the floor and my mother helped my dad to a chair, he seemed to settle down, although his face still had a tic, his mouth moving up and down in round O's. He sat stiffly at our kitchen table, the back of his hand thrumming uncontrollably on the table. I saw drool escape from his mouth. My mother wiped it just before it reached the end of his chin. I stared at him, imagining the drool globbing into a long drizzle of flowing water that pooled at his feet, a tributary feeding a small, spreading pond. Then I snapped out of it as my mother commanded again, "Brie!"

"The captain has the conn," I announced, a phrase from my childhood to cede control to whoever had the keys to the front door. My mother, always the captain, took control in her crisp, efficient way. I went out to the porch to sweep up the glass. I saw her scoop up the turkey, add some more juice from a measuring cup, and pop the bird into the oven.

"It'll be alright," she announced to nobody in particular. "Not to worry, dinner will be fine." I watched the glass pieces mixed with leaves and twigs from the porch fall slowly into the garbage can as I brushed out the dustpan.

I drank too much at dinner. So did my mother. Store-bought wine, I noted. I thought we had an endless supply of my dad's homemade wine. When had he stopped making it? He wasn't drinking either. My mother had to help him a few times, cut up the turkey and such. Where was my supervisor dad, who used to do all this with a laugh and hugs all the way around? I didn't ask.

We passed the time without incident. But I remember every detail, every clink of a fork, slurp from a glass, and, most of all, the heavy silence that hung over us like the gray Amherstian sky outside.

My mother took my father up to bed early that night. She stayed upstairs. I stayed downstairs, drinking, thinking about Neal, wishing I were with him rather than here. The house grew quiet except for the occasional creak. *Are you keeping a secret from me?*

As I made my way upstairs to my childhood bedroom, I stopped to look at the pictures on the wall of the three of us: at the beach over many summers, on a cruise to Alaska when I was 12, playing in the leaves with my dad when I was six. *Memories.*

My mother had folded down the corner of the handmade quilt on my single bed. I remember when she made it. The Coho had started its version of a quilting bee. In hippie-style, everyone contributed to everyone else's quilt. Some of them turned out to be a ghastly hodgepodge of designs and colors. Mine turned out kind of sweet with natural greens, blues, and browns. "The green to match your eyes," my mother told me when she first put it on my bed. "The blue is for the sky and the brown is for the earth. And you see the green sandwiched in between? That's you, my belle."

I used to ask her about my green eyes. "How did I get them when you and daddy have brown eyes?" I had learned in school about dominant and recessive genes.

"Ah, some things cannot be explained by science," she would say ambiguously. "Not by science…"

As I was falling asleep, I thought dreamily about my father's weird seizure. It's not a seizure, I told myself sleepily. I've seen something like it before. It's like chorea…" I know that I said it out loud. Chorea! Bolting upright in bed, banging my head again on the bedpost, I realized where I had seen that kind of jerky set of unruly movements before. "Gadzooks, I don't believe this." I unzipped my backpack and brought out my laptop. I opened it on my childhood desk and began to research.

"Mom?" I asked at breakfast. "Can we talk?"

She looked at me and then softly said, "Yes, Brie. After breakfast." The meal was interminable, and washing up seemed to take a month, what with the slow sudsy water and me wiping each dish. Far be it for my groovy parents to have a dishwasher. "I prefer the old-fashioned approach," she said, reading my mind. "The warm water makes me relax, and I can think."

My dad was dozing awkwardly in the study by the time we finished the dishes. We sat down with cups of strong Peet's. "It's Huntington's isn't it?" I asked.

Chapter 10
That same year

My arms felt funny moving all the time
and sometimes my head didn't feel like mine
kept telling myself it was the Ballantine Ale
and them jugs of wine on the writing trail
I prefer a disease you can sober up from
Woody Guthrie

My father, George Whyte Prince, was 55 at diagnosis over a year ago. Dottie Grace Prince, my mom, had noticed physical and emotional changes starting a few years ago. "He starting having small tremors, mood swings, temper flashes, totally out of character. I – we – didn't know what it was for a long time," she told me. "We thought it might be everything from early Alzheimer's to Multiple Sclerosis. We spent over a year going through test after test. All the time, George, Dad, was getting worse. We didn't think Huntington's for a long time. There was no history, you see. But one day your dad was talking about his mother, you know, Granny Prince? He mentioned her cancer, and it hit me. It wasn't cancer at all. They really had no idea. She was never diagnosed. They just assumed. She went so quickly. Unusually fast, according to what I now know. They saw the jitters, but they never connected the dots. It was a different time…"

I fingered my grandmother's pearls around my neck. "You mean she had Huntington's and they never figured that out?" So stupid, I thought. But, of course, if my dad knew, he would never have married my mom. He certainly never would have had children. I just wouldn't exist, that's all…

My dad has Huntington's Disease. And what I saw yesterday is chorea. That was only the beginning. I'd probably see it again before I left, 48 hours from now. And it would get worse.

. . . .

Been on this road for a mighty long time,
Ten million men like me,
You drive us from you' town.
We ramble around.
And got them 66 Highway Blues.
Woody Guthrie

I already knew a lot about HD by the time I knew about my dad. Errol had published extensively on this subject. I had read all of his papers. He would quiz me to make sure I had actually read them. "I'm counting on you, Brie," he'd say.

At Quixotic I needed to write about what we did and create presentation materials. Errol took me out on the "Random Scoot" to explain it to me, "just the two of us." As we drifted in neutral, he peered at me over his glasses and continued, "I'd like for you to understand the science, Brie. You have a background in neuroscience. You'll get it. And," he stopped to smile broadly at me, "You'll be able to explain it to anybody – to your parents – after I explain it to you!" *Little did he realize…*

I oversaw the development of the video about HD and how our drug could cure it. Errol had dubbed the drug that he discovered in his university lab, the one that was licensed into Quixotic, "HD66." The 66 was named for the famous Mother Road, Route 66, which went from Chicago to California. Woody Guthrie, who died from Huntington's, traveled the famous road and wrote about it in the lonesome, sad song, "Highway 66 Blues."

Besides the research that I did on my own, I picked up a lot from the scientists at Quixotic. In addition, Errol let me observe his patients as he treated them and talked to the families. "This is my intern," he would explain to the patients and families. I watched. And now, I remembered.

The images of the Quixotic video haunted me Saturday night as I lay in my childhood bedroom. HD damages the nervous system by promoting apoptosis, or cell death, of neurons in the brain. We show this through animation. Ani-frigging-mation, I thought ruefully. As we ate a simple dinner of Thanksgiving leftovers that night, I imagined my dad's brain cells dying with little pops, one by one, pop, pop, pop, taunting me and my inability to help him, or to stop the steady and painfully slow march to incapacitation, and the silence that will take over at the end.

"Typical symptoms of HD include emotional instability, personality change, loss of memory, dementia, declining motor skills, anxiety, and paranoia," I had told my mother that afternoon. She had read about all this, but she was impressed. With my father, we have not yet run the full gamut. I know what will come; I am loath to share my knowledge with my mother. But she has done her own research, and I will not intrude to tell her what she does not need, or does not wish, to know.

She looked at me with hooded eyes before I went to bed that night. "I'm sorry, Brie," she said. "I'm so sorry." Just as well I never had any siblings. Thankfully, I did not say that out loud as I traipsed up the stairs to my bedroom.

I couldn't blame her for not telling me sooner. What would that have accomplished? She didn't know that Quixotic was focused on HD. A year ago we weren't even in clinical trials. Knowing wouldn't have helped. Still, I felt cheated. How and when was she planning on telling me?

Now, I realized. Now is as good as any. How ironic; Thanksgiving is the perfect time to tell me. She didn't plan for it to happen exactly this way, but she did plan for it to happen this weekend.

As I lay unsleeping that night, I reminded myself that the progression and symptoms of HD vary widely on an individual basis. We don't know how fast the disease will progress in my father. My affable and warm father, who would hug me at the least provocation. A softie at heart, he was a favorite amongst my friends. He coached soccer, softball, and ping pong, even though he wasn't great at playing any of them. He goofed off with my mom, showing his love with embraces around the kitchen stove and what I was sure were wet kisses. George was never wildly successful in his career. He and my mother had moved to Amherst from Berkeley, where they had migrated after attending Reed College in Portland, Oregon. George was an environmental psychologist. Most people looked at him strangely when he said those two words together. But he had received his PhD from the University of California at Berkeley and, from there, found a research position at the University of Massachusetts, where they settled, just in time for my birth.

My mom is a strong spirited type who studied philosophy, art, and the obligatory calligraphy at Reed. At Berkeley she got a master's in architecture. Once they settled in Amherst, she opened her own office, and stumbled upon the idea for co-op housing, a communal living environment for grown-ups. Amherst was one of the earliest co-op housing developments. Now they are popular all over the country. My mom designed several of them. She's been on television and has been featured in national magazines and newspapers. We're not well off financially, but we're comfortable.

She's very good at what she does. She'll do what it takes. She'll take care of my dad in the best way possible. When it comes to the final steps, she'll know what to do. She's just that way. *I didn't get that gene.*

I had seen chorea, the Tourette syndrome of the body, before. When I saw it in my father, it became personal. The next day, he knocked a lamp over. On Sunday, when I had to leave to go back to Pittsburgh, he fell in the bathroom. I noticed that someone had removed the lock on the door. It will only get worse.

It's not supposed to happen this way, not to me. Your work and your family are not the same. Quixotic is a business. We can save lives, sure. But my father's life? Mine? There is no separation now. I think about how everyone talked about the passion of an entrepreneur in grad school. *They have no idea what that really means.*

. . . .

I got this thing called chorea in my head
wanna walk but I fall down instead
folks say "Woody, he's just drunk again"
but I haven't had a drink since I don't know when
besides...I only drink when I'm alone...or with somebody
Woody Guthrie

On the plane on the way home, I glanced over some recent articles. "HD symptoms can sneak up on you," I read. "The healthier a patient is, the more he successfully fights the onset of the disease," another article said. My dad's symptoms seem to have bucked the norm and were progressing rapidly.

HD affects only about 30,000 new patients each year in the U.S., so it's considered an orphan disease. This terrible disease is a business opportunity for Quixotic. "The HD66 treatment will mitigate the symptoms and terrible desecration that happens to a person with HD," I wrote in the most recent business plan.

I remember Errol's description at a conference, "The science behind HD66 is simple. The magic of chromosome four. The misfortune of HD lies within a solitary gene, HTT, which, is, as you know" he said, looking at the audience of scientists and physicians over his glasses, "an excessive repeat of a DNA sequence – CAG. If you have more than 40 repeats of that one little CAG sequence, the codon, then you are doomed. You WILL develop HD. Your future is foretold and unavoidable." I remember Errol pausing and looking at the crowd. "The longer the repeat of the CAG codon, the earlier and more severe the onset of the disease. The symptoms of HD are relieved only in sleep, and, ultimately, in death. The brilliant machinery of our bodies can be undone by this tiniest of faulty cogs, a repetition of a bad sequence lodged on every chromosome four in every cell."

A betrayal of the body, I called it.

I know that the data on Huntington's is unequivocal. It's genetic. The mutation that causes Huntington's is dominant. The disease does not skip generations. Anyone with more than 40 CAG repeats on chromosome four shares the same fate. No amount of love, religion, or hope deters the disease from its course. What's in store for my dad is athetosis. His fingers and toes will become crimped and rigid, and the ever increasing chorea will overwhelm him, leaving him writhing on a bed that he will never leave.

The HD gene is passed from generation to generation. If a parent has it, you have a 50-50 chance of inheriting the mutant gene. The conundrum is that, if you don't know you have it, you might pass it on to your children. It's a vicious cycle. Now, I know the extent of the viciousness. There are no instances of HD appearing without family lineage. Today, with the genetic test for the disease, that will occur less and less. If you know a parent has it, then you too can have that test. So you can know. *I can know.*

My dad's mother and her family didn't have a clue. It was the 1970s. Granny Prince died in her early 60s. In a family of ranchers in Eastern Oregon, she wasn't the go-to-the-doctor type. Her decline was painful to watch, my dad told me years ago. But she couldn't have known that it was Huntington's unless she knew that it came from her parents. The mutant gene of Huntington's wasn't found until 1993. There were tests prior to that, but they involved multiple family members and they weren't even that accurate. Post mortem, an autopsy could reveal that the caudate on both sides of the brain lacked the normal convex shape, the typical and healthy bulge into the anterior horn of the lateral ventricles. But who ordered that kind of confirmation?

On the ranch outside of Bend, where I have only been once, it was Darwin's law all the way. "I didn't get to complain," I recall my dad telling me. "In fact," he told me, "none of us got to do much of anything outside of help with the cattle and mending fences." I had two uncles. The eldest died in Vietnam. The next one was a renegade and, I think, ended up in a Canadian jail. Dad was the youngest. His father passed away before I was born. So did Granny Prince. There was no one left to know that the repeated gene resides in him. And, possibly, in me. I feel the soft weight of her pearls around my neck.

Errol loved Woody Guthrie's songs. He sang them all of the time when he thought no one could hear him. Woody got HD from his mother. Two of his daughters have it. Woody's wife, Marjorie Guthrie, founded the

Huntington's Disease Society of America (HDSA) in 1968. Woody wrote a song about Huntington's. I had heard Errol sing it. It had new meaning as I listened more carefully to the lyrics playing on my phone.

If you can't remember how I died remember how I lived
and if you can find it in your heart to forgive
know that the piece of brain that had to fall
never affected my love for you at all
I'm gonna play this thing 'till they find a cure.

Should I get tested? Yes is the obvious answer. If I do, and am found to have that gene, what do I do?
I've read stories about people with HD, including emotionally-charged articles about some who have committed suicide rather than suffer the ignominy of the slow death and loss of control that comes with the disease.
How do you live your life if you know you will have that kind of end? How do you deal with having no future? The only drug that is currently on the market for HD helps to alleviate symptoms; it does not target the CAG repeats in the huntingtin protein directly. The drug was approved by the Food and Drug Administration in 2008 and addresses chorea by increasing the amount of a neurotransmitter in the brain called dopamine that is important in motor functions. The drug also has unintended side effects that include insomnia, drowsiness, nausea, and restlessness. My dad is not taking it. I probably wouldn't either.
How do you marry? If you know that you have it, you can't morally have kids. I didn't call Neal from Amherst. No one at Quixotic either. I can't see that their knowing will help. But I will sure as heck find out if my dad can be part of any clinical trial. *Is it too late for that? Can HD66 cure him?*

Chapter 11
That same year

As I squeeze into the shuttle that takes me to baggage claim after that Thanksgiving weekend, I resolve not to tell Neal about the Huntington's in my family. Not until I am ready and have some answers for myself. I'll tell him that my dad is sick, but I won't fess up as to what it is, or that it is hereditary. I'll buy some time to debate with myself if I should tell him and when *Should get tested first?*

I met Neal at CMU while we were getting our MBAs. He's of Indian heritage but born and raised in the U.S. by expatriates from Allahabad. We took a vacation last fall in India to visit some distant relatives. They took us to the Ganges where they performed spiritual rituals. We went to the Taj Mahal, and I can still see that striking white building when I close my eyes. It's an extraordinary structure, with its embedded gems. It was the first time Neal had seen it too, and we spent hours there in spite of the heat. It was there that I thought about spending the rest of my life with Neal. *But I don't know. I'm focused on my career, on Quixotic. I don't know if I want to settle down with one man, have a family, all that stuff. My life at the Coho in Amherst was not exactly normal; I don't know what normal looks like. Now, there may be no normal anyway.*

Neal works for his own startup, CivicEssence. I've told him a million times that's a terrible name, but he laughs at me and says, "So come up with an alternative, Miss Marketing." All of his employees are CMU and Centre-Pitt alums. He's been able to bootstrap his startup, raising a bit of capital from high-net-worth individuals, angels. He's not gone through painful institutional funding rounds like we have at Quixotic.

Most of our classmates ended up in New York City or San Francisco. But Neal loves Pittsburgh. "That's because you're from Detroit," I once taunted him. "Pittsburgh's a step up!"

But Neal was unfazed. "Look at what you can get here in the way of houses," he retorted.

He's right. Pittsburgh houses are beautiful – big, old fashioned charm. I think about the Google ad to recruit employees to Pittsburgh when they opened up its office here, which is one of their largest offices outside of the Mountain View, California. All the ad said was "Five bedrooms, hardwood floors, fireplace, large yard, great schools, $250,000. Apply Google Pittsburgh." They got so many applicants they had to take the ad down.

I get what Neal is saying. I love it here too. And him? Isn't this what you're supposed to have in a partner – synergistic goals and views on life? Love? *Who beats two entrepreneurs, two companies, one family?*

. . . .

I see his little blue Honda approach outside of baggage claim. As he jumps out and we embrace hello, I realize that it's easier not to think about my dad, my own dilemma. We hug for a long time, and he kisses me. I never want to let go.

"I missed you so much," he says into my hair.

"I missed you too."

"No more vacations apart, OK? Let's find a way to do them together. What about December?"

"Sure. But I'm tired. Let's talk about that later."

"Soon, OK?" He puts his fingers on my pearls. I cover his fingers with my hand.

As we drive to my apartment I look over at him, his steady and handsome face. I can't tell him. I can't not tell him. It will come up. Neal has made it clear that he is a one-horse kind of guy and that I am it for him. He has hinted before that we should spend Christmas together, not go to our separate families, but go somewhere special. I suspect that he wants to pop the question, to give me a ring. I know him, and I know this is the way that he would plan it. He will get down on his knee, I am sure. I suspect I would say yes. *What if he wants to be traditional and talk to my father?*

Late that night, another sleepless one, with Neal breathing quietly and peacefully on one side, and Arwen purring on the other, I debate with myself. My struggle is the same as millions of others in similar situations. Personalized medicine can give great freedom – we can predict our own futures – but it also causes great ethical dilemmas. Given that there is no viable treatment for HD, diagnosis is a death sentence. Who wants that? *Do I want Neal to be my Dottie? Is that fair? Would he sign up for that? Can HD66 stop this cycle? For me and others?*

As the clock reads 2 a.m., Arwen stretches and rolls on her back for me to rub her tummy. My thoughts circle round and round. Will Neal still want me if he knew that we couldn't/shouldn't have children? He sighs in his sleep. I reach over and kiss him, knowing that I can't face hurting him. He is number three of four kids; he loves his siblings, his family. He'll make a great dad.

"Hey beautiful," he says, eyes half open, and reaches to pull me to him.

Chapter 12
January 10, that same year

Dawn is still an hour away as Errol stood at his bedroom window looking out at the soft snow that fell during the night. The dream haunted him – again. The Voice.

Luna whined. "Sh," he told her, softly lifting her off the bed. He didn't want her thumping off the bed and waking Amy. He had removed her collar so that her tags wouldn't make any noise. He picked it up from his bedside table, and it clanked. "Shit, sorry, honey," he said in response to Amy's grunt.

He made his way carefully downstairs, struggling with the squealing dog in his arms. As he let her down she yelped in excitement. "Sh!" Errol opened the hall closet and reached for his cross-country skis. It had been snowing for two days; now it was deep enough. He strapped on Luna's blanket and hooked on her long leash. She walked on her hind legs whining with excitement as he laced up his ski boots. She barked impatiently. Errol clamped his hands on her jaw, prompting a shriek of surprise. Both hands on her muzzle, he heard his skis clatter loudly to the floor. "Shit!"

"PLEASE, Errol," Amy begged from upstairs.

"Of course, love. I'm out the door. Go back to sleep." The sleigh bells on the front door were still jingling as he stepped out onto the front porch. Luna skittered ahead down the steps, pulling him. Their prints were the first on the sidewalk, and they jogged down the hill and up the steps at the end of the block to Highland Park. The snow gleamed, pristine and pure. Errol strapped on his skis, turned on his headlamp, and started the rhythmic strokes – glide, push, skate, push. He entered the park's running path, which was illuminated by the street lights that circle the drive around the park. Luna was ecstatic, her airplane ears flapping and baying as she leapt in and out of the drifts. When they arrived at the back entrance to the zoo, Errol punched in the security code to open the gate. Dena, the zoo director, had given him that code a few years ago. The code still worked. He didn't come to the back door of the zoo very often, but, when he did, he appreciated his easy access. *Dena was a near miss. I'm glad I didn't do that to Amy.* He grimaced as he saw Luna leaving little yellow signs along the way. *Oh no, there's a brown sign.*

Errol steered towards the polar bears. He knew that they'd be out and happy in the snow. "Just the bears and us," he told Luna, and she bah-roo'd her agreement, pulling Errol down the path.

He had been bothered for weeks. He was experimenting with a new molecular design for HD66. Not for Huntington's, which was well on its way to commercialization, thanks to Quixotic, but for Parkinson's Disease. Errol had worked his whole life on solving conditions related to the basal ganglia in the brain that play a central role in many neurological conditions, including Huntington's. But they also figure in Parkinson's, which involves degeneration of the dopamine-producing cells in the substantia nigra, a component of the basal ganglia. Parkinson's represented a much bigger market than Huntington's. That was not the only reason he was interested in the disease, he told himself, planting his poles and stopping to watch the polar bears frolic in the snow. But still, it would be a great additional asset for Quixotic if he could make it work. *If.*

His interest in Parkinson's began about a year earlier with his colleague, Maya Pendyala. She had been researching Parkinson's for the last few years. Maya was convinced that the siRNA approach that Errol was using with HD66 – maybe a variation of the treatment, and injectable – could work on a key Parkinson's protein, alpha-synuclein.

He was skeptical, but she had insisted. "There is evidence of the proteins interacting," she had informed him with a burning passion that reminded him of a younger self. Maya was in her mid-30s, thin and dark with long gleaming hair and deep brown eyes with flecks of gold. She was intense.

"You know that it's generally agreed that each aggregation-prone protein is characteristic of a specific disorder. But we know now that aggregation-prone proteins can co-aggregate and modify each other's behavior, suggesting this process could contribute to the overlap in clinical symptoms across different diseases. It's possible that once your treatment for HD is in the brain, it will work with any protein, including the Parkinson's alpha-synuclein. I think it will work. I need your help!"

"I don't know if it will work," Errol had responded truthfully.

Shaking her black ponytail, she looked into his eyes, "Errol, please."

"It's a stretch, but we can try," he had agreed, noting her big smile of appreciation.

Since then, Errol had been working with his students on chemical variations of HD66 to impact the substantia nigra in the brain. So far, nothing worked. It was frustrating to see so little progress. "Don't give up," the Voice had told him.

Note to self: *Change protocol and work with lengthened carbon chain.*

He dialed a familiar number. He needed to talk to the only one who would understand.

"Errol, what is it?" murmured a sleepy Brie.

....

12 days later, January 22

It was midnight; Errol couldn't sleep. Cautiously, he went downstairs to make tea and read over his lab notes. Luna followed him, her tags jingling noisily as she thumped down the stairs. He had given up taking her collar off. Either way, he seemed to wake his wife. He ignored the moan of frustration from upstairs and studied his notes. He was stymied after two weeks' work on expanding the carbon chain and testing on mice. No net improvements found. "Do not look back; look forward." The Voice was never far behind.

He'd met with Maya last week. They continued discussing MPTP, which she had explained causes Parkinson's by destroying dopaminergic neurons in the substantia nigra of the brain. "MPTP, which chemically breaks down to 1-methyl-4-phenyl-1,2,3,6-tetrahydropyridine, is a sad story," she had elaborated, gesturing with her lovely brown hands. "In the 1970s, a chemistry graduate student in Maryland tried to synthesize a similar compound, which is the synthetic opium-like drug, MPPP, or 1-methyl-4-phenyl-4-propionoxypiperidine. Unfortunately, he accidentally synthesized MPTP as an impurity in the MPPP. Within days of injecting the drug, the young man exhibited signs of Parkinson's." Maya paused and shook her long hair. Her soft brown eyes were so sad Errol thought he might drown.

"There is another case," she continued. "In the 1980s in the San Francisco Bay Area, seven young people were diagnosed with Parkinson's after having used MPPP contaminated with MPTP. The neurologist, J. William Langston, tracked down the cause to MPTP. He made the case famous with his publication of 'The Case of the Frozen Addicts.' It's terrible, Errol."

"I know. I want to solve this, Maya, I really do," he said looking at the passionate young scientist.

"I think about my monkeys," she replied sadly, and swept her arm towards the closed door to the animal lab. "I know that some variation of HD66 will work on the protein and reverse the neuron damage. Please don't give up."

I never do. I can't. The Voice won't let me.

. . . .

Later that week, Gigi had exacerbated the situation when she asked, "Don't you have some other programs that we could license into the company? For some other conditions besides Huntington's? Maybe a disease that has a higher incidence, a larger market? It would be so helpful for our funding."

Errol had stalked out of the conference room. As he slammed the door he heard Matt chide her: "Damn it, Gigi, don't goad him. He's a scientist for fuck's sake."

Errol shook the memories from his mind. He was scheduled to meet Maya in her lab this morning. *What will I tell her? She will be disappointed in my results, in me.*

Luna started to bah-roo at something she heard outside. "Stop!" he heard from upstairs.

"Sorry, honey. We're outta here." He gathered a few things and called to the beagle, "Come-on Luna. Let's go down to the river!" As always, he was drawn to the water, the source of his creativity. *The river will help me think. It's where I started. I have to keep going. I cannot look back. The Voice, ever present, makes me keep going.* Luna jumped into his truck, whining with impatience as Errol threw his running shoes into the passenger seat. "I'll make a quick call," he said to his canine companion.

Note to self: *Commence experiments with shortened carbon chain. Confide in Brie. She is the only one with no agenda.*

. . . .

Two weeks later, February 5

Errol was not hungry. Outside, the snow and ice had melted. Deciding to skip lunch, he donned his running clothes, left his university lab, and started towards Schenley Park. It was raining, and his shoes squished in the mud. Typical Pittsburgh weather – the sky was steely gray. The drops fell off the trees, and he was soaked as his lanky form brushed the low-hanging branches. He shook the rain out of his eyes, missing Luna. *I hate running without her. She'll smell the run on me when I go home.* He picked up his pace.

He couldn't stop obsessing over why his experiments were not affecting the Parkinson's protein. He reviewed the different chemical constructs in his mind, mixing them, confusing them, seeing Maya's face, recalling his own patients. He shuddered the rain off of his face and ran faster.

Soaking wet, he forced his mind to return to the core problem. The shortened carbon chain had resulted in only minor improvements in DNA disruptions. He had spent hours researching the primate studies for MPTP. He had watched again the two NOVA productions that PBS made based on Langston's book. *I want to help her.* He sloshed through the mud, running full out. At the end of the trail, he stopped, doubled over with exhaustion, rain and sweat streaming off of his face making tiny rivulets of water in the wet ground.

Note to self: *Check lab notes from the students. Something overlooked?*

. . . .

11 days later, February 16

He had just left Maya's animal lab. Walking back to his office in a light drizzle, he couldn't get over it. It was awful. The monkeys were so immobile they had bedsores. They had to be fed by a tube through the nose. *I won't be able to tell Amy, let alone my kids. They would be horrified.* Errol had explained to his family why animal testing is necessary. If we don't test on animals, we would have to test on humans. But they oppose it. He argued that animal testing was not cruel. "We don't mistreat the animals; we care for them. As scientists, we try to be as humane as possible."

Sam had been somewhat sympathetic, "I know, Dad, but it's too weird for me."

Ariel was more blunt, "Gross, Dad. I don't want to ever do that."

Amy had just looked at me, "We don't need to know everything, Errol." *If she knew everything it would kill her. Only Brie would understand.*

Maya had made some creative suggestions for the chemistry. Errol resolved to commence a new series of experiments. He would put Shala in charge. She was excelling as his post-doc, and Errol was proud of how far this quiet Asian had come along.

As he arrived at his clinic to see an afternoon of patients, Errol decided to go back to the lab that night and continue working on the Parkinson's project by himself. *The students must be doing something wrong. A cure can't be so elusive. I'll start again with the mice. I won't stop until I have found it.*

"Where are you? How can I catch the fish without you?" The Voice did not answer.

Chapter 13
July 1, two years before the incident

It was late at night. The lab was quiet. Shala quickly tidied up, throwing away paper plates and used napkins. She was bursting with her news.

Dear Pliya, my darling sister,

Guess what? I have made a friend! My first real American friend. Dr. Errol introduced me to a Brie Prince who works at the company that he has made called Quixotic. She is very nice. She is typical American, and I like that. She is very smart, yet she is fun and not so serious like me. I met her in the lab, and we met for coffee. Can you imagine? That is what the Americans do. They meet for coffee at places like Starbucks! These places are everywhere. Oh yes. Here there are many coffee houses. They are nice places with air conditioning and soft chairs. It is funny, Pliya, because there are sometimes coffee shops next to each other or opposite sides of the street. You have choices. You have to pick which one you wish to enter. So much, they have here.

All is going fine in the lab. Dr. Errol. He tells me that I am in charge, but he does all of the talking and telling what to do. I am getting more comfortable being here, and the young men working here are nice to me.

I think of you often, my dear sister. I am sorry that you cannot write to me but I understand. I do not forget. Never. I send you all of my love.

Your almost American sister,
Shala

Chapter 14
March 14

I wake up in the middle of the night. My mind is buzzing. I have an idea. I hurry to make coffee and wait for the sunrise. I don't want to tell anyone, even Neal, because it's a just a hunch. A theory, I tell myself. But something worth investigating. When I doodled on my pad last night, a little drunk, I drew the river. And the lock. The lock building with the flag and all, which I had seen crossing the bridge many times. I had seen it that morning when Gigi and I descended the path behind the Creamery. *The lock*!

I leave my apartment as soon as it's light and drive to the Highland Park Bridge. I drive across it looking downriver, but I can't see much. I'm on the upriver side of the bridge. I take a left off the bridge and another left to get to Silky's Marina. I park and walk out onto the piers. There are only a few boats docked, given the early time of year. It's cloudy and cold, and I shiver as I walk past a houseboat. Some people live for being on the water, no matter the weather. I walk out to the furthermost dock and stand there looking at the wall of water flowing off the weir. Then I look over to the lock just across from me. There is actually a boat waiting downriver. I see a light near the lock and the boat disappears into the lock. About 20 minutes later I see the boat come out on the upriver side motoring towards whatever destination the pilot has in mind.

Getting into my car, I drive back over the river. This time as I glance to my right, I can see the horizon where the water meets the sky. They are both gray. The shadow of the bridge looks like the twist of DNA. I never noticed that before. I wonder if Errol ever noticed that?

I park in the same spot as that morning with Gigi. The path down to the river is much easier in the light. Turning right, I make my way to the lock. I am sure there is another way by the road, but I don't know it. When I reach the building, I see the stairs leading up to the door. Is this the front door, I wonder? At a lock, where is the front door? Facing land or the river? I don't have time to wonder as the door is opened for me and a booming voice emerges from a short red-faced man in a cap. "Hallo, little lady!" The voice from the small man is loud, but it's friendly and inviting. "Are you comin' to see me?" he asks. "If so, you're at the right place, and how do you do!" He chuckles and then introduces himself, "I'm Captain Bob."

Captain Bob, where did I hear that before?
"I'm the lock master. And what may I do for you, an unexpected, but not unpleasant, guest?" His face gets redder as he laughs, and he invites me in for coffee. I see a tray of donuts; he is clearly used to people stopping by. Boaters I guess. I can just imagine Errol being here and the two exchanging stories.

I explain who I am and why I have come. "Oh," his face looks suddenly sad, "I am so sorry about Mr. Errol. You were his friend?"

I nod. "Actually, his colleague. We work at the same company."

Captain Bob asks me to sit down. He is quiet for a moment. He sips his coffee. "I was on shift that night, that morning, of Mr. Errol, you know, but I left my shift after radioing to him. I told him he was getting too close to the falls. But he does that sometimes. They all like to fish too close above the falls, too close below. Drives us crazy. Mike, my second, comes on at 3 a.m. I didn't think much about it. I knew Mr. Errol was warned and he's very, well he was, very experienced."

Captain Bob pauses and looks at me. His face is even redder than a few minutes ago. "I didn't know, Miss Brie," he says quietly. "Like I said, Mr. Errol, he was very experienced. I've been on the "Scoot" myself. We fished together and..." He pauses again. I don't know what to say. "You see, once we had the radio contact, I just didn't think anything about leaving the shift and going home. I didn't know until the next day, well until that night, on the news. Mike said he talked to the police; there was nothing anybody could do." He pauses, and we sip our coffee.

I follow Jim's instructions, "Let the silence happen. Don't fill it with meaningless chat or questions."

"I feel terrible about what happened. I liked Mr. Errol very much. We were friends. He used to come here all the time and we'd trade stories. I know where he comes from..." he trailed off and wiped his face with a red bandana.

"Did you notice anything about him, his voice, the boat?" I ask, finally.

"Well, we didn't have a long exchange, you see. There was another person on the boat. It was dark and I couldn't see who it was and..."

"There was someone else with Errol on the boat?" I ask incredulously.

Chapter 15
March 15

I've spent the morning in my office writing on my whiteboard. No one came in, but I kept the door shut just in case. There are surprisingly few emails today. The halls outside my office are quiet. I need to think. There is a big question mark in the middle of my white board. Shooting off from this symbol are lines leading to circles. In each circle is a question: When? Where? Why? How? Who? Shooting off from each circle are other lines, some of them connecting together into a series of squares. Each square contains a list. My thoughts that might answer the fundamental questions. It's a mind map. I learned about this technique in my MBA program, when I took a class on creativity in business. But I've never applied it to anything so serious. Like a murder.

Everything has changed. It's no longer speculation. *Errol was killed by whoever was in the boat. And, whoever that was, stopped Errol from getting me a cure for my father. I WILL find out who did this.*

I tell no one of my discovery of a second person on the boat. Everyone is a suspect. My colleagues' names are on my whiteboard under "Who." I hear a noise in the hallway outside my door. The handle turns. I jump up, not wanting anyone to see my whiteboard. It's Gigi. "Can I talk to you?" she asks wearily. "I'm so tired."

"I'm tired too," I answer, standing in the doorway and blocking her from entering.

"We're all dazed," she tells me, reaching out as if she wants to pat my arm. She looks at me for a long moment like she wants to say something. Her skin is white and drawn. Then she shakes her head and shrugs her shoulders. "Never mind. I'm going home. I can't do this."

She smiles a tight smile and then closes my door with a click.

I walk around to Jim's office. He's not there. Neither is Matt. Quixotic feels ghostly. I peek in the lab on my way back to my office. It's empty. I return to my office and close the door. The sound reverberates in the emptiness of the building.

I call Straler and leave voicemail to call me back. Then I get to work transferring what's on my whiteboard to my note pad.

I don't know where the day has gone, but I glance up and it's dark outside my window. I check the time on my phone: 10 p.m. No return call from the detective.

My thoughts wander. *Did I do the right thing not telling anyone when I first found out about my father?*

. . . .

18 months earlier

The positive results from our Phase IIA and B trials for HD66 were supposed to make our Series B financing go smoothly. At least, that was how it was supposed to work. So why was it taking so long? "Oh, there is always lots of drama around financing," Gigi told me. "It's much harder than anyone realizes." In preparation for an investor presentation, she had asked me to draw a flow chart of the clinical trials for HD66 on the large whiteboard in the back conference room. I drew three big boxes: Phase I, Phase II – broken into two smaller boxes for Phase IIA and B – and then Phase III. Gigi wanted me to add dollar figures to each box. How much did each stage cost?

I remember stepping up to the board and drew a red circle around Phase IIB. No one would know the meaning behind the circle. I had just found out about my dad having HD. The shock of my dad having HD and me being in a startup bringing to market a drug that could cure him consumed me for weeks. The timing was off – to get him into the trial that we were doing – Phase IIB. It was too late. If I had known a few weeks earlier, could I have gotten him into the trial? *Could I have saved him?*

"What does it take to get someone in the trial?" I had asked Gigi after that fateful Thanksgiving.

"Oh," she told me, "A bunch of paperwork and protocol. It's all about the PI," she continued. By PI, she meant principal investigator of the trial, the doctor who manages it. A trial could have multiple PIs, which meant that they were testing the drug on their patients – with their consent, of course. "We recruited our PIs through Errol's network," she added.

The next day, I ran into Errol, "What does it take to get a doctor in your trial? Do you have anyone from Baystate?" I asked innocently. "Like, you know, assuming that you know folks from home…" Baystate is the hospital near Amherst.

"Nah, we didn't go outside of the majors," he replied. He saw my questioning look, "Like Harvard, and a few of the big hospitals. Baystate could be considered for Phase III," he said matter-of-factly. As he headed off down the hall, he added, "Especially if we know anyone from home that has Huntington's." I am pretty sure that he did not look back and see the shock on my face.

It was too late for my dad and the Phase II trials. But it wouldn't be next time, I'd promised myself. Little did I know how impossible that would be.

We were raising money now to bide time to land a strategic partnership with a large pharmaceutical company that had the resources to take our drug through a Phase III clinical trial. I wrote the figure "$30 million" under the Phase III box on the whiteboard. I put a blue star above the words. Even with a $60 million Series B institutional round, we wouldn't be able to do that on our own. We would need a partner. I was frustrated by how long the funding round was taking. I had told no one about his condition, not yet. Not even Neal. There was no point until I had a plan.

. . . .

My office phone rings, jarring me back to reality. It must be Straler. "Hello?" I query. "Thanks for calling. I have something to tell you."

"Me too, Brie. I glad you still there." The voice pauses. "Hello, Brie? You there?"

"Who is this?" I ask, flustered.

"Dis is Boris. Can I see you? I have something to tell you. Is important," he adds. I don't know what to say. "Don't worry, Brie. I am not murderer. I not harm you."

How does he know that I might be thinking about a murder? He's come right out and said that he is not "the" murderer. Do I believe him? "OK," I say, after a pause. "But not here."

I hear him chuckle a low, foreign-sounding laugh. "Yes, I know dat. Ritter's Diner on Baum. It open late."

"Yes, I know Ritter's," I tell him, having been to this local legend diner several times. While some call it "Critters," I appreciate that it's not that far away, that the parking lot is well lit. My stomach is growling, and I realize I haven't eaten all day. "Give me 20 minutes."

There is that laugh again. "I already here. Booth at back, near corner." I feel like asking which corner, since the restaurant is an L shape and there are booths in three out of the four corners. But I realize that it's moot; I'll see him when I enter the front door. "You want coffee black or white?" he asks with another chuckle.

"Cream, please," I reply.

"Thought so," he starts, and I don't wait for the next chuckle before I hang up.

. . . .

In the diner, Boris is sitting at the back corner on the long part of the L, where the window looks out onto the street, so he must have seen me walk up the sidewalk from the parking lot in the back. There is a cup of steaming coffee on my placemat, next to a small pitcher of cream and a spoon on a napkin. Boris looks up and smiles. Crooked teeth. No chuckle. "Thank you for coming," he says. "I not know who to talk to," he pauses and stirs his own coffee, which is deep black. I see a pile of empty sugar packets next to his cup. His phone is on the table. "These Popov guys," he begins. "They very bad people."

I remember Boris introduced us to the Russian venture capital firm. Of all the VC firms that I had to research for our funding round, Popov Brothers from Moscow had made me the most uncomfortable. "Is Popov the same family as the vodka?" I asked Gigi once as she walked into my office, snapped up a document from my desk, and plopped her pert fanny down on my loveseat.

"No," she replied, like she was talking to a child. "It's just their name. No connection to vodka. Although I might enjoy that," Gigi snorted.

"Damn Popov. They're not even related to vodka," Errol said dismissively as he swept by my office door, trailing his long arm through the door jamb.

"Be quiet, Errol," Gigi said arching her eyebrows at me. "We know that YOU love vodka." She smiled at me, her dark eyes dancing. "Popov isn't even Russian vodka. It's English," she quipped, curling her upper lip.

The next day, I saw Boris in the kitchen, making coffee. He must have known I'd been asking about Popov.

Without asking, he assured me, "They will be investing. They like Parkinson's program."

I had asked, "How do they even know about that? You know Errol hasn't even, well we don't have... Anyway, how do you know they will invest? Why are they so interested in Parkinson's? WE are focused on Huntington's. We need the investment for the Phase III trial." Boris had stared at me, big blue unblinking eyes. Then he wheeled and stalked off towards the lab. He forgot his coffee.

When I mentioned the interchange to Jim he laughed it off. "These Russians; they're like the Mafia — they all know each other. Nothing to worry about. I think he's right, by the way. They seem very keen to be in the round."

"But are they interested in Parkinson's or HD? We're not going to slow down our HD efforts, are we? You know I hear a lot of stories about corruption in Russia. Maybe we should..."

"Oh, money is money. We just need to get it in the door. And don't worry; we'll still move forward with HD. But we need other potential drug candidates too. It lowers the risk for investors to have multiple programs."

Jim is right. Even so, I'm concerned. Popov Brothers is thousands of miles away, and something about them just doesn't seem right.

Gigi didn't seem troubled either when I told her. "You know, they seem much more interested in Parkinson's than HD. They talked to Matt about some sidebar agreements to accelerate development in Parkinson's."

"Don't worry." she admonished with a sniff of her perky nose. "I'm on top of them."

"But they're so secretive. It's like they don't want us to really know them, to know what they do, or who they do it with."

"Hmph," Gigi retorted. "It's good for us that they're that interested," she said. "Who cares if it's HD, Parkinson's, or another condition? It's money that we need. We're a startup, right? We need money to survive." She flounced away with a dismissive wave of her hand.

My background research on Popov had proved to be a challenging task. The firm consisted of three brothers, although we have dealt with only two of them. Alexei seems to be the only one who speaks English, but Grigorii had also been on the calls. They were constantly talking to each other – in Russian. I found Alexei hard to understand. "It isn't only his accent, it's his attitude," I told Jim after one of the calls. "As an investment firm, they seem experienced, but they're obscure. I can't find what companies they've invested in. There's no information on them. I can't figure out what industries they prefer. Their website gives me nothing except short biographies with no specifics. I've searched and searched, and I find nothing."

They told us during our third call, after a lot of emails and documents passing back and forth, that they were in for $3 million. I knew that we would take their money. It would help get us to the final clinical trial.

Boris brings me back to the present. "Popov, they very bad. Errol, he knew how bad."

I remember how adamant Errol was that he didn't want them as investors. "Did Errol know them from before?"

"Yes, that is so. Not from me. This was before me. But he know them, yes." Boris tells me about his dealings with the firm. With the principals. I can tell that he both fears and hates them. Apparently, Popov has a vast network of pharmaceutical drug representatives. I don't understand the finer details of the Russian economy, but I gather from Boris' story that there's a lot of corporate pillaging and graft. The companies, the reps, as they are called, and the purchasing folks in the hospitals all receive money that ranges from bribes to over-pricing. There is no transparency. Everyone is on the take. Popov Brothers feature largely in this ecosystem. Apparently, wherever there is a need in hospitals, clinics and practices for drugs, Popov is involved. They have an acute interest recently in drugs relating to Parkinson's. Boris doesn't know why that is. He tells me that they knew about Errol's work. They wanted access to a Parkinson's drug. They wanted to distribute it in Russia. *Was Errol standing in their way?*

Boris pauses. I can tell that he wants to say something, but waits while the waitress – Ethyl, who has been at Ritter's a hundred years and probably owns the place – pours steaming coffee into our cups. He resumes his story as Ethyl walks away. "Popov tried license Errol's Parkinson drug direct from university. They not welcomed there. But they tried anyway."

"You mean that they wanted to license the Parkinson's drug out from under Errol? I ask. "And us, at Quixotic? I'm not even sure it was a drug – yet. Errol told me he hadn't..."

Boris chuckles. I gather from what he said next that their scheme didn't work, so they wanted Errol to license the Parkinson's drug into Quixotic where Errol could finish developing it. Then they could license it out, for a fee of course. What they didn't figure was that Errol would not play ball. By the time they realized that, they were already investors. They had been looking for a cure to Parkinson's for some time. Errol's work was the most promising. *Did they know that we really didn't have anything for*

Parkinson's yet? That Errol was still working on it? Didn't they care about our almost-certain cure for Huntington's?

Boris keeps silent for a few minutes. I had ordered French toast, which came loaded with butter, a side of bacon, and a large pitcher of syrup. Full of high fructose corn syrup, I'm sure, but, glancing at my phone, it was 1 a.m., and I didn't care. Boris watches while I munch. My mind is going a hundred miles an hour. If Popov Brothers are as devious and scary as Boris intimates, then they could have killed Errol to get him out of the way, so that they would have a clear path to get what they wanted.

"OK, Boris, I get the picture," I tell him as I sop up the last of the French toast with leftover syrup. This is huge. But I still am confused. "Why are you telling me?" I ask, genuinely wondering, why me.

Boris slurps his coffee noisily and gestures impatiently to Ethyl for more. I wait, fork paused. Syrup drips slowly onto my plate making small pools. "Errol, he gave me the job. He knows my skills. When I send him my resume, he called me. Errol gave me the chance in the U.S. I am grateful, thankful for this man to have done this for me."

"Wow, Boris, that's great – for you. But, can I ask, why me? Why are you telling me and not someone...?" I ask, stirring the pools of syrup with my now-empty fork.

He takes a big gulp of coffee. "You found me in office that night, morning really it was, and I, thinking to myself, you might think I killed him – Errol. I wet, Errol die on river. You put two and two together – you get five. I know these things. How mind works." He looks at me intently. His clear blue eyes look troubled. "I did not kill Errol. I owed him. I wish I could have..." He puts more sugar into his coffee even though it's half gone and stirs.

"I tell you because you wondering how-why this happened. You are the person, Brie. I trust you."

I am honored by his words. I pause and sip my coffee, which is cold. Boris waves his hand at Ethyl and points at my cup. Burnt coffee a minute later. I ask, daring to lift the cup to my lips. "Why were you wet, Boris?"

"Rain." That's all he says.

In a heartbeat I realize that he is telling the truth. And he just told me who killed Errol. "What now?"

"I leave for California tomorrow, umm today," he announces glancing at his phone. "I will not stay here. But I give you this," and he hands me a folded scrap of paper. "It my cell number," he says. "Not known." He pauses. "Not to them. To nobody. Just in case."

I glance at the phone in his hand. Brand new. Holy crap, Boris is leaving. He just told me who murdered Errol, and now he is leaving? "Boris, I..."

But he is already standing. He puts a finger to his lips and dons a beat-up leather jacket. "Brie, I sorry to do this, but I will not leave without telling you. You are smart," he says with a smile. There is that chuckle again. It gets louder instead of softer as he makes his way out the door. A few minutes later I hear a motorcycle rev up, and I see him zoom past the window.

Will he get a helmet by the time he arrives in California, I wonder? How the heck will I explain this to Jim?

My cellphone buzzes. It must be Boris. "Boris," I say into it, "Look..."

"Who's Boris?" Neal asks.

"Oh, sorry, honey," I say. "That's someone at work, you know, one of the scientists, with Errol. You remember, I've mentioned him to you. The Russian who works for, worked for, Errol."

There is silence on the other end. "Where are you?" he asks hesitantly.

"Ritter's. I'm just wrapping up." The line goes dead. *He doesn't trust me.*

My phone buzzes again. "Neal, I'm coming home. Don't be…"

"Neal? I'm sorry. This is Detective Straler Henrik. Do I have the right phone number for Brie Prince?"

Chapter 16
July 20, three years before the incident

Shala looked around the lab. Furtively, she opened the door into the hallway, and peered right and left. No one. She moved to the computer and logged in.

Dearest sister,

I have been so lonely and missing you. But I have done something to make me forget that I am missing you. This will make you laugh. I am in a rowing club. Ha ha! I wish that I could see your face as you read this. Are you not amazed?

You cannot imagine how much fun this is. We go out on the river. In boats! We all row with long wooden oars. Very fun! Ha! Can you imagine, we have so much water here in Pittsburgh? Three rivers! Another rower told me that there is even a fourth river running under the ground! You cannot see it, but it is there. So much water here.

Ha! I am now strong from rowing. Imagine, your sister rowing a boat on a river! Is very much fun and I wish that you could see me on the river. You would laugh and I would laugh, and we would know that only in America can we be having so much water that we can be rowing all the time! Ha!

I am thinking of you in my thoughts.
Your happy now sister,
Shala

Chapter 17
March 17

I'm late getting into the office the next Monday. My thumb hurts from cutting myself making a salad to bring for lunch. Rubbing my clumsy bandage, I review my game plan. I still haven't told anyone about the second person on the boat. When Straler called last night we talked about Boris. I was really late getting home and Neal wasn't speaking to me. He left in a huff this morning. *Although he made me coffee, so he can't be that upset.*

The voicemail from Errol is another secret. I know that it's a cure. *I have to find the killer to find it.*

I email Matt, Jim, and Gigi for a huddle in the small conference room. "It's important," I write. I text Straler.

"What's up?" Matt asks as he takes his seat at the head of the table.

All eyes turn toward me. I dial Straler's number, explaining that he needs to listen in. I gulp and begin. I tell them about Boris and what he told me about Popov. "I think that they killed Errol," I conclude.

Straler talks through the speaker phone, "If we're right – that it's **H** – then our department would be willing to entertain any information or leads you might provide. We do appreciate that you have information beyond what we can access," Straler says, speaking what had to be the uniform language of cops and detectives – his newness to the force mitigating his excitement. "The Popovs are definitely persons of interest."

"If this is true, I wonder how they," but Matt doesn't have time to ask the question.

I interrupt by handing out a sheet of paper to each of them. "Straler, you have this by email. This is my suggested bullet point list of how we should proceed." I explain my logic: "Look, they are not from here, they don't know the U.S. or our ways. We want to be very careful that we don't reveal anything on our side. We let them do the talking." I nod at Jim who smiles at me with one eyebrow cocked.

"Do you agree with this approach, Henrik?" Matt asks into the phone, glancing at me with a frown. Gigi stares darkly at me.

"Yes, completely," Straler agrees. "We want to judge their reaction. Step by step. As a detective, I want to proceed slowly but thoroughly. Have you let them know anything about Errol? Do they know that he has died even?"

"No," I respond. We wrote something but never sent it out."

"We wanted to wait until this phase is over," Jim said quietly, looking at Matt.

"So, for the Russians, no accusations, no tipping our hand that we suspect them," I finish.

"We have to tell them that he's dead," Matt states evenly, "but we don't need to... what's the term? Cast aspersions?"

"That's right," I say. "Let's just say that there has been an accident and let them ask questions. Only tell them what they need to know." Jim gives me a tight smile, both eyebrows raised – does he think I'm too involved with this, that as a marketing executive I have no role here? I glance at Matt, "Not any more than they need to know."

"OK, Miss Sleuth, you're on," Matt replies.

I check my email on my phone. "There's a response from Popov." I had emailed them yesterday about a call this morning. "10 a.m. our time. That gives us a little over 30 minutes."

Matt's face tightens. "Tell everyone to meet in the conference room just before 10."

"I'll be there," says Straler and signs off.

Left alone, I toy with my notepad as I think through the different scenarios. Why would Popov want Errol dead? What would that accomplish? It only makes sense if Errol was in their way of getting something. What could that be? They wanted something from him. Did Errol say no? If he disappeared would they get it? Errol had something for me, but I can't find it because he's dead. Why would it be different for Popov? Even if they did get something once Errol was out of the way, what good would it do unless it was finished? Did Errol have something that was worth his death? Worth killing for? My phone buzzes. I'd set the alarm. 9:55 a.m.

Jim, Gigi, and Matt stand uncomfortably in the conference room. Matt motions for me to move and sit at the head of the table. He takes a seat on the side. Gigi looks at him with a frown.

Straler shows up a few minutes later, slightly out of breath. "Thanks for waiting." He nods to us, and signals to Jim that he doesn't need a chair. "We ready?" Straler asks.

"Yes," Jim replies. "Since Brie contacted them, we want her voice to be the first that they hear."

I hand out revised copies of the briefing document. Straler looks my way and smiles. I ignore the little flutter in my stomach. Nerves, that's all it is, I tell myself.

At precisely 10 o'clock I dial the international number. Alexei's secretary, Marina, picks up. "Oh yes, Brie, Alexei and his brother Grigorii are awaiting your call. I transfer you."

A few clicks later Alexei booms into the phone, "Hello Quixotic, Miss Brianna. Who do we have on your end?"

I want to correct him, tell him, "it's Brie, like the cheese, not Brianna," but I can't bring that up now. "Hello Mr. Popov. Jim, Gigi and Matt are here. I'm putting you on speaker phone." I pushed the orange button and nod to Jim.

"Alexei? Jim Reichert here. How are things in Moscow?"

"Peachy," Alexei replies. "We are fine. What is new with you and why this urgent call?"

"We have some news on our end. Important news." Jim pauses, a bit too long, before continuing. "Alexei, I have bad news." I can hear Russian on the other end. Swearing perhaps?

"It's not about the Parkinson's is it? You know we are very interested," he hastily adds. "We have plans. But we can wait; you know we Russians have much patience." I hear what sounds like laughter in the background.

"No, it's not about the Parkinson's drug. You know, of course, that Errol was working on that in his Centre lab, and we have taken the necessary steps to secure the asset through an exclusive option." He pauses.

"That would convert to an exclusive license for the new indication," Matt clarifies. "For Quixotic. Any dealings about that drug would have to go through us. I think you know this, but I want to be clear," Matt finishes firmly.

"Good, very good," Alexei says. "Of course we know this when we invest." I hear a deep-throated chuckle. "It makes investment more possible."

My mouth drops open; I can't help it. I hear more Russian on the other end, then a booming laugh. Then he clears his throat and in a more commanding voice says, "We read about NGX and HD cancelling. This not good for Quixotic. Investors are not happy. Things go wrong, eh? But now clear way to focus on Parkinson's, eh? We can help. Is this why you call?" More Russian in the background, voices rising, laughter booming in the background.

I think of Boris; where is he by now? Indiana, maybe? I shudder. I have read the Russians, Tolstoy, Dostoevsky, and Turgenev. I am fascinated by the histrionics depicted by the authors – the men weep, laugh, swear, and kill, all within the scope of a single page. We've gone from laughter to criticism to intimation. Could they have gone as far as murder?

"No Alexei, this is not about Parkinson's and it's not about HD66. It's about Errol." Matt pauses as if gathering strength. Gigi strokes her arm; Jim blinks. "Alexei, there's been an accident. It's Errol." I hold my breath. I don't want anyone to say anything. This is a crucial moment. I look at Straler. He is leaning forward, his forehead furrowed to listen. Would they tip their hand?

"My got," Alexei breathes into the phone. "Errol? What has happened? Is he alright? Where is he? Can we send flowers?" I hear more Russian. There are several voices. Shouting. Sounds like arguing. Damn that Boris isn't here. "Please tell me and my brothers, what has happened? Is he OK?"

There is a long pause while Matt gathers his wits. "No, he is not OK. Not at all OK." Matt tells them that Errol is dead. We hear a gasp. Then more shouting in the background. Is he translating what we say for the other brothers? Matt continues, "Alexei, we are wondering if you have had any contact with him in the last few weeks?" There is a huge silence. We hold our breaths.

"My got," Alexei chokes. He sounds genuinely shocked. "I am so sorry; we are so sorry. I not know what to say," he fumbles.

"I'm sorry that we didn't let you know earlier," Jim states. "Quite frankly, we've all been in shock and we are only starting now to get the word out."

"This is terrible. I am so sad. We have differences, Errol and us, but we are friends, like true Russians. We mourn for him and family." I hear a muffled sound. Is Alexei crying?

I can't remember the rest of the conversation. All I know is that if they killed Errol or ordered him killed they are fantastic actors. But we only heard from Alexei. I think of Boris and his obvious fear, so great that he had to leave town. And all that Russian being spoken in the background. Who knows what was being said?

I glance at Straler. He is scribbling in his notebook. He looks at me and smiles broadly. His eyes twinkle. He's having fun, I realize.

. . . .

"What you probably don't know about detective work," Straler says, into his third cup of coffee that afternoon at Ritter's, "what I have learned – through training, mind you – is that it is never, and I mean N-E-V-E-R," he says spelling out the word, "the first suspect who is the killer. That's Detective 101."

Clearly I am a neophyte. But someone has to say it. "Detective," I start. "They might not…"

"Look, Brie," he interrupts, "You know that I'm new at this too. I'm leveling with you. I didn't know. I really didn't. It was a good try. I really wanted it to be them. To prove the saying wrong, you know. Hey, they'd probably have my badge if they knew what I just said. But I appreciate your help. I can't solve it on my own. You were the one to finger the Popovs. I wouldn't have known. You're trying; you're helping. That's good." He pauses and I see a pink flush on his cheeks. "You've got guts, Brie.

You've already gotten further than I did. Together, we make a great team." He smiles, his eyes crinkling. They are a crystal clear blue.

"We aren't ruling them out," he says, and brings out a little book and pen. "I brought my own, today." He clears his throat. "99% of this process is instincts. Yours are obviously strong, and I believe in that." He smiles again.

I ignore the flutters.

"My boss warned me earlier; it's usually getting stuck on the wrong guy – or gal – that proves the problem." He looks at me and smiles as he takes a sloppy gulp of coffee. "So, we're not crossing them off of our list. Not yet. Just that we have to examine all angles. Right now, my investigation will stay neutral."

OK, I think, taking the last bite of my donut. If this keeps on, I'll gain weight.

But Straler is not done. He takes a slurp of his coffee and flips to a new page of his notebook. "Let's talk about some other possibilities," he begins. "Starting with who could have been with Errol on the boat."

I know that I look shocked. "I do my homework too, you know," he says with a chuckle.

. . . .

Walking back to the office, I wonder about my conversation with Straler. Popov Brothers could be the killer, but Straler encouraged me to trust my instincts, and they screamed at me during the call that Alexei was genuinely shocked and distressed. We really don't know Grigorii so he's an unknown, and, therefore, not above suspicion. There's also a third Popov brother. The one that Boris knew. Speaking of which, Boris is not above suspicion either. They're all still on my list along with Gigi, Jim, Matt, and even Amy

I think about the other investors, how Errol was not happy about the VCs. I didn't like Jeb Brooks from Sanguine. He was dismissive and arrogant. He couldn't even remember my name, even after I told him, "It's Brie, like the cheese." I remember driving him from the airport when he came that first time. He wouldn't look up from his cellphone, like he was super important and I was super not. He didn't react as we emerged out of the tunnel to the glorious view of downtown. He didn't say a word when I pointed out the three rivers, even when I mentioned that there was a fourth river that ran underground. Usually people are interested in the Pittsburgh story. Outsiders coming to Pittsburgh for the first time have no idea what to expect. Most know about the steel heritage and the decimation of the industry – Pittsburgh as the center of the rust belt. But Pittsburgh has emerged from its smoky, dark days of the past to become the best little city in America. "Rust built," Errol called it. And Errol was right; VCs are jerks.

The others seemed to not care. Jeb invested $5 million. One of their partners had a mother with HD. Did he get the test, I wonder? I wasn't able to find out. Errol did a funny parody of Jeb and his relationship to his phone, I remember. We had all laughed at his antics. Is Jeb on the list? They all are. *We're on the list too.*

I was disturbed by Straler's questions at Ritters about Errol's students. I'm embarrassed at my outburst. "That's ridiculous," I snapped. "They're his students. They love him; I've met them; they worship Errol, um worshipped. They cried at his memorial service. No, we're going too far now. If Errol knew that we suspected his students, he'd go ballistic."

"How well do you know them?" Straler queried.

I didn't respond. *How well did I really know anything or anyone?*

"Look, you're probably right," the detective admitted. "But we have to investigate all angles. I'm going to pay them a visit tomorrow. Unannounced."

I didn't agree right away, but he encouraged me, "Brie, you know them. You know a lot more about Errol than I do. They'll be more comfortable if you come. It'll really help. It'll help me." He smiled. *Who could resist?*

. . . .

That night I sit at my kitchen table with a half bottle left of Merlot. Could the killer really be one of his students? I think of lovely, warm Shala Mukerjee. Errol had introduced me to his post-doc some time ago when he invited me to visit his lab. "Shala," I said and extended my hand. Shyly, she gave me a light handshake. "What a beautiful name," I had said, giving her hand a slight squeeze. Her smile lit up her face. Since then, I have grown to love her heavy accent and lilting voice. She has gorgeous thick black hair almost down to her waist. I doubt she knows how beautiful she is. She's usually dressed in a baggy t-shirt and jeans. We've met a couple of times for coffee since then. She's sweet and kind, and she was proud of her work in the lab.

She introduced me to Errol's other students. "Brie, this is Yahya Kazmi."

"Hello Miss Brie," he said politely with a thick accent and a cold look. He must be Middle Eastern, but I'm not sure from exactly where. He did not put his hand out to shake. I dropped mine.

"Very pleased to meet you, Yahya."

A young man stood next to Yahya. "This is Patrick," Shala told me. "He's new."

"Hello Patrick. I'm Brie."

"Hallo," he said. I couldn't place his accent, but it was obviously somewhere where English is spoken. Scotland, maybe? Australia? "Nope; the north," he guessed my thoughts. "Northern Ireland. You know where that is?" he asked, and pointed to what I assumed was north. His accent was lyrical but nasal, very Irish, now that I heard it clearly.

"Yes I do," I answered, taken aback. "I've been there, actually."

"Ach, you must be one in a million, 40 million actually, who call themselves Irish in America. You know, we've only five million total in all of Ireland: one and a half million in the North; three and then some in the South. But only a few know that there even is a North. So we feel very small indeed." He smiled, but his eyes were angry.

Errol had interrupted then, shaking his head, "Guys?" I remember that the three students turned simultaneously to look at him. He gestured to them. "Back to work, eh?" They nodded in unison. They looked like his beagle, totally devoted and loyal. *Disgusting.*

I pour another glass of wine and contemplate the journey of a startup.

Chapter 18

May 3, one year before the incident

"Damn! To hell with this!" Errol exploded in his university lab. "We're getting nowhere trying to find a Parkinson's drug. Take a break. All of you, go home. We'll reconvene in the morning. I'll work on it tonight. See what I can figure out." Errol dismissed his students with a wild wave.

"Oh, Dr. Errol, I am so sorry. I know that I have made mistake. Please..."

"Out now!" Errol commanded. "Mistake or no, I'm going to fix what I just saw happen here."

Yayha looked at Errol with a dark scowl. Patrick shrugged his shoulders. Shala's hands shook as she gathered her things.

"Come back in the morning. We'll see what we have by then." Errol almost pushed them out the door and turned his back as they left. As the students hustled down the hall, Errol got out his lab notebook to record what happened. He looked at what he had just written:

"We killed the mouse. Instantly. A complete failure."

How could we be so far off? Errol glanced up at the clock. It was 10 p.m. He called Amy.

"Hi, babe. What's up?"

"I'm at the university lab. What are you up to?"

"Oh, I'm having a quiet night. The kids are reading. I'm in bed. What's going on?"

"I'm having trouble with one of my experiments. It might be a long night."

"Wow, that's a first," she said, chuckling.

"OK. Sorry, but I just can't let it go."

Amy yawned, "I know, Errol. Don't jingle the bells when you come in. I have a big day tomorrow. It's a $50 million ask."

"Big fish on the line, huh?"

"You could call it that. I gather that you are still fishing?"

I can't seem to find the fish anymore.

. . . .

8 a.m. the next day

Shala opened the lab door. "Oh, Dr. Errol," she said, obviously surprised to see that he was still there.

"Didn't mean to startle you," he responded. "And sorry about exploding last night. I was just frustrated. I have something for you all to see. We'll wait for the others." Shala dutifully got out her notebook to record whatever it was that Errol would show them.

They heard shouting in a guttural foreign tongue and then Yahya yanked open the door holding his cellphone to his ear. He stopped shouting abruptly when he saw Shala and Errol. He said nothing, cutting off the call without another word and slinking into a corner to take off his coat and backpack.

Errol knew that Yahya was from Syria, but he didn't know much else about him. Yahya never said much. Errol felt sorry for him, knowing that things were really bad in Syria. He had read how the people's revolution had been co-opted by those with political agendas. It had become a flat-out war with extremists on both sides and no signs of an end. Errol had noticed that recently Yahya seemed distant. He had been taking time off for long weekends. Normally, he didn't question his students about what they did with their time. As long as the lab ran smoothly, the experiments were done correctly, and the science was advanced, he let them be.

Patrick was the last to arrive. Seeing the others, he immediately launched into a rapid-fire excuse, "Sorry, got detained by a bomb in the subway. All the officials saying it was Johnny's work, but I know that it was Sean's. You see, a Sean bomb is…" he stopped talking long enough to see that Shala was staring at him in horror, and Yahya looked like he might jump him. "Hey slow down the crew," Patrick said. "No offense here. Just joking an' all. You know there is no subway here…"

"OK, guys, we've got serious business to do. I've got something to show you. Shala, I don't know what you've done, but you're not going to believe this." He gazed at them with a professorial air. "You know that we start with low doses, anticipating potentially negative effects?" They nod. "And, of course, if that happens, we continue to lower the dose?" They nod again. "Watch, lady and gentlemen." Opening a small cage with a flourish, Errol extracted a mouse. Picking up a small syringe he injected the mouse. Within seconds, the mouse began to gasp, its little mouth opening and closing, then its body began to spasm. It was all over.

"Holy shite!" Patrick exclaimed.

"Yep, that's my reaction exactly. Holy shit indeed." Errol peered at his students over his glasses. "That was 100 microlitres."

Shala added, "And five seconds, Dr. Errol."

"It's a killer," announced Yahya, looking at the dead mouse on the benchtop. Shala retrieved the body and lowered him gently into the animal disposal container.

"Lower the dose," Errol commanded. "By one half."

"50 microlitres," Patrick stated as he squeezed the dropper. Seconds passed. "Holy crap, again!" Patrick yelped.

"Killer," Yahya said quietly. They stood for a moment, silent in the shock of what was happening. Shala picked up the second dead mouse with a grimace.

"Lower the dose," Errol commanded again. "The same, by one half."

"25 microlitres," Patrick announced loudly.

"Why is it doing this?" Shala asked. "We have many dead mouse."

"Not sure," Errol told them honestly. "I was as surprised as you."

"You always tell us that science is not a science but an art; I see that this is what you mean now, Doctor Errol."

Errol frowned and balled his fists. "This is not art," he barked. "This is a mistake!"

"Oh, Dr. Errol, I am so sorry," Shala began. "I must have mistaken…"

"Not now, Shala. We have to focus on what we are doing wrong. TO FIX THIS," he shouted. Shala dropped her head, Yahya glared, Patrick turned white. "LOWER THE DAMN DOSE!"

"12.5 microlitres," Patrick whispered. "Shite, it's doin' it again. Is there no limit, no amount small enough?"

Yahya's dark eyes burned. "It's a killer."

Shala didn't look up as once again she lifted the dead mouse. "Oh, Dr. Errol, this no drug here, I am so sorry, I change…"

Errol took the mouse from Shala and held it up turning to face the three of them. "Look, I've been working all night on this. The same thing over and over. Nothing changes, no matter how small the dose. It's just a failure, that's all. This won't cure a damn thing."

Yahya mutterd, "A killer."

Patrick looked at him and laughed a deep, nasty sound, "Failure? Ha! Not if you're looking for a weapon of mass destruction, a WMD, I believe you call it."

"What the?!" Errol shouted. "You think this is a joke? This could be the end of the line, you nitwits. This isn't a fundable invention. This isn't a viable path we're going down! You may all have to abandon this lab and go home if we can't figure out what we are doing wrong!"

Patrick and Shala looked shocked, but Yahya glared angrily at Errol, who continued his diatribe. "Look, something is terribly, terribly wrong. I can't stay right now. I have patients to see and a few things to do at Quixotic. You guys have to turn this around. It's important. We cannot fail. We cannot lose the fight!"

With that he stalked out and slammed the lab door. As Errol stormed to the bike rack, he thought about what had happened. *Is death by invisible small doses a huge mistake? Or a discovery?* An idea began to take shape.

. . . .

3 a.m. the next morning

The university lab was empty except for him. Errol had sent everyone home – again. He couldn't believe the series of events that had led to this moment. He was appalled that they had failed so miserably. *How is this possible?* Errol reviewed what happened as he wrote in his lab notebook: "Have achieved LD50." The abbreviation was for "Lethal Dose, 50%," or median lethal dose. It is the amount of a substance required, usually per body weight, to kill 50% of the test population. "We've killed 100% so far. No matter how small the dose. Tried picolitres, even femtolitres. All efforts have failed. The treatment is a failure as a drug for the brain. A complete and utter failure. Like me."

Errol stared at the page, noodling as he thought. Could a highly lethal death injection be of any use? Maybe I should think about this discovery differently? The others are about disease. This is not. Until now, my inventions have been to save life, to make it better. But this is not a life-saving device; it's a killer. What to do with it? Certainly not as part of Quixotic. It doesn't fit. Does it have any value? Probably. Somewhere, not in my world. Who would want a death agent? What would it be worth? The opposite of the term for medical prescription, RX... Oh, that's perfect. It now has a name – DeathX.

He decided to keep quiet about this for a while. Above all, he didn't want anyone else finding out about it. Until he had a plan.

Note to self: *Remind students to keep this confidential. Keep lab book home for now. Just for safe keeping.*

Chapter 19
May 8, that same year

Dearest sister Pliya,

I am very worried. I think that I have done something wrong in the lab. Dr. Errol has told me this. We have experiment going very wrong. I cannot tell exactly, but I am making mistake and the mice are dying. They are not living. It is my fault. I am not synthesizing correctly the chemicals. If I am not smart enough to do experiments correctly then I will not be able to stay in the United States. Dr. Errol has told me that if I cannot fix the mistake he will not keep me in the lab. Then I will have to come home. And I would love to see you so much, my dear Pliya, but my heart will be broken from being sent home. I want to stay in the United States, so I work all night for three nights to fix my mistakes. I do not want the mice to die. This is sad and wrong. I am hoping that I do not write to you next with the date of my arriving at home. I am hoping and praying that I will fix my mistakes. And the mice will not die.

Please pray for me my darling sister as I pray for you every day of my life.

Your sister who is mistake making,
Shala

Chapter 20

Christmas, three years before the incident

"OK, I'm nearly packed!" I yell at Neal from the bedroom of my apartment. I go to the closet to get out my suitcase. "Two minutes."

"Great," Neal says. "I'll just help myself to a glass of scotch, OK?" I know he's ogling The Balvenie Scotch, which he had given me as a present. I had kept it for special occasions. Well, I tried. It was half gone I saw as Neal poured.

I take all of the articles I have accumulated about how to get a non-FDA approved drug to patients and stuff them into the bottom of my suitcase. I grab a few clothes. *Oh my, we're going skiing. Think, Brie. It will be cold.* I open my chest of drawers and throw in a few sweaters. *Where's my silk long underwear? Do I have ski pants? These old gloves will have to do. Shoot, these goggles are missing a strap.* I throw them all into the suitcase.

"Brie, honey. We have to go!"

"I know, I'm nearly ready." *Gosh, where is that pretty nightie? I'd better have one.* I throw a few other things into the suitcase and slam it shut. "I have to bring my computer, OK? I have to work some while we're there." I think about the research I am doing, hoping to find a way to get my dad our HD66 drug, pre-FDA approval and not part of a clinical trial. I found out too late for our Phase II clinical trials and too early for Phase III.

"I figured you would need to work some," Neal says as he walks into the bedroom and lugs my suitcase off of my bed. "Come on, honey. We have a plane to catch!"

We are heading to Vail. We ended up with Colorado because I didn't want to take the time off go to Europe, and it's a bit early for Canadian snow. It could be early for Vail too, but it's a charming village, even if the snow is not great. Plus, it's a direct flight. And we can spend a couple of days in Denver. I have cousins there, and I love the mile-high city. "The Denver Art Museum is top notch, Neal. I can't wait to show it to you." *It will be easy to connect to the Internet at their house. In case I need to do more research.*

"Can't wait to see it, Brie. With you." He gives me a long kiss.

"Hey, we have a whole week for that," I say, spying another article I had printed out. As he releases me, I grab it and stuff it into my purse.

"Yep, can't wait for that. Looking forward to it!" He looks at me with a lascivious grin. Today is actually Christmas. We elected to leave on the holiday itself to save money and to avoid the issue of where we would spend it – which family. Our plan was to stay at Vail through New Year's Day. Neal is splurging on a ski-in-ski-out condo. "This will be so special," Neal reminds me.

I am both dreading and looking forward to the trip. I have done nothing about getting myself tested for the huntingtin gene. I can't get any perspective. Finding out is permanent; once you know you carry a dreaded disease, there is no turning back. It will flavor the rest of my life. I am not up to that. Not yet. I reason with myself that I have actually decided – I WILL get tested. The question is when? In my darkest moments in the middle of the night I am consumed by the fear of being rejected because I carry a mutant gene. I don't think that Neal would drop me because I am defective. But it's scary just the same. I'm not ready to test it, to test him, to test us. I want it all to go away for a few days. I want to have fun in Vail, to postpone the inevitable. But I suspect what he wants to ask me… I shiver with excitement and dread.

"Come on, Brie, time to go!"

. . . .

Four days later, December 29

Little did I imagine what "postpone" meant. "It's never icy at Vail, not compared to East Coast skiing," I had assured Neal, as I took off down the slope on our first run. "Brie, wait," Neal had called after me. But it was too late. I have been on skis since I was five. You do that in New England. I'm no racer. I don't do moguls, but I can ski passably well, and I love the speed. But the conditions that day... I can excuse myself by saying that Colorado ice at 10,000 feet is not like Vermont ice, but it doesn't really help.

I broke my tibia they tell me at the hospital. After the X-rays, during the consultation, I hear the word "surgery" before I pass out. When I wake, Neal is there. He tells me that they had to install pins and plates in my leg. Titanium.

"The screws will outlive me," I grin at Neal. He looks so worried.

The crisis consumes us for three days. We had to rent a wheel chair upon leaving the hospital. I learn that you can't really access ski-in-and-ski-out unless you can climb stairs, ride the chair lift, and walk from the parking lot to the condo building. Neal talked to the manager of the resort and tried to change rooms, but it was too close to New Year's Eve and they were solidly booked. He had to carry me across the threshold. "Oh, honey, how romantic," I said as he staggered through the door, nearly dropping me.

On the couch, with a glass of Merlot in my hands and Percocet in my blood, I tell him to relax, that we can manage, but he is stressed. I have escaped a very difficult conversation, and he is way too busy tending to me to be romantic and propose. I know it's ridiculous to feel so relieved but I am. He catches me laughing to myself. "What on earth are you finding that is funny?" he demands.

"Don't worry, honey," I cover. "I was just imagining all of the jealous folks thinking that we are on the slopes, and little do they know..." And so it goes.

"Thank God the Quixotic office has an elevator," I chuckle. And then I think of what Errol will do when he sees me. He will be merciless, I think with a smile. I glance over at Neal. He is sound asleep on the recliner. I reach into the bag next to me and pull out the papers that I have been waiting to read.

Chapter 21
February 6, that same year

Snow flurries waft down from the gray skies of Pittsburgh. Winter has been settling in since early January – quietly, silently, but firmly. It seems like it will never end. My leg is healing, but slowly. I still have to use crutches. I sip my Peet's coffee and stare out of my kitchen window. The weather reminds me of "Beclouded," the Emily Dickenson poem we all learned in third grade because she wrote it in Amherst:

> The sky is low, the clouds are mean,
> A travelling flake of snow
> Across a barn or through a rut
> Debates if it will go.

So far, I have not come up with a strategy about my dad and HD66. I have to wait for the final clinical trial. I'm impatient. It's taking a long time to get there. Everyone thinks that startups move quickly, that everything happens in a rush. That's partially true. The sense of urgency in a startup is paramount. What most people don't know is that a startup is like anything else – it takes the time it takes. It's slow. *Like making a movie. Or writing your first book.*

Matt and Errol have just come back from an international conference on neurological diseases. They presented our data on HD66 – the positive results of the Phase IIA and IIB trials. That morning, at our on-the-same-page meeting, they told us what happened after they presented.

"Oh it was like Canadian geese landing after a long migration flight," Errol started. "There was a flurry of 'em, and they kept coming. Squawking and chattering, they all wanted to know who we had talked to, who we were talking to, and would we be interested in..." Errol starts acting like a goose and picks up my crutches waving them around like wings.

"We wowed them, it's that fucking simple." Matt stated. "Now we have their attention. Stan, prepare your playbook; we are going in!" Matt has one of my crutches and he thrusts it like a sword.

Stan laughs, "I've already started." He parries with the other crutch. The meeting goes on, and the mood is positive.

The next few months will be taken up with negotiating a deal with a big pharmaceutical company that has the resources to pay for the Phase III trials. The Phase III trial will have hundreds of HD patients who will be enrolled for a period of many months. *I want one of them to be my dad.*

Assuming HD66 comes through that trial, our theory is that we will be acquired. Everyone would make money, from our investors to us. And patients would finally have hope. I hear Clov from Beckett's *Endgame* in my head: "Finished, it's finished, nearly finished, it must be nearly finished." This is the game that entrepreneurs play – build value and exit. *Only it's not a game for me, my dad, and the thousands of patients with HD.*

Matt and Jim are talking to all of the major companies focused on neurodegenerative diseases. They'll be flying all over the world for these discussions, "Asia, Europe, Japan," I listed their itinerary to Gigi after I had made the flight arrangements.

"Wow, Brie, you made these awfully close together. Will they mind?" *No they won't mind. They'd do it even faster if they knew how desperate I was.*

"There's no one who doesn't know about Quixotic. The timing is right. This is tight, Brie, but it's good." Matt said when I delivered the travel documents to him. "You're right to hurry us up." *Little does he know.*

"What will happen is a bidding war between several companies," Jim told me when I explained their itinerary.

"Won't that take more time?"

"Of course. It will prolong the deal, but it will mean that we get the best one."

"Is there no way to do a deal quickly?"

"And why would we want to do that?" Gigi asked with a red-lipped smile. "This will be so much more fun!"

"What does Errol think?" I ask.

"Oh, he wants to hurry it up too," Matt said. He had been standing at the door. "Errol is really no help now. We're not taking him on these trips. He's fucking brilliant, but this is business. Plus his schedule makes it hard for him to travel."

"It's challenging for him to get away," Gigi remarked. "But not impossible..."

Hurry up and close a deal! I went back to my stack of papers. *Somewhere there has to be an alternative. I don't want to wait.*

. . . .
The following week, February 15

"Darn!" I throw down the article I was reading in disgust. *Another plan down the drain.* I couldn't slip my father the drug on the side. First of all, I didn't really have access to it. While I knew some basic things about the science of HD66, I didn't know my way around the lab. I didn't know the exact formula and, while I figured much of that was in the patent language, there was additional know-how that Errol had in his head. His lab technicians might know part of this, but it was unlikely that they would know all. That's why they call it a trade secret.

Secondly, giving my father the drug would be unethical. From my research I learned that it would jeopardize Errol's medical license. Without an Investigational New Drug Application to the FDA and Institutional Review Board oversight, neither of which we could get for a single patient, it would be unethical. Given his MD status, if a random patient were to receive the drug, and the authorities found out about it, he would be penalized. At least that's what I surmised from some cases in different diseases. The doctor associated with the case I had just read about had been prosecuted and prohibited from practicing medicine for the rest of his life. I couldn't risk that. *Errol would kill me.*

Even if I ignored those risks, and Errol agreed, it could blow our chances of FDA approval. "The notoriously fickle FDA," Errol told me, "holds the key to our future."

I know that, if we don't get FDA approval, our company would be toast. If I did this on the side I might wreck the path to value creation and exit. I could be sued by the shareholders. *They would all kill me.*

. . . .

The next day, February 16

"Oh my gosh!" The implication struck me like a lightning bolt. I jerk my leg in surprise and wince in pain as it bangs my desk as I read the tagline below the YouTube video I found as a result of my research.

"Compassionate use is a designation by the FDA whereby a patient can receive a drug that is not yet approved."

I pick up another article I had printed from my Google search and read:

The designation of compassionate use means a company with a new drug can treat a patient with a serious or immediately life-threatening disease who has no comparable or satisfactory alternative treatment options. Compassionate use is reserved for diseases for which there is no cure.

"HD fits the criteria of no cure," Jim tells me when I question him a few minutes later. "Why do you ask?" Jim looks at me quizzically, his fuzzy eyebrows furrowed.

I am careful how I phrase my reply, "Oh, you know, just thinking about patients."

Jim gives me a kind smile. Sometimes I think that Jim can see into my soul. I am not ready to tell him, not yet. Besides, Jim has not been around a lot lately. He has lost weight and looks pale. I don't want to bother him with my problems. "You're thinking of Errol's patients?"

"Of course. This would be good for them. And others."

"Hmmm, let me see what the others say," Jim ponders.

"We could give it to all of my patients!" As a seasoned investigator, Errol knew the tenets of compassionate use trials, but he had not considered it for HD66.

"Yes of course," Gigi admits. "But from a theoretical point of view. I hadn't actually considered it. For us, I mean. I don't have any direct experience, never knew anyone who's done this. Jim, did you know?"

"I've heard of this, read about it generally. It's not new. But no, I never realized that we could do this. Brie brought it up. Matt, what do you think?"

"What? Compassionate use? Fuck that. We can't do that. We have a company to run. That's a dead end street."

"What do you mean?" I ask.

"Stan will tell you best," Matt responds. "Hey, tall boy," he grabs Stan who had wandered by, probably having heard all of us talking. "What the hell do you know about compassionate use and why the fuck aren't we doing this for Huntington's sufferers?"

"Well, I can tell you the legal issues for a start. It's a challenging designation to actually implement. The first problem is liability. Since there is no guarantee of being cured, the patient has to be informed that there is risk that the drug doesn't work, that it might have side effects, that it might not be safe. That creates legal paperwork as you can imagine." Stan pauses and stares at the ceiling for a moment. "The only way to know that a drug is effective, that it works, is through a controlled study. Giving early access to patients outside of this is very risky."

I don't care about the risks of the drug not working. I know I could convince my father and mother to not care as well.

Stan's gaze returned to horizontal. "Secondly, the risk of early access is that we could have a safety issues in an uncontrolled setting that could hurt our chances of approval. You could wreck your chances of advancing the drug, which defeats the purpose of what we are doing."

He looks out the window. Returning his gaze to us, he continues, "A third issue is picking who gets the drug. What's the criteria? How do you say 'yes' to one patient and 'no' to another?"

"What if we could address some of those issues?" I ask. I know I sound too earnest. "I mean, we all believe that HD66 works. That it cures people. Can't we find some way? To not let a few legal issues get in our way of our mission?"

"Oh Brie, that's beautiful and noble and that's why we love you, but understand that there is an inherent contradiction in the compassionate use designation," Gigi states. *She is treating me like a child.* With pursed lips, she continues, "Stan can best explain about how the designation favors big companies."

"She's right. The designation favors large companies with deep pockets. The exception to FDA approval for humanitarian use has financial implications for the company that produces the drug. Companies can either donate the investigational drug to severely ill patients, or they can charge for the direct costs associated with manufacturing the drug." Stan stares at me closely. "There's no reimbursement, no real payment."

"There's no business model in doing this." Gigi says firmly. "As painful as it is, a company like Quixotic cannot afford to embrace compassionate use. We'd go broke."

"The main issue is that, legal issues aside, once you have that designation, you have to comply. You can't give the drug to one qualified patient and not to another. Do you say yes to everyone?"

"Imagine the bad press this could generate," Matt interrupts.

"He's right; we'd be overwhelmed by requests," Gigi says shaking her head. "How would we pay for that?"

"We couldn't get our investors or the board to approve this, anyway," Matt concludes. "No fucking way."

"I can't stand this conversation," Errol says and slams the door behind him.

"Brie, I'm sorry," Jim says quietly. "You don't know how sorry I really am." He looks at me long and hard.

I blink back my tears. *They have no idea. They think I am just a bleeding heart trying to save people that I don't know. I'm trying to save someone that I do know. Maybe even me. And none of you are helping!*

"Errol's not really angry," Gigi tells me with a downward smile. *How condescending.*

"I know. He's just sad." *Me too.* I limp off to get a glass of water from the fridge. I know that technically Quixotic could apply for an individual case for my father, but his disease had not progressed to the point where it was immediately life threatening. That means that the FDA would likely say no. From what I just learned, the request would open up a whole can of worms for our company. We'd have to open up to every request. Like Matt said, we just can't do that. I get the rationalization – the painful reality of a startup which has the capability to help but not the capacity. Knowing that didn't stop me from crying all night. Arwen stays glued to my side, purring my tears away.

Lying next to me, Neal knows that something is bothering me. He never presses if I don't want to talk about something. "I love you," he says and holds me close.

"Just a bad day," I cry into his chest.

I am glad that I hadn't told my parents. *How ironic. I cannot help my own father even though we probably have the only thing on the planet that can help him.*

Chapter 22

June 5, that same year

I am ecstatic. At last. The deal is done. We signed three weeks ago. We have the money. The clinical trial will start soon. *NOW IS THE TIME. I am going to tell them. All of them.*

I enter the room for our weekly on-the-same-page meeting. "The Phase III trial for HD66 will include almost 1,000 subjects and will last 12 months," Matt announces. "NGX is paying for the whole thing. That's fucking beautiful."

"What will it cost?" I ask.

"It's probably about $100 million," Gigi estimates. "We are getting paid to have them keep on paying, Brie."

"My life as a startup," I chuckle back to her.

I had taken a week off to spend time with my folks. I wanted to tell my mother first. To let her know about Quixotic, the trial, and the risks. "It could be good for Dad if he actually gets the drug," I explained. "It might be bad if he gets the alternative, the control, which is a placebo. There is no way of knowing which he will get." I carefully warned her, "Our drug is unproven, it might never make it to market, and there are the usual risks of side effects."

"Brie, you sound like a television commercial," my mother laughed. "Those commercials where the bottom of the screen has warnings…"

"Like 'Perpatrol may cause internal bleeding, heart attack, aches, diarrhea,' and so on," I joined in the fun. I really did end with the ubiquitous "Ask your doctor about it." My father wasn't going to be any worse off than he was right now, I reasoned.

My mother was beyond happy. "Oh, Brie." She wept when she dropped me off at the airport to return to

Pittsburgh. She promised to talk it over with his doctor. If he agreed, then we would tell my father together.

. . . .

It was not an easy process enrolling him, however. In fact it was impossible. First I had to tell Quixotic about my dad having HD.

"I thought something like this was going on with you. I'm so sorry." Jim looked at me and then immediately busied himself with paying the bill for our lunch. I thought I saw a tear escape down his chin. "We'll make it happen." That's all he said. He smiled at me. I couldn't look at him. I couldn't even manage a thank you. *He had known!*

When we got back to the office, I walked down the hall to see Matt, who was shocked when I told him. "Wow, you are in luck, my dear," he exclaimed. "The world is so small; what are the chances that you would be working for a company trying to solve a disease that you didn't know you might have..." he broke off. "Oh, fuck, I'm an idiot. Sorry; I didn't mean to imply..." He was clearly embarrassed, an emotion that I had not seen in him before.

Errol was harsher. "Good that we know," he said accusingly. "I didn't think that we kept secrets at Quixotic. But always good to know in the end." He wandered off down the hall.

I was pissed. How could Errol be so insensitive? Of all people!

Gigi was sympathetic. "Oh my God, Brie. I am sooo sorry." She hugged me lightly. "You should think about getting tested." *The clinical response.* "I assume that you haven't done that or I would be able to see by your face..." She caught herself. "Never mind, Brie. We're all here for you. And of course for your father."

"Can we just focus on my father and the trial?" I asked. "I would like to see that my dad gets into the trial."

"Oh dear, that may be more difficult that you anticipate," she said quietly.

"Oh, don't worry. I will make sure that he fully understands the risks that he might not get our drug. I've already told them and they are hot to go."

"That's not what I meant. I have to talk to the others. It's not as simple as you think." With that she ushered me out of her office. "I'll get back to you. As soon as we know something."

What does she mean "not as simple?" Who cares? This is finally my chance. Nothing can stop me now. I've waited and waited and now I want my father in the trial. Don't they understand what's at stake here?

I saw the trio later that afternoon, Matt, Jim, and Gigi, huddling over the whiteboard in the small conference room. Errol stormed in and back out in five minutes. I was not sure if they were discussing me, my father, or something else entirely.

Errol pointed at me as he stomped down the hall, "You…" But he disappeared into his lab.

What I learned the next day was that, because he is my father, he created a conflict of interest for Quixotic. "If he provided you with inside information during the trial that would, or could, crater objectivity," Matt explained.

"No worries, Matt. I resign, effective immediately." He looked shocked. Indeed, it would break my heart to leave Quixotic, particularly at this exciting time, but I couldn't possibly not do that for my father.

"Matt, if he has a chance of getting access to our drug before it comes on the market, it's a life-saving moment." Matt looked like he would burst. "To be able to do that for my father…" *The chance to save a life?* Matt looked like he was going to explode. "He would do the same for me. It's not really a choice."

"Fuck, Brie. Does Neal know?"

I cringed as I admitted that I had kept all of this from Neal. "No. I couldn't... I couldn't tell him. Not yet. Not until... I have to get tested. Then I'll tell him."

"You'll know then, about you." He looked at me, a cold blue stare.

"Yes, right. I'll know then. Definitively. Matt, I want to tell Jim, Gigi, and Errol myself about resigning. I'll get you an official resignation letter after I tell them, OK?"

"Suit yourself," he shrugged.

He was certainly not making much of an effort. I decided to tell Jim first. I invited him for a second lunch that month.

"Resign? Has it come to this? I'm so sorry," he lamented. "But I understand. We are fully supportive of you, Brie." I quickly ordered dessert so that I wouldn't start crying. "I'll see what we can do," he added. "It may not be necessary; let me do some checking. I've been looking into this myself." I looked at him wondering if he just said what I thought he said. But he was busy with the bill and his wallet.

Gigi was adamant, "I do not accept this, Brie. And remember, you work for me!" She pointed to the door of her office. I slunk out.

Later that week Jim and Matt met with me to tell me that my leaving Quixotic wouldn't fully solve the problem. "You see," Jim explained gently, "you have vested options in Quixotic, which means that there is still the potential for conflict since you are technically a shareholder."

"But I haven't exercised my options, and I won't. The company can have them back."

"We thought you would say that. I'm checking with Stan," Matt replied. "It's complicated," he added. "But not necessarily unsolvable. We'd like you to stay on, obviously. You're an invaluable help to us all. And God knows, we need all the help we can get."

"For the moment," Jim added, "we'd like for you to not make any final decision about leaving."

"Not until we have some definitive answers," Matt added. "Let's make sure we cover all options. So to speak." He smiled grimly.

"OK," I acquiesced. "You know that I don't want to leave."

"We know," Jim concluded quietly. "We so very much know."

I was sulking in my office when Errol gave me a call. "Brie, I want you to know something."

"Don't, Errol," I responded. "It's not necessary. Everybody is so darn sorry. I get it, Errol, I really do. There's nothing that we can do."

"Never say that to me again," he said and hung up. *Darn him. Everyone is against me. All I want to do is to help my father. Why is it so difficult?*

Gigi came to see me that afternoon. "We are not accepting your resignation," she said curtly. "This is not a viable option." She too smiled at the pun. "These conflicts happen, and we will figure it out. Conflicts are only bad if you don't disclose them. Don't make any plans that can't be changed," she stated as she swept out the door. The air had a wake like Errol's Scoot.

I will not give up. There has to be a way.

．．．．．．．

Six months later, December 5

"The honeymoon is over! NGX realizes that they didn't get everything that they wanted," Matt announces at our weekly meeting, slapping the table forcefully.

"They realize how much they left on the table," Stan informed us as we look at the table.

"They will so fucking get over it," Matt stated confidently.

Stan, however, looked worried, "They figured it out. Hate to say it…"

"Then don't," Matt snapped.

Jim was concerned too. "Big companies can do big things if they are crossed."

I was counting on NGX and the clinical trial for the drug to get approval. For my father. *The last resort. Now even that might be taken away from me. By them.*

The next few months I hardly saw Stan. I noticed a lot of big books on his desk. Like he was back in law school, he appeared to be reading a lot.

As Jim had predicted we had kept all assets outside of HD66 from NGX by forming a new company, Quixotic Labs. We put $10 million from our upfront money into the new company so it was a well-funded startup with valuable intellectual property. We had other drugs in the pipeline. Gigi kept talking about Parkinson's and glancing at Errol. Maybe he was getting closer? The Russians were pressuring us about Parkinson's too. I sometimes got the impression that no one cared about HD anymore.

I was relying on HD66 making it through the trial that NGX was sponsoring. I figured that NGX would want complete control over everything associated with Quixotic. I had thought the deal structure was very clever once I understood it. "To stop us from continuing our other programs with similar drugs based on the core components of HD66, NGX would have to buy Quixotic in her entirety," I told Neal.

"That's clearly a dangerous strategy," he countered.

"The question is, what will NGX do now that they know?"

"What does Jim say?" Neal asked. Neal really liked Jim. He never said that he didn't like the others but I sensed hesitation in him when I talked about Gigi and Matt.

"He agrees that NGX will have to buy the whole company. 'It's an insurance policy,' he told me."

"You mean that NGX would have to buy the whole company or else you can do deals with other companies for drugs like the one you have for Parkinson's?" Neal is smart. As an entrepreneur he got it right away. "So, you could just keep on selling off assets, one drug at a time?" He sounded smug.

"Yes, I think that's what they had in mind when we crafted the deal."

"Wow, a lot of money could be had. NGX would have to pay more if they wanted all of the assets. More than the $300 million specified in the existing contract. That's huge, Brie."

"Yep, a lot of money."

"No wonder I love you" he told me kissing me and squeezing me tightly. "Come on, let's go to bed…"

In the middle of night, while petting Arwen, I recalled how silent Errol was about NGX. After his big explosions early on, and his blatant satisfaction at the favorable terms of the deal, he seemed to move on, ignoring anything to do with NGX. Unusual for Errol to be so reserved.

. . . .
The next week, December 10

I get an email from Shala asking me to stop by the lab. She says that she wants my opinion on something. Something that they have discovered in the lab.

"Hey Errol, I announce as he sweeps by me in the hall looking preoccupied.

"Hey, beautiful? What's up?"

"Oh, I just want to stop by the university lab and see what you are up to."

He peers at me over his glasses and frowns. "Of course, stop by anytime. You'll be very interested in something that we've done. I haven't told anyone else. It's different than other discoveries. Something very unusual. At first I thought it was a disaster, but it's fascinating. You'll see. I'm sure the gang would love to see you. Shala in particular looooves you." With a swoop of his hand, like he is sweeping long hair back from his face, he imitates Shala, "That lovely Brie friend. She is now my good friend too, Dr. Errol."

I laugh. "Is it something that we could commercialize?" I ask.

"Hmmm, maybe," Errol replies thoughtfully. "You can bet that someone would pay a lot for this one," he finished. "Anyway, glad you are coming," he adds with a twinkle in his eye. "I have a little something extra, for you."

I'm sure that I look surprised. "For me?"

"Something very special and only for you," he says with a chuckle. "You will understand why when I tell you. But… not yet!" and he swishes out my door, shirttails flapping.

He's been teasing me for weeks about this. *What does he have that is so special? Is it something for my father? I've almost given up.*

. . . .

2 months later, March 1

The trial is over. The relationship with NGX has gone from bad to worse. In couple terms they are not speaking to us. This morning the bubble burst. Without warning, NGX stopped the trial. Stopped. Dead in the water. Now we'll never get HD66 to market.

We always knew that there were three potential outcomes of the trial. The one that we all expected, that our investors wanted to happen, is that the clinical endpoint was met, meaning that the drug worked. In this scenario, because HD is an orphan disease, we could go immediately to the FDA for fast-track approval. I had been counting on that. A second scenario would be an outright acquisition of Quixotic by NGX. A third option, the one Matt told us was the most probable, is that the data from the trial would be good, but not good enough to go straight to the FDA. In that case, NGX would have to extend the trial to include a Phase IIIB. That would add another 12-24 months to our plans. That would be OK with us because "moving forward is still moving forward," Matt told us. The fourth scenario is one we never considered or discussed, at least not out loud. That would be a failure to meet our clinical end point. In other words, if patients showed no improvement, or there were serious adverse side effects. Then we'd have a problem – a big one. Our drug would not make it to market – ever. *And my dad would die a horrible, inevitable death.*

The pathological optimism that you have to have in a startup precludes the ability to consider the fourth option. Plus, we genuinely didn't think that could happen. We were so careful in Phase II A and B. We studied the data from those trials to make sure that there was nothing hidden, nothing that we didn't know about. We were confident going into Phase III. Who wouldn't be? After all, NGX clearly believed that we had something, $300 million worth of something.

So, their press release this morning came as a surprise. "Holy fucking shit," I heard Matt scream from down the hall. It was the middle of the morning, 10:30 a.m. Gigi and Jim poked their heads out of their offices. So did at least a half a dozen other Quixoticers.

I follow Gigi and Jim into Matt's office. "NGX has cancelled the trial," he informs us in a strange monotone. Like the quiet before the storm. He proceeds to read from his laptop:

> NeuroGenex, Inc. has halted development of an experimental drug to treat the devastating neurodegenerative disorder known as Huntington's Disease, saying Wednesday that it proved ineffective in a late-stage clinical trial.
>
> The decision deals a blow to an estimated 30,000 Americans who suffer from Huntington's, a fatal degenerative condition for which there is no cure.
>
> 'There were a lot of people wishing for a positive outcome, who were hanging onto this as their hope,' said Martin Nextburg of Orono, Maine, who was diagnosed with Huntington's in 2008 and who had been featured on a national Public Broadcasting Station special about the disease.
>
> It was also a setback for Cambridge-based NeuroGenex and its chief executive, Martin Stronghold, who had bet more than $300 million on the high-risk Huntington's program earlier this year when he licensed HD66 — the drug — from Quixotic, an early-stage company based in Pittsburgh, PA. Shares of NeuroGenex, which trades under the symbol NGX, fell nearly 5% in post-market trading Wednesday evening, losing $1.89.

While most drug candidates fail in clinical trials, HD66 made it to a Phase III clinical trial, which is typically the final step before drug companies seek approval from the Food and Drug Administration to commercially market a treatment. That raised the expectations of Huntington's patients and their families.

'Getting this to a Phase III clinical trial was of huge importance,' said Molly Mohab, executive director of the Pennsylvania chapter of the Huntington's Association, a nonprofit working to find better diagnoses and cures for the disease. 'We were stunned today. The news came out of left field, and we are shocked and disappointed.'

'The experimental treatment had earlier shown 'some minor effectiveness in a smaller clinical study, conducted by Quixotic,' Dr. Stronghold said, but there were 'no observable benefits in function or survival for Huntington's patients or any subgroup in the larger NGX-sponsored Phase III clinical trial. We are sorry for those who continue to suffer from this devastating disease,' Dr. Stronghold concluded.

"Fuck this," Matt declares and stops reading. Jim lets out a long, slow breath. We had all been holding our breaths, trying to hear every syllable and word as Matt read the NGX press release.

"Has it hit the press yet?" Gigi inquires.

"Not sure," Matt replies and his fingers are already pounding his keyboard in an obvious search of the Internet. "Yep," he informs us. "Seems like the *Boston World* – of course – and some others have picked it up. It's all over the Internet," he finishes.

"Oh my God, we have to call Errol!" Gigi says. "He'll just die at this."

"He already knows," Jim says quietly, glancing at his phone. He looks around at all of us, the shock resonating around the room like a wave off of a cliff. "Don't panic," Jim cautions.

. . . .

It's like a bad dream. I can't go back. I can't go forward. Reminds me of my bee dream. I can't escape. I drain the last of my glass of Chardonnay.

Chapter 23
March 18

I'm scheduled to meet the detective at 9 a.m. at the Soldiers and Sailors Garage. From there it's an easy walk to Bocci Hall where we are heading to talk to Errol's lab students. I see Straler waiting for me by the ticket booth. He's frowning into his phone. He heaves a sigh of relief when he sees me. "Brie," he greets me brightly. "Thanks for coming. I was worried that you might not show. You're friends with Shala and I thought…" He looks at me rubbing my arm. I bumped it on the door to my deck. It'll be a bruise by now I am sure.

I nod and we start walking up the hill and then left to walk along Centre past the engineering building to the newer health sciences wing. The building is mostly glass and was designed by a Centre alumnus architect who works in Atlanta. While some of the university's buildings are cement structures from the 1960s, and others are historical buildings, this newer one is hyper-modern, with all kinds of features. "You know, this building earned a green building award when it opened four years ago," I inform Straler. "It has a living, green roof. All kinds of things are growing up there." Straler looks at me, tilting his head like a dog. *I've impressed him!*

As we enter the shining glass doors at the front, I glance longingly towards the Tazza D'Oro café on my right. Janeen, the owner, also has the café in Highland Park, near Errol and Amy's house. I have been there several times to meet Errol. The first time I looked at the coffee menu, I noticed the usual lattes and macchiatos. But it also listed an Italian Cappuccino. "What's that?" I asked the young woman behind the counter who sported tattoos and a nose ring.

"Oh," Errol said before she could answer. "An Italian Cappuccino? This will change your life." He promptly ordered two of them and I caught him winking at the girl behind the counter. Indeed, it did come pretty close to changing my life. Because I joined Quixotic. The coffee meeting was another non-interview. I've craved Tazza's Italian Capps ever since.

Straler must have noticed my glance. "Brie, it's still early; would you like to get a quick coffee first?"

"You're in for a treat," I say with a smile. When we were in line, I point out the Italian Cappuccino.

"What's that?" he asks the young pierced man behind the counter.

"Oh, that," I quickly say. "An Italian Cappuccino? This will change your life." And I order two of them, winking at the barista behind the counter, who grins.

Straler laughs, "Well I definitely need one of those!" His blue eyes twinkle at me. I feel the heat in my cheeks.

20 minutes later we are on the fifth floor. I am walking fast to keep up with the detective's lanky gait. I had learned that he moved from Pattensen, Germany when he was young, had two siblings, both younger, was a University of Pittsburgh engineering alum and had studied criminal forensics. He had a loose, easy way about him. He was unabashed about this being a big assignment for him to prove himself to his boss. "I appreciate your honesty," I told him. "You said that I care; so do you. That matters."

The lab door is closed. This is not unusual, given that labs deal with chemicals and experiments. As we knock and then immediately open the door, I see the students clustered together by the window. They're in an intense conversation. I hear Yahya say a loud, "No, not agree." Then they notice us. I hear the inhales of surprise.

Shala looks at us; she looks frightened. Then she recognizes me and her eyes lower. The other two look at me, then to the detective, and then back to me with wide eyes. Yahya is frozen; his arm half lifted from when he was talking. Patrick looks angry, but quickly changes his face into a forced, tight smile. Shala sneezes and covers her face with her hands. I nod and smile at her. She gives me a sad smile in return. She must miss him terribly. She knew him the longest.

Straler introduces himself, "Hello, I'm Detective Henrik." He nods towards me. "You already know Brie, here." He tells the students that I am helping him with his investigation. The students stand perfectly still, shock registering on their faces.

"About Dr. Errol?" Shala asks, her mouth hanging open. She sneezes again, grabs a tissue from a nearby desk and blows her nose. Poor thing. She has a cold on top of everything else.

"Yes," Straler replies.

"Shala," I say gently, knowing how much she cared for him. "We're visiting everyone who had a connection to him." Her eyes grow even wider, and her pretty face is distorted by grief. She looks like she will burst into tears. "This is routine, it really is," I assure her.

"Shala? Brie has told me about you, about all of you. She's right. This is just a routine visit, not to worry. We don't know how Errol died, and we're investigating the circumstances, trying to figure out what happened to cause his death. For our report."

"Investigating?" Shala asks. "Like on television?" Patrick shoots her a dirty look. Shala starts coughing and covers her face with her hands again. Yahya stands there, his brow furrowed, in a brooding silence.

"Are ye thinking that there was something wrong about what happened?" Patrick inquires in his broad Northern Irish accent. "Something not natural?" Shala coughs. Both Yahya and Patrick look at her; she looks down, her long hair covering her face. Her rounded back heaves with a silent sob.

"I'd like to ask you a few questions. Can we please sit down?"

Patrick nods in the direction of a table and he brings over another chair. We sit down. There are crumbs on the table. Shala sweeps them neatly into her hand and deposits the crumbs in the sink. This is where they eat their lunches. There is complete silence as we all take a seat.

Straler clears his throat, "To start, I'd like to ask if you three would tell me a bit about yourselves, how long you've been at the university, whether you've worked with Errol the whole time, when you graduate, that kind of stuff. We'll just do this as a group, and it will be short, I promise." He turns his head. "Shala, Brie has told me that you are a post-doc, that you've been here the longest. Can you please give me the basic information about when you started working with Errol?"

Shala blinks and relates her information. "I came here seven years ago to complete my PhD here in this lab. Dr. Errol was my thesis advisor. After my PhD is awarded, Dr. Errol, he gives me opportunity to stay here as post-doctoral researcher."

"What are you working on here at the lab? Is there anything in particular? Anything important?"

Shala looks surprised. "Detective, we are scientists. This lab is science. Everything is important. And working with Dr. Errol, it is very important. We have made important discoveries. But maybe that is over now," she finishes sadly.

Patrick butts in, "Detective, what Shala says is true. We like to think that everything that we do is important," he pauses and looks at Shala. "The work isn't over, is it now? But I don't think we have anything that really relates to, you know, to anything that could have happened to Errol."

Straler turns to Yahya. "Can you please tell me your full name, where you are from, and the other things about your education here and working in the lab?"

Yahya remains silent, his black eyes gleaming, his jaw set. We wait a moment. Just before Straler opens his mouth to speak, Yahya starts, "I am Yahya Kazmi. I am from Syria, Damascus. I am here three years. Before, I attend university in my country." There is something very stilted about his speech, more pronounced than just his accent. I don't know Yahya well, but I don't think that he usually sounds like this. Straler glances at me. Yahya notices this and glares.

It's Patrick's turn. "My name is Patrick Bailey. I come from Northern Ireland, a place called Portadown. I'm new here'n all. This is the first year of my PhD. I went to university in Belfast. And here now, while we are happy to answer your questions, Detective Henrik, we really didn't have anything to do with what happened. I mean, I'm here because of Errol. He recruited me. Along with the others here as well. We worked for him, with him. We'd never allow anything..." Yahya glares at him and Patrick stops talking. "I'm sure ya know what I mean."

Straler asks some general questions about the work they do in the lab. I can tell that he has trouble understanding the answers because the students answer with technical explanations. I explain that this is a diagnostics lab where they look at different disease states and what triggers them and then try to find solutions that un-trigger the disease. It's overly simple I know, but what does he really need to know more than that? Does he need to understand the intricacies of RNA? I doubt it will help him in the investigation.

Since we sat down no one has mentioned that Errol's death might not have been natural. It doesn't seem right to me, but Straler had warned me that he didn't want to trigger a panic among the students. He's cautious in his questions. He asks them how they are coping and whether they will continue as before? After they answer he asks what will happen now, moving forward.

I am curious about this too. Do they stay on? In this lab? Will they be reassigned? Will a new Principal Investigator, or PI, step in and take over from where they are?

Patrick explains that they are in a holding pattern while the department figures this out. A PI has been assigned to them and they are continuing with the work – Errol's work. "For me it's OK," he explains. "I'm the newest. I'm early in my PhD, and I could go to another lab, no problem," he says. "But I don't fancy that. I like the work here and, even though Errol is gone, we'd like to stick together. It's been quite a shock you see," he pauses. "We were discussing what to do when you all came in," he explains. "And we decided that, unless we are forced to disband, we'd like to stay together. We've got some interesting discoveries that we're on about now. Sometimes that can take years, you see. We're committed to developing what we've got to the next level, don't ye know?"

Yahya is quiet and looks down as he says, "I already commit to thesis. I like to finish. Here. Yes, new PI has step in. Dr. Rees her name. We can continue under supervision of her." He looks intently at Straler.

Shala dabs her nose and then says, "We not know for certain. Maybe we stay together not such a good idea. Maybe Yahya and Patrick have new assignments. I think maybe other new PIs." They both look at her and frown.

Straler puts his notebook away and stands. "So, will you all be here for the next couple of weeks? In case I have any more questions?"

Shala and Patrick nod. Shala looks at Yahya. He glares back. "I not here weekend."

"Oh?" Straler asks. "Where are you going?"

"New York City," he answers with a glower.

"What's in New York?"

"Nothing, I need go there." Yahya answers ambiguously.

"He goes four times in the last two months," Shala announces.

I could see Yahya tighten his whole body like he wants to react, but he holds himself in check. "Well alright, just give me the exact dates and where you'll be," Straler tells him, adding, "please. And for all of you, I'd like your cellphone number, home number, if you have one, Pittsburgh address, and email address. Just in case we need to get a hold of you individually. Please email the information to me." He hands them his business card.

As we walk towards the garage, Straler asks me, "How well do you know them?"

"Not much," I respond. "Except for Shala. We've had coffee a couple of times. She's sweet. She adored 'Dr. Errol' as she calls him."

"That Yahya…"

"Yes, he's kind of weird. I mean he's from Syria and all that. I think Patrick's kind of on the edge as well."

"Yes, agreed. Yahya said he would be in New York from Thursday through Sunday. I don't get it," Straler said. "Why now? What's in New York?"

Chapter 24
November 10, one year before the incident

Dear Pliya,

Please do not be alarmed from what I wrote to you two months ago. It not a mistake that I made. It is a new thing that we have discovered. A very dangerous thing. But not my fault. So I am off a hook as they say in America. I am writing quickly to you so that you do not worry that I arriving home any second. I not arriving home because I am still staying in the lab and in the United States. I have a plan now. Dr. Errol, he is part of this plan for me and for the future. You will be very happy, I assure you.

Your sister who is not mistake making,
Shala

Chapter 25
March 18

I get a call from Amy that night. She tells me that she didn't want to bother Matt, Jim, or Gigi, but she has something and could she drop it by? I look at my phone for the time. 9 p.m. My apartment in Shadyside is not far from her home in Highland Park, but I offer to meet on neutral ground – Tazza D'Oro. Twice in one day. I long for the Amherst scotch bar, but the Pittsburgh coffee house hasn't made the leap to alcohol. Maybe eventually, I hope, as I walk out my apartment door.

She's already there when I pull up and park. I can see her blond hair through the window. Luna is tied up outside. She wags her tail and whines as I smile at her and extend my hand. "Out for walkies?" I asked the beagle in my best Barbara Woodehouse voice. My father had loved the British dog trainer, and I had grown up with a series of golden retrievers, all of whom we had trained the Woodhouse way. "I'll bet you miss your master," I told her as I stroked her silky coat and gazed into her soulful eyes.

Amy hugs me and we sit down after ordering some herbal teas. Then she hands me something out of a plastic bag. I can see at a glance that it is a lab notebook. It must be Errol's. *Oh my gosh, maybe this contains what Errol wanted me to know?*

"He brings these home sometimes to write in them late at night or early in the morning," Amy tells me. "I didn't think it was important, but, since I don't believe his death was accidental, it might be... important," she adds hesitantly. "You know I'm not a scientist, and I can't make it out." She pauses. "I didn't want to turn it over to the students. Or even to the detective. I haven't told anybody else about this, Brie. I want someone to take a look, to make sure, just to see, if there's anything. I don't know," she ends miserably.

"I'll take a look," I tell her gently. "It might be, well, relevant."

We exchange chit-chat about the kids, trying to avoid the obvious. I don't want to look too eager. But I can't wait to get home and go through the book.

She doesn't know that there was someone else on the boat. I don't tell her. *Everyone is on a need-to-know basis.*

. . . .

I stay up half the night reading the lab book entries and doing some research on the Internet. I don't find any references to Huntington's or my dad. Nothing that will help. But I do read about the science behind a terrifying discovery. He called it DeathX. Errol discovered something that is lethal and entirely non-traceable at nano-scale doses. That a postage stamp quantity, applied directly to the skin, could result in death without identifiable causation. That it could be applied by a naked hand as long as the chemical remained on the other side. A deadly nerve agent. *Wow. That's significant. Who else knew? Did he disclose it to the university? Certainly his lab students knew about it. They didn't mention it to us when we interviewed them. Were they hiding something from us? Why?*

I can't help myself. At 3 a.m. I pour a glass of The Balvenie. I need something to calm my nerves, to help me focus, to channel my thoughts. What Errol discovered is clearly dangerous. In the wrong hands it could be used in terrifying ways. It could harm on an enormous scale. It's odd that Errol never mentioned any of this to any of us at Quixotic. He wasn't the secretive type. *Why didn't he tell us? Was he hiding it – from us? Does someone know and they're just not saying? Jim? Gigi? Matt? Does Boris know?*

. . . .

I research nerve agents that afternoon. Chemical weapons, I learn, are cause for much concern because they are indiscriminate. Chemical weapons can't tell an old lady from a soldier. They can injure or destroy people, animals, plants, and anything living that is in the chemical path. In the U.S., we frown on the use of chemical weapons – publicly that is. However, we dropped napalm on Japan, killing more people than the atomic bomb. We used the toxic defoliant, Agent Orange, in Vietnam. During the Cold War of the 1950s and later, we stockpiled liquid VX and sarin – both deadly.

We supported Saddam in Iraq as he gassed Iranian soldiers and villages in the Iran-Iraq war of the 1980s. *Washington Post* reporter Michael Dobbs wrote in 2002 that the Reagan administration was aware that materials we sold to Iraq were being used to manufacture chemical weapons. Dobbs noted that Iraq's chemical weapons' use was "hardly a secret," with the Iraqi military issuing a warning in February 1984: "The invaders should know that for every harmful insect, there is an insecticide capable of annihilating it… and Iraq possesses this annihilation insecticide." In 1988, Saddam used chemical weapons to quell Kurdish resistance forces within Iraq. Two decades later, the George W. Bush administration, led by Secretary of Defense Donald Rumsfeld, cited Saddam's use of chemical weapons against his own people as a justification for invading Iraq.

This is all in spite of the Geneva Protocol of 1925, which banned countries from using chemical weapons first in a conflict. The Protocol was a result of almost 100,000 soldiers suffering the horrors of German mustard gas in World War I. In 1993, the world passed a tougher treaty, called the Chemical Weapons Convention, which sought to prohibit the production of chemical weapons and mandated their destruction. Many countries – 189 to be exact – signed the agreement, although two countries (Burma and Israel) signed but didn't ratify the treaty, and five states (Angola, North Korea, Egypt, South Sudan and Syria) didn't sign it at all. Syria, I note. Yahya's country.

As I finish reading, I reflect that chemical weapons have been around for a long time. If Errol really had invented a new one, it's one more addition to an arsenal that many countries would value. Who, how, where – those are the questions for which I have no answers. A new page in my own notebook.

Curled up on my couch, it seems like a stretch from the safe base of my cozy apartment to be thinking about all of this. What did I know about nerve agents beyond what I just read? *Can I really help figure all of this out? Should I call Straler? What would I say?* "Oh, by the way, Errol discovered a deadly nerve agent. He might have gotten in over his head. Because it could be worth a lot of money to the right buyer." It's far-fetched, I caution myself as I sip the scotch.

Arwen jumps into my lap and purrs. I carry her into the bedroom and get ready for bed. I wish Neal were here, but he is out of town. I am almost dozing when an idea pops into my head. I recall that Errol had made a few trips over the last couple of years to the Middle East. Conferences were the reasons for these trips. But what if there was something else? Come to think of it, some of the locations seemed baffling. Why would you want to go to Saudi Arabia under any circumstances? I had seen two references to trips there. They were not too long ago. I didn't think that they were important. What if they were outside of his university work?

Maybe I'm being harsh, but, in the dark of my room, I see Errol in a different light. What if these were not innocent trips but demonstrations of a product? Of a deadly product? To people who would value a death agent? It could be worth a lot of money. The salary of a research scientist, even a successful one, is nothing to write home about. The lure of the almighty dollar. Would he turn to the dark side? *Maybe I never really knew him.*

I punch my pillow, sleep eluding me. I go back to my desk and stare at my notebook. What do I really know? What would tip Errol over the edge? *Think, Brie.*

I start a new page in my notebook. Who could be customers for a deadly nerve agent? What is the market for such a product? Is there competition? How would you price it? I pour myself the last of my scotch and laugh with the irony that I am approaching solving the murder like a startup:

What is the problem?
What is the solution?
Who are the customers?
Other stakeholders?
What is the value proposition?
What are the channels to market?
Who is the team?

My notebook page looks like an outline for an investor PowerPoint deck. I cared about what happened to Errol before this because I cared about Errol, Amy, and Quixotic. He had trusted me. He wanted me to make sure that his work would continue. And I need to find out what Errol had for me. I'm deeply hooked on solving his murder. I have to get to the bottom of it. "The bottom," I say out loud, grimacing at my empty glass.

. . . .

Early the next morning, I am groggy but awake. I know that I need more information from the lab. The students, they know about this. The only one I trust is Shala. I send her a text message to ask if she can meet me at the Starbucks in the Whole Foods parking lot at 8 a.m.

....

Shala is already sipping tea when I walk into Starbucks the next morning. We exchange pleasantries, and then I get down to the reason for the coffee. "Shala, Amy had Errol's lab notebook and gave it to me last night to read."

"Oh," she says in her singsong tone. "Did you find anything interesting?" She coughs into her hands.

"Yes, I found something very interesting. Something very important. Something that happened in the lab. That you must know about."

"Oh, what would that be?" she asks me innocently. Her eyes are oval and moist. "You know Dr. Errol is, was, such a smart man, a great scientist," she says. "Much work that is done in the lab is very important, very good science," she says and wipes her nose.

"Yes, I realize that," I say. "But I am talking about a discovery, something that seems to kill even with small doses. Do you know anything about this?"

She takes in a breath and looks a little alarmed. Her brown eyes gleam. "Yes, I know about this. We call it DeathX. It is joke. Bad joke maybe. But it very important." She stops talking and seems like she wants to say more.

"Shala, if you know anything about this, about ideas that Errol had about using it, or selling it..." I end slowly. Shala looks panicked. "You can trust me," I add. "I want to help."

"I must go now," Shala says quickly looking at her phone. "They will be missing me at the lab. I open up, you see." She gets up and fumbles for her things. "Brie, I email you later. I have some thoughts. I will tell you in the email. OK?"

"Of course," I respond and give her my gmail address. "Send it to this address, not to Quixotic, OK? Thank you for meeting me. I appreciate your help, Shala. I do. It's important."

She walks slowly out the door, glancing back at me with a strained smile.

. . . .

That afternoon, I get an email from her.

Dear Brie, I am thinking all day about our talk. First, let me tell you we all surprised at this "discovery." This not what we expect, what Dr. Errol expect. We didn't think it at first a discovery. We thought it was mistake. I thought that it my fault that it was something I do wrong in the lab. I try over and over again for days to make it work, to not kill the mouses. But I am not successful. Dr. Errol, he try over and over. Then we realize that this was new thing.

Patrick starts joke about it, about it killing. He talked that it might have value to bad people. Dr. Errol, he listen. And, I have to tell you, Yahya also talk about discovery. He want to repeat experiments, changing doses even after Dr. Errol gone. Why this? He is strange. All of these travels to New York. I don't understand why he goes.

We argue about what to do. Patrick says that we not say anything about this. He says that no one knows, then not matter. He tell us that we should move on to other work and leave death agent behind. Yahya says good idea – no tell anyone about DeathX. Why does he think this, I ask? And why is he doing experiments at night when he alone?

Brie, I do not trust Yahya. I do not trust Patrick. I do not say this to detective. But I trust you, so I want you to know my bad feelings. You will know what to do.

Thank you for the coffee and goodbye for now until I see you next time.

Your friend,
Shala

. . . .

I go back to the lab the next day. Alone. No Straler. Shala looks better. She must be over her cold. She seems very glad to see me. Patrick, however, looks worried; Yahya glowers behind dark eyebrows. I try to loosen him up by teasing him about New York. "You staying in the city?" I ask. "A girl?" He looks shocked. "Oh, sorry," I quickly cover. "Just teasing you, Yahya."

"I go to friends," he tells me.

"Oh really, what part of the city? You driving or what?"

"I take Megabus," he responds reluctantly. It cheaper than train. And quick too."

"Yes, I've taken the Megabus too, but to DC. It's great." I pause. "Where are you staying?"

He pauses, as if to think of the answer. He does not look at me. "I stay Hell's Kitchen. With friends. You know New York?" he asks, looking up at me his brows knitted.

"Yes," I conclude. "I lived there for a job for a bit. I know the Hells' Kitchen area. Well, have fun!" Shala looks at me but quickly looks away as Patrick tilts his head listening.

The idea had hit me last night like a brick. Yahya knows about the nerve agent. It's valuable, particularly on the black market. Given where he comes from, Yahya could be doing some kind of deal. I have to go to New York. To see for myself. If I find out anything important, Straler can take over.

Back in my office I look at the Megabus schedule for Pittsburgh to New York. It takes eight hours. I can make it quicker by car if I leave really early. His bus leaves at 6 a.m., I realize grimly. To make sure I can beat him I should leave at 5 a.m. Ugh. I have to find parking too. But it's a good plan. I'm curious more than anything else. My biggest concern is whether I tell Neal. Should I mention it to Jim? Straler? I'm not doing anything wrong, I reason. I won't tell anyone because I don't have a good reason why I would go. I recall Jim's admonition: "It's better to ask for forgiveness than permission." He was talking about entrepreneurs. But then, I'm being entrepreneurial, aren't I? I'll tell everyone that I need a few days peace and quiet and that I am going home. They should only contact me if it's really important. Knowing the situation with my dad, they won't question me. I'll put an away message on my email. I better mention it to my folks, so that we don't get our wires crossed. I'll tell my mom that I am visiting a friend in New York.

. . . .

When I arrive home, I am halted in my tracks by a sticky that I left on the kitchen table from last night. All it said was "Amy?" Checking my phone for the time, I realize that I would catch her at home. She picks up right away, sounding a bit anxious. "Amy, I read Errol's lab book. And well it's…"

"It's important, isn't it, Brie? I thought so. Otherwise why would he bring it home? I mean he does things like that, bring his notebooks back and forth, but not that often and I just thought..." She trails off.

"Amy, Errol discovered something that he documents in that notebook. I don't know who else knows. We didn't know anything about it at Quixotic. At least, I think that's the case. I have to check to make sure of that. Anyway, I am not sure that this relates to Quixotic. You see, it's out of his lab at the university. His students knew about it."

"Oh," Amy says quietly. "Is it important?

"I don't know," I reply honestly. "It's a new invention; it's really dangerous." I let some silence happen over the line. "It's something very powerful, very strong – and lethal. It could be of great value to someone somewhere..." I pause again and take a deep breath to get the next part out. "Because it could be used as a kind of weapon, a chemical weapon. I don't know the details of how it's made or how it could scale, but someone would be able to take this and do terrible things with it."

I hear Amy sputter a bit. "I don't believe that Errol would..."

"I know that this is a lot to take in, Amy, but I have a couple of questions. Can you handle this now?" I ask.

"Just a minute, Brie." I hear Amy talking to someone in the background. Of course, the kids are there, and she doesn't want them to be a part of the conversation. It sounds like she changes phones, "OK, I'm in the office now," she says. I remember that they have a lovely home office at the front of their house. Errol had custom-built the desks, and he had big windows looking out onto Sheridan Avenue.

What must she be going through? Does she have anything to hide? "Amy, I need to ask about Errol's travel to the Middle East in the last couple of years. What do you know about these trips? When, where, who, that kind of thing?"

I pause. No response. The silence is long and painful.

"Um, Amy, sorry to keep persisting, but did Errol have any contact with people, maybe even innocent contact, with people that might be interested in this kind of discovery?" I wait.

"Do you mean that you suspect that Errol would try and sell this product to someone?"

I breathe for a minute before I answer. Very important to be calm here and not alarm her. "Amy, I am not implying anything. Maybe he did nothing about this at all. Or maybe he did something legitimate. For all we know, Errol could be trying to enhance our own weapons, in this country. I mean, it is feasible that someone as smart as Errol would realize that, if this got out beyond our borders, it could be very dangerous to our whole country. Maybe he talked to people in Washington DC? Or maybe elsewhere? I'm just trying to understand."

I hear a sniffle on the other end. "I don't know, Brie. It's so unlike him. I mean conferences, yes, he went to many of them. But doing business, selling an invention? I can't imagine him… What would he wear? His Hawaiian shirts? Oh, it's laughable." And she chuckles, a soft, sad laugh.

"Amy, let's just consider this. Maybe it's nothing. Objectively speaking, no assumptions, can you make a list of his travel in the last couple of years? I'll do it on the Quixotic end. And I can ask someone at the university if they can give me any information about his speaking engagements and conferences. Then, at least we have some data. No assumptions. Just fact collecting. That OK with you?"

"Of course. Let's make sure we do this thoroughly, Brie. I want to rule this out, not in, you understand? But I get what you are saying. Examine all angles."

Chapter 26
March 3

The black cloud appeared on the horizon, and he knew that they had to hurry. His grandfather sees the cloud too and shouted the boy into action. He hauled in the nets, too early he thought; we don't have a full hold of fish. He glanced into the deep well, less than half full of thrashing fish bodies. He needs more fish. We will have to come out again. His grandfather's needs were simple and pure. The boy was here only for the summer. But his grandfather was here for all time.

As he lashed the net to the port gunwale and secured the fish hold, the old boat lumbered to full speed. He was angry at being cheated out of what they came here for. We will get you, he raged. He was only a child, but he knew how to handle the unexpected at sea. His grandfather had taught him well.

The boy looked, but his grandfather was not at the wheel. He entered the wheelhouse to take charge, to do as he was taught.

"Always forward," his grandfather would admonish. "Never go back. No matter what." The boy had promised many times. He knew that his grandfather was to starboard, securing the fishing lines so that they wouldn't get fouled in the propeller. He started to turn the boat around. He was the captain now. He recalled the stories his grandfather had told in his native Greek – of their forebears, and how their blood runs in the boy's veins. He was scared, but he drew upon the courage of generations. The storm crackled and danced around the boat.

The boy strained his head seeking his grandfather. The Kataigida has been his boat for as long as the boy could remember. It was named after the Greek word for storm. "This boat belonged to an ancient in my village who sailed alone to flaunt Mother Nature. When he died, the boat passed to me. She taught me well. Her name comes from *The Tempest*, the Shakespeare play that starts with a storm." He would quote the first lines of the play:

Heigh, my hearts! cheerly, cheerly, my hearts!
yare, yare! Take in the topsail. Tend to the
master's whistle. Blow, till thou burst thy wind,
if room enough!

The boy's thoughts were interrupted when a wave crashed over the starboard rail of the boat. He concentrated and brought her around and into the wind. But he could not see his grandfather. Suddenly afraid, he knew that stories wouldn't help him. He rushed out of the wheelhouse. His grandfather was not on board. The boy was alone. He dare not go back. He had failed. It was his fault.

Errol awoke from a cold sweat, shivering from the Voice.

. . . .

"Captain Bob, are you up there?" Errol shouted from the depths of the lock hold.

"Sure I'm here. Whadda ya want, soldier? Comin' back so soon?" Captain Bob smiled at the "Scoot" from 50 feet up as he dropped the rope down for the second time that night. Errol tied his long line to the shackle and Captain Bob pulled it up. Walking along as the "Scoot" slowly made its way forward, he said, "Ya up for any fishing?"

"Not tonight," Errol responded. "Busy," he said as he gestured towards the bow.

"Ah, aye, aye, cap'n," he said, and saluted Errol as he pulled the last of his rope and coiled it neatly before stowing it in the "Scoot's forward seat cabinet. "Watch the ice up river, eh?"

"Will do." Errol motored slowly out of the lock heading upriver.

There were still small slabs of ice on the river. He had no trouble when he launched the boat and took her through the lock earlier that night. There had been a thaw last week and no new snow. The temperature had been unusually warm for this time of year. Which is why Errol had dared put the "Scoot" in the water and head out for a ride. *I need to think.*

I don't understand what's wrong, he had mused grimly as he had turned around to come back. It had been an unusually fruitless boat ride. No solutions. "Hell, I discovered a cure for Huntington's," he told Luna as she whined. "At least I thought it was a cure. Even if it's washed up now. I can't believe that NGX cancelled the clinical trial. Now HD66 will never make it to market. My patients will still suffer. All that work, all that money, all that time – empty, useless. Like me." *Where are you Voice when I need you?*

Errol steered the boat around a small floating piece of ice. Luna shook her tags, wagged her tail and looked at him. "Working on a cure for Parkinson's has been painful and frustrating. And I haven't found the answer. What if I don't? They'll never have a cure." The Voice was silent. Errol knew by heart the classic statements about the disease:

> Parkinson's disease is a progressive disorder of the nervous system that affects movement. It develops gradually,

sometimes starting with a barely noticeable tremor in one hand. A tremor is the most well-known sign of Parkinson's disease, but the symptoms worsen as the condition progresses over time. There is no cure for Parkinson's disease, although existing medications may improve a patient's symptoms.

He had never felt this bad before. So hopeless. So far from the Voice. From something that worked. *There is no cure. And mine is nothing. My invention is not reversing the signs and symptoms. Is it only hubris that tells me that I can change that? I did it before. But now, all I do is kill mice. Instantly and irrevocably. DeathX. It's not a cure. It's a curse. I don't have it in me anymore. I am used up. I am tired. I don't have any more ideas. I keep trying but nothing seems to work. In fact, it's not even close. I'm finding the opposite happens. Shit, I am done as a scientist. I've fucked up. The university will know. I'm losing my funding. I won't get tenure. My family. Oh God, I really fucked up this time. With her too. I shouldn't have gotten her involved. It's too late. I can't go back. She'll kill me. The pressure. I can't do it anymore. I give up. All these years, I have kept moving forward, never looking back, grandfather. They have all been for naught. I was wrong to not turn the boat around. I could have found you. I left you. I am sorry. It is my fault. I killed you.*

A hand touched his shoulder. He wished he could turn the boat and go back for his grandfather. But it was too late. Now he faced the end. He was forced to go forward, too far, too fast, too late. There is no going back. Ever. The falls loom ahead. His destiny. Through his blackness he hears Luna howl. *What have I done?*

Chapter 27
March 21

Gosh I love the Internet. Last night, I was able to reserve a parking space in New York City just a few blocks west of where the Megabus leaves their passengers at 7th Avenue and 28th Street. From Pittsburgh, it's a seven-hour drive to get through the Holland Tunnel. If I leave at five, it would put me in the city around noon, a couple of hours before the Megabus arrives. I don't want to take any chances with traffic, getting lost, and finding parking.

I pack haphazardly at the last minute and arrive in the Big Apple just before noon. Parking was a cinch. I send a text to my CMU friend Suzanne, who lives in the city. We plan to get together. That way I am covering my tracks, I reason. I walk a few blocks to Macy's at Herald Square. I have to buy some essentials. I need to disguise myself. Yahya can't recognize me.

At 1 p.m. I scope out the intersection where the Megabus picks up and drops off, a few blocks from Penn Station. I want to find a place where I could see the bus disembark its passengers but that wouldn't be obvious in case Yahya was looking around. I have to smile because I feel like I am in a Nancy Drew novel. I know that I'm an amateur, that I am not a professional crime solver. I'm just trying to eliminate a suspicion that Yahya is up to no good here in the City. But I'm dressed the part after my purchases. I emerged from the ladies room in trench coat, black boots, floppy hat, and "Men in Black" sun glasses. I snap a selfie on my iPhone. Neal will get a kick out of this when I show him next week.

I inhale deeply. There is no smell in the world like that of New York City. I love this city. I lived here for a brief spell, after college, before moving to Pittsburgh. I had taken a job at a life sciences accelerator for six months, a sort of prolonged internship that was run by a fellow Hampshire College alum. I lived on the Upper West Side and commuted up to my job, north of Harlem. That experience had led me to Pittsburgh. One of the companies in the accelerator was run by a young woman who graduated from CMU and had gotten her PhD at Centre. She raved about Pittsburgh. Her enthusiasm certainly factored into my places to look when the urge to go to grad school came knocking.

Hampshire College had been the first path on my journey. New York had woken me up. But Pittsburgh seemed like a place where I could stay and make a life. *My life in a startup.* In spite of its recent entrepreneurial activity, Pittsburgh was still struggling to get to the next level. Investment dollars are scarce, and it's fiercely competitive. "What we need is more success stories – exits," I had read on Jim's "NewVenturist" blog. "The more exits, the more money that gets invested, which, in turn, creates more exits – a virtuous cycle. Investor returns have been slim in Pittsburgh. Quixotic is the tipping point. If the company is successful, it will make a significant difference – not just to Quixotic's investors and staff, but to the whole region." Jim is right. *We have to succeed. For all of us.*

I buy a Nathan's hot dog from a street vendor and slather it with sloppy yellow mustard. I have no trouble poking around NYC for an hour. As I munch I watch the people of New York and feel the vibrations of the City in my soul. It's like no place on earth. I think that Neal and I should come here for a long weekend, take in a show and the Indian food on 6th Street. We could visit some of my old stomping grounds. He'd like that. It would be nice to make it a surprise for him. For his birthday in June.

It's time to take my place behind a food stand across 7th Avenue. I have a view of where the bus will stop and am pretty hidden to anyone across the street. I buy a newspaper and open it, pretending to read. I haven't thought too much past this point although I made my high-level plan on the long drive this morning. My strategy is to observe, to stay out of the way, to make sure that I'm not seen, but to find out what Yahya is up to. If I can confirm that it's something bad, then I'll let Straler know right away. I figure I can call him on my drive back.

Now that I'm executing my plan, I realize that there are some holes. Here I am in NYC, and nobody knows that I'm here. My intention is to follow Yahya. But how do I actually do that? *I'm an idiot.* But then I see the bus pull up. Passengers start to disembark. I see Yahya step off the bus. He looks around furtively, but he can't see me. He has a bag slung over his shoulder and he hurries up 7th Avenue.

I feel like I'm in a mystery movie. Yahya is walking fast uptown, me trailing him. He turns left on 34th. As I make the turn I know that Hells' Kitchen is a few blocks away. I follow a safe distance behind, around a half a block. He doesn't seem to notice me, and even if he did, he wouldn't recognize me.

He turns right on 9th Avenue and then left on 37th, weaving his way into the thick of Hells' Kitchen. Then he glances around, turns onto 10th Avenue, crosses the street and enters a building on 10th and 39th. Crap! What do I do now? My heart is pounding. *Calm down!* I wait for a few minutes, but he doesn't come out. I wait a few more minutes, and then, my heart in my mouth, I approach the building. I can get in the foyer, but the inner door is, of course, locked. I don't know which apartment he went up to. Shysta. I'll have to wait. I hate to admit this, but I'm in a stakeout. Is that the right term? I cross the street and stand on the corner, reading my newspaper.

As it turns out I don't have to wait long. Yahya comes out with several other men. Yahya still has his bag with him. They all look to be around the same age. They look like they might be Arabs, but what do I know? They walk up the street, and a few blocks later they enter another house. I mark the address, wait a few minutes, approach the door, but the same thing – the inner door is locked. It's 4 p.m. There is a coffee shop a half a block up. I go in and order a latte. No Italian Cappuccino here, I note.

A couple of hours go by. I have actually read the newspaper cover to cover, checked my email and doodled in my notebook. It's 6:30 p.m. It'll be dark soon. I can't be doing this on my own on 10th Avenue. Yahya and some others come out a few minutes later, and I see that he doesn't have his bag on him. Good, I think, that means that's where he's staying the night. They wander east, and I follow at a safe distance. They're pretty easy to spot because there are five of them. Yahya has his arm around one guy. They are laughing and all talking at once. They turn on 8th Avenue and pretty soon I see them duck into a restaurant. I can't decipher the name of the restaurant as it's in Arabic, but it also says "Good Wholesome Middle Eastern Cuisine."

OK, I think, they are in for a while. I am tired. I have booked a hotel uptown, so I walk back to my parking garage and get my bag. I hail a cab. As I sink into the hotel bed I am glad to be away from the watch. I have tomorrow, I think, and yawn.

. . . .

The next morning I show up early to the place where I think that Yahya has spent the night. I get into place just in time to see him and another Arab-looking man emerge from the building. They seem to be arguing, loudly, but of course I can't understand what they're saying. Once they are a few steps away from the front door, they quiet down, but it looks from their body language that they are still in the midst of a heated discussion. The other man is taller than Yahya and has full black facial hair. They walk quite closely together and I wonder if they are friends, relatives, or whether they know each other from Syria or the US? I am in a quandary about whether I should follow them or not. Once they are a block away, I decide to follow them, but not closely. They don't seem to be up to much, so I feel OK about going for what I hope looks like a casual stroll.

I see the companion glance around a couple of times, but not really back, and not at me. They go into a corner market, and I busy myself at a newsstand until they come out with a couple of parcels. Breakfast, I guess; looks like fruit and other items. They are coming back my way and I cross the street at the corner, while they are still a half block away. They don't notice me. They are talking animatedly, it seems, from their gestures, and I hear an occasional guffaw, so I assume that the argument is over. When they get back to the building they enter, and there I am again, a half a block away and at a loss for what to do. *Should I wait?*

I don't have to wait long at least. About 15 minutes go by while I check my email. Not much has come in, probably because of my away message. A group, including Yahya, emerges from the building. They are talking and gesticulating and a couple of them glance around. One casually looks in my direction but I don't think he sees me. I am at a bus shelter and look like anyone else waiting for the bus. I decide not to follow them this time, and a good thing too because they walk a couple of blocks up to the newspaper stand where I was a little bit ago to buy a magazine. They buy several papers; I had noticed that they had a lot of foreign papers at the stand. They split up into two groups, one coming back my way and pretty soon they go back into the building. The other group disappears around the corner. I sit down on the bus bench and am looking at my phone when they walk by. They don't glance at me, and I'm pretty covered with the raincoat, droopy hat and sunglasses. I don't glance up once I realize that it's them, so I don't know if Yahya is in that group. I am petrified to look up even after they pass, so I don't see if they all go into the building. I assume so. A full five minutes go by before I dare look up. A bus comes by, and I let it go, but then I get on the next one that stops. I just figure that I should. I get off two blocks later and continue to walk uptown, towards my hotel and away from Yahya and his friends. I am exhausted even though it's only late morning. I will give this one more try I think, but tomorrow, not today. And then home.

Neal calls me in the afternoon wondering how it's going with my folks. I tell him that I don't feel well and that I am going to take a nap. He seems to accept that, and I feel better about the white lie rather than making something up about my folks.

I had arranged to meet Suzanne for dinner. She works downtown near Wall Street, and we agree to meet at 7 p.m. at a restaurant in the Village. I take a cab downtown but ask the driver to round the block and head up past the building on 10th Avenue before heading downtown. He obviously thinks it's weird because my destination is downtown not uptown, but he does it without complaining. New York cabbies know better than to ask questions.

There is no activity around the building. I see a light on in an apartment on the third floor and a person at the window that looks like Yahya or one of his cronies, but I can't be sure. In any case, we go right, and then right again heading downtown. I check my phone and notice that I missed a call from my mother. I'll call her tomorrow.

I'm looking forward to an evening with Suzanne. She always has a lot to say, and it will take my mind off of my own situation. I don't have to tell her about what I am up to, about Errol, about DeathX, about Straler. I want to tell her about Neal. She knows him and knows that we are an item. It'll be fun to tell her about how he dotes on me. She's been dating a guy from India too. We can compare notes. I put on my pearls, looking forward to a stress-free evening with a friend.

. . . .

I wake on Sunday morning feeling refreshed. Detective work suits me, I think. I order a big breakfast at the café downstairs and then head out for 10th Avenue. I take up my same haunt. About 9:30 a.m. I see Yahya and a few of his friends head out. They are walking and talking really fast. Again, they split up into two groups, and I try to tag the group that I think still contains Yahya, but I am not sure. It sounds terrible even to me, but it's hard to tell them all apart. How Jurassic of me. I spot Yahya when he turns sideways. My phone rings. It's my mother again. Darn, I think, I forgot to call her back, and I can't do that now. My eye catches the headlines of a newspaper as I walk by a stand. I catch my breath and back up a bit.

"Syrian chemical attack kills thousands." I quickly buy a paper and scan it. Apparently, the Syrian government launched rockets that had warheads filled with deadly chemicals the day before, Saturday. March 22. I read about sarin gas, "a powerful neurotoxin, a nerve gas." The article went on to say, "The gas used may be a new form that has never before been used. More deadly than other gases…" I am shocked. I read that in spite of the attack, the death and injured toll was relatively small, "roughly equal to the average number of fatalities in an ordinary week in the civil war. Since it started, the war has claimed more than 100,000 Syrians killed by conventional means. Also documented in the last year and a half is a large number of verified war crimes, including the indiscriminate shelling of civilian neighborhoods, summary executions, and the torturing to death of captives."

Oh, no. This just got a whole lot more complicated. My mind jumped to conclusions. That attack could have used DeathX. Yahya is selling Errol's DeathX to the Syrian government. Or, Yahya is a rebel, and is selling DeathX to the rebels. Nerve gas is part of the civil war in Syria, and now Yahya has access to a new type of agent that can be turned into a lethal gas that no one else knows about or can replicate. The reality hits me. *Yahya is a terrorist.* Of course that's why he comes to New York all the time.

My mind races as I read some articles about the Syrian conflict. The civil war is two years old, and many rebels have adopted the same brutal and ruthless tactics as the regime they are trying to overthrow. It's become a criminal environment populated by gangs, kidnappers and killers who are adopting an extremist stance. Some have openly allied with al-Qaida and the Islamic State, ISIS. Oh my gosh, Yahya is part of one of these groups. *I better get out of here. I'm playing with fire.*

My phone rings. It's Jim. I better take this, I think, and I turn the corner and enter another bus shelter, covered with graffiti. There is no one there waiting for the bus. I cower against the dirty glass and say hello to Jim.

"Where are you, Brie?" he asks anxiously. I don't answer right away, and he continues, "Your mom called yesterday, and again a few minutes ago. She says she can't get a hold of you. We all thought you were in Amherst with them? Where are you? Are you OK?"

I take a deep breath and quietly answer, "Jim, I came to New York. There was something I had to do, wanted to do."

Jim interrupts, "Brie, we talked to Detective Henrik. He told us about the visit to the lab and about Yahya going to New York. You didn't follow him there did you? I mean, we have no idea what he might be tangled up in..." He trails off. "I think you should come home. Brie? Brie?"

I don't answer because my phone has fallen to the ground. Well, it's been knocked to the ground. I watch it fall in slow motion. I have a thought at the back of my head that I am glad that I have the Cell Helmet that will stop it from breaking – a local Pittsburgh company, started by a Pitt grad, sells a phone cover that is also an insurance policy. Then a hand covers my mouth, and I am grabbed in a bear hug. I hear what I assume to be Arabic. It sounds like swearing, but I really have no idea. I see small white dots scatter to the pavement at my feet. The white dots roll, and my eyes swim. My pearls. Granny's pearls.

There are suddenly two men on either side of me hustling me to a standing position between them. They both grab me, and I can hardly move. I glance around but there is no one there. I open my mouth to scream, to cry for help, but a voice near my ear says "Shut up; do not yell or we will kill you." I see someone bend over to retrieve my phone. They will realize that I was on a call. I am terrified of what this will mean. But I have no time to think.

They walk me towards the building. When we arrive, they hustle me inside. One of them grabs my hands behind me; another one pushes me up the stairs. Three flights of stairs. I was right. They shove me into the front apartment where I noticed the person in the window.

I am in a disheveled living room. To my left, I see a small kitchen with take-out boxes and garbage on the floor. There are flies. Someone slams a couple of doors behind me, to bedrooms, I assume. I don't want to imagine what happens next. I concentrate on memorizing my surroundings. I see cracks in the dust colored wall. The window is dirty. I am pushed into a chair. I look around, hoping to see Yahya. But he is not there.

"What are you doing?" a voice growls at me from behind. "Why are you following us for two days?"

Shoot, they know. I am terrified. *Why did I come?* I wish I was back in Pittsburgh. What an idiot I am, pretending that I can solve a murder. I try to speak, but I can't find my voice.

"Answer!" the voice commands.

I stutter and spit out, "I'm, I'm looking for Yahya. I work with him."

"Yahya!" they exclaim. A few exclamations in Arabic. "He is not here. Why do you care? Why would you come to New York, and he has no idea you here?"

The man has his hand raised. Is he going to hit me? Am I going to be tortured? "I don't know anything," I manage to squeak.

"We will see what you know," the man promises.

I hear voices outside the front door of the apartment; I hear shouting in Arabic. Then I hear the door burst open, and the sound of feet, hard soles, like boots, on the scuffed hardwood floor. "Who is this?" someone asks harshly. "Why did you bring her here?"

Someone shouts something, but I don't understand it. I don't even know if it was in English or Arabic. Then I see Yahya come into my vision. He looks at me and his mouth drops open. He grabs my hat and yanks it off. "Brie? What is this?" He glances at his compatriots and then scowls at me. "Brie, what you doing here?"

"You knows her?" someone inquires loudly.

"What she doing here? Why here now? Who she is?" someone else asks with heavily accented English.

I realize that I better speak, and quickly. I am trying not to cry, but I know that my voice is trembling. My whole body is shaking, but someone has their hands on my shoulders, and I can't rise out of the chair. "Yahya, I am so sorry, I don't know," I take a deep breath, "You told me and the…" I didn't want to say the word "detective." I hurriedly continue, "Mr. Henrik, remember, that that you were going to New York. You told me that you were taking the Megabus to the city, and I thought maybe there was some connection, something that I would see, that I would learn. About, you know," I took a quick breath, "about Errol."

"About Errol?" Yahya asks me.

"Yes," I manage to mumble. "We think, we don't know, Amy is sure, we think it wasn't an accident. That's why I came to the lab. To ask you, to find out if you…"

Yahya stares at me.

"I read Errol's lab book. I know about DeathX."

Yahya mutters a string of words that I don't understand. A bunch of the others all start talking, loudly, gesticulating. I see what look like threatening gestures, but I have no idea what is being discussed, only that it involves me and possibly my life.

Then I see something that I wish I had never seen. Yahya takes a pistol out of his jacket and points it at me. I'm going to die, here in New York, and no one will know. My family. Neal. My dad will surely die now. And I will never get to say goodbye.

I start to cry, and make no effort to stop. "Yahya, I don't know why you did it, but please stop. Don't make it any worse now. One murder is enough... I saw the news. It's terrible." I leave off because I am blubbering and I am speaking gibberish that I can't understand myself.

"Brie!" Yahya says sharply. "Stop. Now."

I don't want to look at him. When I do, I see that the gun is not pointed at me. It is pointed above my head, at the guy behind me I guess. Then Yahya swings around and levels the pistol at each one as he circles. It is a full 360 degree circle that he makes, arms outstretched, the pistol level with his wrists. *What is he doing?* I vaguely wonder through a thick fog? My mind can't take this in. I feel like I am on another planet looking down on me in this room on this chair.

I realize thickly that Yahya is threatening everyone else. He is protecting me. I start to cry again. I can feel the tears on my face, but I cannot hear anything except a dull roar in my ears. The Arabic swearing starts like a wave that crescendos over me like a blanket. I don't faint, I don't feel the slightest like fainting, which surprises me. But I am holding my breath, for a really long time. I exhale and hold it again. I feel like minutes pass. Then I hear someone say "OK." A bunch more exchanges, and I hear doors, lots of doors. They have vanished, into the bedrooms, out the front door of the apartment, I don't know. Maybe they all crowd into the bathroom? But they are gone.

Yahya pulls a chair in front of me. We are alone. "Brie," he says gruffly. But I detect a gentleness in his tone. He does not touch me.

. . . .

He tells me to wait right there. He looks at me for a long moment. "You not move, right?" he asks. "Please do not. You will be safe, but I have to get you out. I be back, OK? Stay put," he emphasizes this last command with his hand. Like Errol used to do to Luna, telling her to stay. Yahya's dark eyes burn. I feel guilty. I have made him do something difficult. I hear voices, but I do not glance their way. I am doing as I was told. *Like Luna.*

I don't want to see what is going on. I have no idea who Yahya is or what he is up to. *Why is he being nice to me? Did he kill Errol? If he did, why is he acting like he is going to walk me right out of here?* It doesn't add up. I'm not thinking rationally, I realize.

Yahya returns. He has his bag. And my phone. "No calls, OK?" he tells me more than asks. "We go now." He helps me up, and I need it because I am a bit wobbly. I don't remember going down the stairs but I remember the sound of Yahya breathing behind me. I want to run but I know I can't. It will only be worse if I do, I suspect. I hear a very strange sound and look up as we approach the front door to exit the building. It's a lilting, haunting sound. With a shock I realize that it is coming from Yahya. He is whistling. I don't recognize the tune. It's not a happy sound; it's mournful, but sweet and quite pretty. I glance back once we are outside. He hands me my floppy hat. He smiles at me, and I realize that I never noticed how white and straight his teeth are. These are the most words I have had with him, I realize, and he just tried to kill me. Or, I correct myself, maybe he stopped them from killing me. I don't know why, but suddenly I trust him. If he killed

Errol, or if one of those fellows did, why would he be whistling, and why would we be walking away from the building?

"We go uptown?" Yahya asks me. Why is he asking me? Is he taking me somewhere? "You stay at hotel?"

I don't say anything. I can't process this. Why does he care where I am staying in New York City?

"OK," he says, "no worry. We walk for a while, no? Yes?" he finishes. He smiles at the contradiction. Perfectly straight white teeth. And his eyes, they seem to smile too.

We walk for a block, maybe more, I have no idea. It's the middle of the afternoon. It's not even night. *Are these the actions of a killer?*

He hails a cab.

Chapter 28
March 24

Buzz! I awake with a start. I had set my alarm for 6 a.m. I want to check out early and get on the road. I have a lot to process. The first thing I did when Yahya said goodbye to me at the hotel yesterday was to call my mother to say that I had taken a spontaneous visit to New York City to visit Suzanne, that I had wanted a weekend away from work, email, and the pressures. I told her I was sorry that I missed her calls, but I had dropped my phone in the toilet. She has known forever how clumsy I am; she believed me.

She doesn't know about Errol. She doesn't really know who Errol is, except from hearing about him from me. She knew that the chief scientist behind our drug was a guy who got his PhD from UMass around the corner. She knew that Errol was dead, but she has no idea that the death might be murder, that her daughter was playing amateur sleuth. She doesn't know the agony that I have gone through trying to get my dad into the clinical trials. All failed efforts. She knows only that I was not successful. She doesn't know about the clinical trial being stopped by NGX. That even if he was in the trial it would be a moot point now. She might have found out on her own about NGX stopping the trial, but I doubt it. She would have asked me about it. I can't tell her, dash her hopes of a cure – not yet. Errol had something intended for me, for my dad. I just have to find it. That's why I came to New York. She doesn't need to know any of this.

I also texted Jim last night. That I was OK. That Yahya was here, that he was not the killer, that he needn't worry. Everything was fine, and I was going to stay an extra night in NYC. I would be back in Pittsburgh Monday night.

Next, I called Neal. "Babe, where are you? No one seems to know. Should I know something?"

I sighed. "Neal, I'm not hiding anything from you, not really. I'm just very involved in what happened with Errol. You know that I've been talking with Amy. And this detective, Stra..." I caught myself. "Henrik, Detective Henrik," I corrected.

"Yea, well you're sure not telling me much about anything." I could see that he was annoyed. He'd be far more than annoyed if I told him I had just survived a kidnapping. That I almost died. That I was with terrorists. I'll have to level with him. But tomorrow, not tonight.

I yawned. "Look, Neal. There's nothing going on. And I'm not playing games. Really. But there are some things that I have to do. I have to help solve this murder."

I heard a slow uptake of breath. "Brie, do you know that it was murder?"

"Yes, Neal, I'm sure." I paused. "You see, there was a second person in the boat."

"Shit, Brie."

"I know, Neal. It's bizarre." I ended the call by promising to tell him the whole thing, tomorrow. He would meet me Monday night at my apartment. He promised to cook. "Mmm, Indian food, please?"

He laughed, "Sure thing. Whatever you want." I hear him breathe. "I love you, Brie. Please come home – safely."

Lastly, I called Straler. He picked up the call before the first ring sounded. "Brie, we've been so worried. Jim told me you were in New York. Where are you?"

"I'm fine, thanks, detective."

"Hey, what's with the detective?"

"Sure, Straler. I know. I'm just tired. You know why I came. I thought I could find something out, you know. It was so weird that Yahya was coming to New York. But it didn't seem like anything definite. I didn't know what I was looking for. Just that I was looking. That's why I didn't tell you."

"I get that," Straler said, sounding miffed. "But it was dangerous of you to go on your own. You could have at least let me know."

He's jealous! I saw some action, and he's a young detective dying to see some action. "You didn't miss much," I said. "Really. I ran into Yahya, well, kind of ran into him. He recognized me, and after a shock, we talked. He has an explanation. I'll tell you the whole thing, promise. But not now. I'm tired. I had some late nights here in the City – with friends. Yahya's driving home with me tomorrow. We'll be back mid-afternoon. He's happy to answer any questions that you might have."

"Great, what time would you like me to pick you up?"

"Straler, I'm in New York City."

"So am I."

"Really, Straler, you're in New York?"

"Yup." I heard a tinkling laugh. "Brie, you might be one step ahead of me, but you are not going to hog all of the fun, are you? What hotel are you staying at? I'll pick you up at 7 in the morning. We're partners, remember?"

Wow, partners.

I ordered room service and crashed. When I wake, the television is still on. There is a story on of a terrorist cell bust in New York City. The sound is turned down, but I am jolted fully awake when they show the front door of the building on 10th Avenue that I WAS JUST IN. I think I screamed out loud because I notice that my hand is over my mouth. I grope for the remote and turn up the sound. But I can't take it all in. Something about a terrorist plot, I hear the word "Syria," and also "rebel," and I see a bunch of people being led out of the building and into a police van.

Oh my goodness, I think. Where is Yahya in all of this? Is one of them him? I get a text message just then. I don't recognize the number, but I certainly welcome the message: "*Brie, Yahya here. Please do not reply to text. Like we talk, you are safe. I am OK. We leave for Pittsburgh, now? Meet me Starbucks 6th and 23rd.*"

I glanced at my phone, 6:30 a.m. I just have time to get ready. I look forward to ordering a double latte at Starbucks. I will need it. It is a long drive home. Straler is waiting for me in the lobby when I step off the elevator. He has an Uber driver waiting for him. I tell him that Yahya is waiting for me. When we get to the coffee shop, I go in first to explain Straler's presence. Yahya looks terrible. He has the saddest eyes I have ever seen.

The Uber driver takes us to pick up my car. On the way back to Pittsburgh, Straler driving, and Yahya slumped in the back seat, I recounted what had happened to me. I told Straler what I had seen on the television. I told him that I saw Yahya's brother being hauled away. We drove in silence for a long time. I turned around and looked at Yahya.

Yahya told us about his brother. The story was a sad one. As we knew, Yahya and his family are from Syria. The current war didn't start as a war, but, rather, as a rebellion against the repressive government. Yahya told us that he escaped through his education. He was ecstatic at being accepted into Centre for his PhD. When he landed at Centre, he thought he'd reached a place where his past couldn't touch him. Where he could be literally free. He followed the rebellion, and he was convinced that it would be a peaceful uprising. But Yahya's brother chose a different path. He's 14 months younger than Yahya, and had fallen in with a difficult crowd in the Syrian equivalent of high school.

The situation only got worse in university, where the brother spent one year before dropping out. For a long time Yahya didn't know the extent of his brother's involvement in the political world, the violence, the incidents, the terrorism that he embraced even before the revolution started. Yahya was already in the States. Relations became strained with his family and with his brother. His mother called him numerous times asking him to help his younger brother, but Yahya didn't know what to do, and he didn't want to leave the U.S. and his education.

Then, a few months ago, he got a call from a New York number. It was his brother, Hasad. He was in New York City. Hasad tried to get Yahya to come to NYC, and, once there, tried to convert him to the cause. Yahya didn't buy into the violence, but he kept going to and from NYC in the hopes that he could extract his brother. But Hasad hated America and hated anything American. "I love America," Yahya confessed to us. "I thought I could convince him of a better way." There was nothing we could say or do to ease his pain.

Yahya will not be making any more trips to New York City. He spent a lot of the trip looking out the window. A couple of times he wiped his face, and I could see that the back of his hand was wet.

. . . .

Tuesday, March 25

Straler insisted on meeting me early on Tuesday morning. I had chosen Ritter's – again. I might gain weight

I reasoned, but at least I am consistent. Once seated, I take a sip of my coffee. Straler, who had been writing notes, pauses, pen in the air. "You did good, Brie. You really did."

I smile at him.

"Now we know it's not Yahya. Cross him off of your list. In your notebook," he indicates my notebook with his pen.

How did he know that I was keeping tabs on the investigation through my notes?

"I peeked, while you were in the ladies room, last time we were here," he admits sheepishly.

I laugh, "You're such a detective!"

"Can we move on?" Straler asks me next. "To the next on the list? What about Patrick? And, what do you know about NeuroGenex?" he queries. "Jim told me Errol was dead set against that deal." He winces at the remark.

"Yes, I know something about NGX," I reply. "Let me get it all together and get back to you. Might as well give you all the relevant information at one time. Give me a few days."

"Sure, of course. Good. Thanks. Really, thanks, Brie." Straler rises to go.

I stare into my coffee cup. I wonder if I will ever feel rested again.

Chapter 29
March 28

The tension at Quixotic is unbearable. Matt snaps at me constantly, asking me questions, wondering what I'm working on. He seems distracted. Gigi is as demanding as ever. She's asked for help on some financial reporting that we owe to shareholders. For me, it's a lot of staring at an Excel spreadsheet with loads of numbers. I'm not very good at it. Gigi keeps harassing me to do it over and over again. Stan is always at his desk, working on something that I don't understand. The lab is quiet and folks come and go. I don't know what they are working on either. Only Jim seems unfazed, and he stops in my office with a kind smile.

"You OK, Brie?" he asks.

I don't answer, but he accepts my nod. "I know that it's tough around here right now."

I nod again.

"Look, Brie, I know what you are going through. With your dad and all this? I know that it's very hard on you. Believe me, I sympathize."

He has aged, I see, from the deep creases in his face. "Thanks, Jim. That means a lot."

He looks like he wants to say something else but then seems to change his mind. "Just don't let any of this get to you. This will pass, I promise. Things have a way of working out."

I don't believe him, but I don't want to disappoint him. "Gigi is riding me to get these numbers done." I roll my eyes.

"I know, Brie. We all ask a lot of you. Just know that I'm here. If you need anything."

Little does he know. He exits awkwardly out my door. He's definitely older all over. His hands shake a little as he waves goodbye from the hallway. His steps going down the hall seem belabored, like he's in pain.

I have a nasty email from Gigi to hurry up. I want to hurry myself. I have something else that I want to finish. I know that my work is not what she wants, but I email her the spreadsheet, knowing it will bide me some time.

Most of what I know about NGX is public information. I did a lot of research. I asked a load of questions. I put the finishing touches on a short overview of the company. I had told Stan that I would pass it by him for review prior to sending it to the detective. He's showing wear too. I never noticed gray at his temples until last week. I guess we've all aged.

Report on NGX
Brie Prince
Quixotic, March 28

Overview. Neuro Phamaceuticals, the precursor of NGX, was formed in the late 1970s in Switzerland by a trio of scientists focused on groundbreaking discoveries for human health, including one who went on to win a Nobel Peace Prize for his discovery of Phenomalia to treat breast cancer. The company is based in Cambridge, Massachusetts, although it has research operations in Switzerland and Germany. The company went public on NASDAQ in the early 1980s based on its numerous partnerships with tier-one pharmaceuticals to take its pipeline of products to market. By the late 1980s, NGX had two products on the market, one for brain cancer and one for Multiple Sclerosis (MS). By 1990, the company was selling a vaccine for cervical cancer through its partners. In the early part of this decade, NGX had one of the largest pharmaceutical manufacturing operations in the U.S., based in Georgia, and was growing rapidly. In 2002, it became the third largest biotechnology company in the world by merging with Genex Labs, a Silicon Valley VC-funded, public company that developed and commercialized monoclonal antibodies. Genex's first target was a treatment for non-Hodgkin's lymphoma. The combined company, renamed NeuroGenex, or NGX, has expanded for the last 11 years and today has annual revenues of over $5.5 billion. Its stock price has almost quadrupled in the last three years from $62 to $246 today. The company prides itself on achieving its goal of discovering, developing, and delivering – to patients worldwide – innovative therapies for the treatment of neurodegenerative and other diseases, including cancer. Recent efforts by NGX are targeting conditions including Amyotrophic Lateral Sclerosis, commonly known as ALS or Lou Gehrig's disease, Spinal Muscular Atrophy, Huntington's Disease, and ovarian cancer.

Quixotic. NGX's 2014 annual report mentions several ongoing trials for new drug candidates. The report does not mention Quixotic but does mention HD66 and the cancelation of the Phase III trial: "Our unyielding commitment to biomedical research that saves lives is reflected in our only clinically unsuccessful project of 2014. In March of this year, we discontinued development of HD66, a drug that was being tested in people with Huntington's Disease (HD). We regret to say that HD66 failed to meet the necessary clinical endpoints in a pivotal Phase III trial, in both the general study population and in multiple subpopulations. Our search for a cure to this terrible disease will continue."

Leadership. NGX's CEO, Martin Stronghold, MD, PhD, is relatively new, having been there only five years, three as CEO. Stronghold had a relationship with Errol prior to our recent relationship around HD66. This relationship does not appear to apply to Quixotic or the rest of the executive management team. Dr. Stronghold used to be at the University of Massachusetts (UMass) at the same time that Errol was there, studying for his PhD. Dr. Stronghold was an associate professor, became a full professor, got his MD along the way, became chair of medical diagnostics, and then was awarded the deanship of the School of Health Sciences while Errol was there (six years). Dr. Stronghold left UMass the year that Errol finished his PhD – he was on Errol's dissertation committee. He became chief science officer of a relatively early-stage company in Boston, named CodeGenetics. Apparently, he brought with him an invention that was licensed to the company from UMass. This licensing transaction appears to have been a relatively standard licensing agreement between a university and a startup, with the usual equity position and royalty agreement. Having obtained a copy of both the patent and the license, I note that the inventors listed on the patent include Errol's dissertation advisor, Dr. Sally Mutase, but do not include Errol. There are no licensing officers currently at the UMass technology transfer office (TTO) who were there at the time of this license (1991), although they were able to pull the file electronically and send me the license agreement and a few side notes of the negotiations. It is difficult to decipher the exact situation, but there is a note from one of the two licensing officers assigned to the case (it appears that the first one may have left the university before the license was signed) indicating that there was conflict between Drs. Stronghold and Mutase about the license and the technology itself. However, there is no mention in the notes as to the details of the disagreement. We can presume that this situation was resolved, as the license was eventually signed.

Unfortunate circumstance. Shortly before the license was signed, Dr. Mutase was killed in a car accident. Newspaper articles about the death mention that she died on an icy road in the countryside, a half mile from her home in Pelham, a small town near Amherst. She was unmarried, no children. Newspaper accounts of the accident give no indication that it was anything but an accident. One article from the university paper, "MassUNews," however, interviewed several folks close to Dr. Mutase, including colleagues and Dr. Stronghold. Quoted in the article, Stronghold expresses his "regret for the loss of a colleague and a brilliant scientist with so much to give to the world through her inventions and innovations." Another junior colleague, Dr. Alise Freundenhofer, had very different comments, "Dr. Mutase was more than a scientist; she was involved in translating that science to the market following the principles of 'consilience,' where many approaches converge across the experiments to reveal something new. Dr. Mutase was on the verge of a very big deal. Her approach was not accepted by many. In fact, she was creating some turmoil in the field. I find it curious that her accident occurred now, just before a big publication that she was authoring and prior to closing an important deal with industry." I have searched for the author of these comments but to no avail. I did find that Dr. Freundenhofer moved to Switzerland about five years after this article was written and conducted research at the University of Bern. However, there is no record of Dr. Freundenhofer in recent years. She has, quite simply, disappeared.

Dr. Stronghold today. Dr. Stronghold remained with CodeGenetics until it was acquired by Life Pharmaceuticals, which then merged with multiple other companies including Neuro Pharmaceuticals. Dr.

Stronghold remained at the company through these mergers. In fact, when Neuro Pharmaceuticals merged with Genex Labs to form the current NGX, Dr. Stronghold was promoted to executive vice president, business development, of the combined entity. Subsequently, he was promoted to CEO in a major management shakeup that occurred three years ago. Most of the executives who were with the company prior to Stronghold's becoming CEO are no longer with the company.

Questions.

A. **The past:** What is the nature of the relationship between Errol and Dr. Stronghold? While we don't know the specific nature of this relationship, it can be surmised that it relates back to their time together at UMass. We know that Errol viewed this relationship in a highly negative way. Is it possible that there is more than just a bad relationship between Dr. Stronghold and Errol? That they were enemies in some way? I recommend that we investigate further, including talking with former colleagues at UMass, and an ex-employee from CodeGenetics, who is a CMU alum. In addition, I have contacted the former licensing officers in charge of the CodeGenetics license through LinkedIn. While I cannot guarantee a response, I have found, in general, that this form of communication can be highly effective. I am continuing to search for Dr. Freundenhofer, who may have additional information that is relevant.

B. **The clinical trial.** Does the relationship, presumed to be a negative one, between Errol and Dr. Stronghold carry over to NGX? Is there a correlation between the fact that NGX licensed HD66 and that Errol and Dr. Stronghold were connected in some way? Did their personal negative relationship have anything to do with NGX's cancelling the clinical trial for HD66? As I get answers to A above, this may shed light on these questions. What I can investigate is more about Dr. Stronghold and his role at NGX. He must have been involved in doing the deal with NGX. How? What was his role in the clinical trial? Did he stand to benefit or gain in any way through the success – or the failure – of the project?

C. **The death.** Is there a connection between Errol's death and the relationship between Errol and Dr. Stronghold? Between Errol and NGX? What about between Quixotic and Dr. Stronghold? Or between Quixotic and NGX?

Recommendations. I intend to keep digging into Dr. Stronghold and NGX to find answers. If there is a connection, we will have to act on it before the trail gets cold.

. . . .

I push send on my email to Jim, Gigi, Matt, and Stan. I blind carbon copy Straler. *I trust no one. Well, almost no one.*

Chapter 30
March 29

My first call in the morning is to Amy. Did she know this Dr. Martin Stronghold?

"Yes," Amy tells me. "I don't know much, and I never met him. I never would want to after how Errol dissed him."

"What do you mean?" I ask.

"Well, Errol disliked him in the extreme." Amy pauses to laugh. How long was it since she has done that, I wonder?

I join her with a small chuckle. "I know what you mean. I'm sorry for this Stronghold fellow." I hear her sigh on the other end of the line. "Do you know why Errol disliked him? Or anything about their relationship?" I probe.

"There was no relationship," she responds. "I mean, you knew Errol. Once afoul of him, there was no going back. The guy would have had to show up at our door with a peace pipe to even begin..."

"And nothing like that ever happened?" I pause. "To your knowledge?" I add. Silence. "OK," I start, but Amy interrupts me.

"I didn't know Errol in those days; that was his UMass career, and I met him when he came here to Pittsburgh, after his PhD. During his post-doctoral research studies."

With his credentials, Errol could have gone anywhere. He stayed in Pittsburgh because of Amy. She was born and raised in the Squirrel Hill area of the city, just up the street from the universities. Errol had come as a post-doctoral fellow to Centre, a leading research university. Like many faculty, he found Pittsburgh to be an inviting home, friendly to scientists with its large university and healthcare base. Eds and Meds they call it. "Pittsburghers never leave here," he once divulged to me. "The City doesn't let you go. They think this is the greatest place on earth. And so you stay. Forever." He gives a low chuckle. "Anyway, Pittsburgh is a great place to raise a family."

Amy is still talking. "That was after his relationship with…" she stops abruptly.

Who was she about to name? And why did she stop? "I'm sorry to pry, Amy," I say. "But these details, any information, you know, is helpful."

"I know, Brie," Amy says, and her voice sounds like she's on the verge of tears. "It's just so hard."

"It is," I sympathize. "But I – we – need you. You were the closest to him, and what you have in your head is, well…" I trail off because Amy knows what happened in New York and why. She knows that it was sparked by her giving me Errol's lab notebook. Before she can say anything, I jump in, "Amy, look, we have to do what we have to do. I can't let this go, particularly now. The detective, well, he needs us."

There is a long pause, and I hear her sigh, "I know, Brie. I can't tell you how much I admire you, and how thankful I am that you're there."

"What I need to know is everything that you know about this Martin Stronghold," I finish. "Can you think about this and then call me back or we can meet tomorrow?"

"Let me jot a few things down," she tells me. "I'll be in touch."

I am about to hang up but stop when I hear Amy clear her throat. She speaks softly, "Brie? I got some information. About what you asked, about Errol's travel."

"Good," I answer. "I didn't get too far at the university. They wouldn't give me any information. I'll have to go a more formal route to get any real information. Detective Henrik would have to lead that effort. But, I did get some success. I got the list of all Quixotic travel for Errol in the last few years. Most of it was domestic, and I suspect that the travel related to fundraising. Then again, Gigi wasn't sure that it covered everything. It only covered what she could look back and find based on expense reports and reimbursements. It's not a perfect system she told me. She might have been holding back, for Errol's sake, somehow. I couldn't get her to say anything more."

"Hmmm," Amy says. "Well, I was able to get into Errol's computer at home. He keeps everything in the cloud. So, I took a look at his schedule of appointments for the last 18 months, basically since the dates that you told me about from the lab notebook."

"And?" I ask. "Anything unusual or out of the ordinary?"

"Well, yes. He had several trips to DC. There are a lot of conferences there of course. We sometimes arranged to go together. We both love DC, and then, of course, there is the Chesapeake. Twice, we chartered a sailboat out of Annapolis and went for a long weekend sail before or after a particular conference. That happened in June and again in October last year."

"OK, that's great, Amy. What else?"

"Well, the rest of the domestic schedule looked pretty banal: San Francisco, Silicon Valley, Seattle. There were two trips to New York City, but I know what they were. The Centre Pathways program put him through some training with Steve Nada and the National Science Foundation's Innovation-Corps program; the onsite trainings were in New York. I went with him for one of them."

"Great, Amy, what else?" I don't want to rush her.

"I looked really closely for some international travel. I went back a little further. There was a trip to Russia two years ago. And there were two trips to Saudi Arabia this year."

"Wow, Russia. And when were the trips to Saudi Arabia?"

"The first to Saudi Arabia was in late January; the second was just a few weeks ago, just a few weeks before, you know..."

"February?" I ask.

"Yes, she said quietly. "I didn't really know where he was going. He was kind of vague. This wasn't unusual because we didn't always keep tabs on the micro details. Sometimes it was too much for me to keep track of. You know he was tired in the last few months. I think that his schedule was grueling between the university, his practice, and you, Quixotic, I mean. It was starting to wear on him. I could tell. He was cranky. Errol just doesn't get like that normally. This seemed new. I caught him a couple of times talking to himself in the study. Like he was arguing with himself. Like he had something that was eating at him. Maybe a decision, I don't know. We'd talked about taking a month in Greece this summer. Without the kids. They would be busy at camp. I thought it would be good for him to get away."

I remember that Errol's kids are involved in CISV, Children's International Summer Villages, a kind of camp around achieving world peace by starting with younger generations. How ironic is it that Errol had discovered something so deadly, and yet wanted to send his kids to a world peace camp?

Amy was still talking, "I couldn't keep Errol's schedule straight. It didn't matter anyway. He always called, emailed, we Skyped. I didn't need to know where he was. I'm the same. I travel. As long as we stayed in contact that was enough."

The Russia trip has to circle back to Popov, I think. And two trips to Saudi Arabia? Right on top of each other. I know that they were not for Quixotic. They were certainly not for his medical practice. Could they have been for a conference? I'll ask Dean Dormer about any recent Middle Eastern events or conferences.

Amy wasn't finished. "Brie?" she asks quietly?

"Yes? Something else, Amy?"

"Not really something. Just a feeling." I wait. "Those times when I caught him talking to himself, and a few other times, when I saw that he was looking at me, when he didn't think I saw, well, I don't know exactly how to describe this, but he had a guilty look on his face."

I hold my breath for a few seconds.

"Guilty? How?"

"I don't know, just guilty. Like he knew that he was doing something wrong. Or bad. He's like Luna. She's the only dog I've ever known who actually covers her face with her paws and looks guilty when she does something naughty." She pauses, and then gives a small, sad laugh.

"How is Luna doing?" I ask to change the subject.

"Oh, she misses Errol. She misses him as much as any of us. She growled at his students the other day. They stopped by and the lovely young Indian woman was so terrified that she hid behind the others. We all miss him so much…"

The phone goes dead. I stare at my phone. She hung up? I haven't moved from my kitchen table. The room feels hot. I am sweating.

. . . .

As I gather my things to make my way to the office, my thoughts turn to Errol going to Russia. The timing was such that he would only have just started working on a cure for Parkinson's. No real data or anything. Nothing conclusive. But, come to think of it, I recall that Errol had given a couple of early talks about new things he was working on. I think that he partnered with a colleague. Myra or something like that, she was called. I'll have to follow through on that.

I walk to the bus stop. My Prius is in the shop and I like to take the bus when I can. It makes me feel like I am doing something to help. I trip in a sidewalk hole and hurt my wrist catching myself. I have a spot on my tan pants now too. I'll have to download the PathVu app that maps sidewalks. I recall that the inventor is a friend of Errol's from Centre who had recently formed a startup to commercialize the app.

What about the Middle East trips, I ponder, as I rub my wrist? What could he have been doing over there? I shiver in the brisk late-March morning. The bus passes me with a splash from a puddle. Now I have dirt AND water on my pants.

I think back to Popov Brothers and my conversation with Boris. It's never been clear how Errol knew them. Had he met them, one or two, or all of them, during the trip to Russia? Why didn't he like them, and why did he have such a hissy fit when we were considering them as investors? How did Boris end up at Quixotic for that matter? A bit too coincidental. I recall that I have the number that Boris left me. Now, where did I put it? I run into a tree while I am fishing in my purse. My nose is scraped. I find the scrap of paper. Then I dig through the outside pockets for my phone. I drop the scrap of paper, which blows away. I run. And trip.

Finally, I dial Boris's number. The phone rings and then I hear a generic voicemail. I leave a short message to call me back. I don't even know if that is still his number. If he was running from something, then he might have changed his phone number again. Maybe we were too quick to let Popov Brothers off the hook? I've got to talk to Jim. He'll know what to do. I swing open the door to the new Tazza D'Oro in Shadyside to get an Italian cappuccino. I need to change my life.

Chapter 31
March 30

It's the middle of the night. I'm restless. Neal is peacefully asleep, but I sneak out to my kitchen to make myself a cup of tea. Checking my email, I see that I got a response from the second licensing officer involved in the UMass Stronghold license. She's willing to talk to me and gives me a date and time. I email back that I can make the time. Which is actually today, I realize. We're confirmed for the call at 8 a.m. That's hours away. I'm asleep on the couch when my phone buzzes me awake at 7 a.m.

"Neal?"

"Hey babe, where are you?" I go in to get my share of love for the day.

"Oh dear," I jolt awake at 7:55. "Sorry, Neal. I have a call. It's important." I stumble to the kitchen and my computer. A few minutes later my cellphone rings. It's her, Jane Lutrell, the former licensing officer, now a staff member at a Boston-based technology incubator. The conversation is short. She can't remember very much, and she is no longer in tech transfer. She tells me that the first licensing officer went on maternity leave half-way through the deal, and Jane took over for her colleague. What she could remember was that it was a "complex deal that was very hard to close and keep all the parties happy."

"What do you mean by complex?" I ask.

"Well, there was some conflict amongst the inventors as I recall. Some kind of dispute as to who was an inventor, and who was entitled to do what. Our job was to keep our constituents happy, which meant all of our faculty, so we didn't take sides. I don't remember how this got resolved exactly – I remember a yelling match between several faculty members, a woman was one of them I recall.

The company, the startup Code something-or-other, had put an ultimatum on the table. They forced it to conclusion." She pauses and sighs. "I saw everything in tech transfer. The ugly side of researchers and human conflict. I don't remember the details of the deal. I think that eventually the university made some money from it. But I was gone shortly afterwards."

"Do you know what happened to any of the faculty involved? Did they join the company, stay at the university?" I ask.

"Well that part was kind of interesting. I remember that the woman faculty member died in a tragic car accident. The timing was weird because it changed immediately who we were dealing with. I mean one day there was all this fighting. Then someone was dead, and it got a lot simpler real quick. I remember now because it was just as I was leaving. I do remember that the one guy, this really loud, kind of obnoxious faculty member – had a name that suited his style, I remember, Strongloud or something like that – he quit the university and went with the company. I always thought that was a bit strange; it's hard for a university researcher to make the transition to a startup, but some do. And he didn't start out that way. That happened, I don't know, maybe after the accident? This guy had a personality that I thought would clash with others. Oh well. Go figure. Why the company wanted him I don't know. Maybe he brought something with him other than university technology and know-how? I don't know what happened to him after that. I got sour on the TTO front, you know. It was difficult to do deals in the first place. On top of that most of the professors weren't living in the real world. It's so isolated there. Amherst is in the middle of…" I think she was going to say "nowhere," but her good manners got the better of her.

"Yes," I told her. "I'm from Amherst so I know how 'nowhere' it is."

"Yeah," she responded. "Anything else I can help you with?" This was a signal that the conversation was ending. I made sure that I could contact her if I needed to.

. . . .

Later that day, March 30

The conversation with Justin Cheray, the ex-CodeGenetics guy that had returned my LinkedIn message, was not much more helpful. Jim was listening in on the call. No one else knew what I was doing, and Jim was the only one I trusted besides Straler. I didn't know the guy directly from my Carnegie Mellon days. But he was from Pittsburgh, raised in the South Hills, a typically boring suburb of Pittsburgh, did his undergraduate work at CMU in bioengineering, a master's at Pitt in the same field, and then interned at CodeGenetics, an opportunity which turned into a job. His profile says he stayed only three years before moving away to get an MBA in New York. Not bad credentials, I thought as I was dialing his number. His email had told me that he's now at a Philadelphia-based startup in genetic sequencing.

He doesn't mince words about Stronghold once I ask a couple of leading questions. "He was a class-A asshole," he tells me within the first few minutes of the conversation.

"Tell me more."

"I mean he came into the company apparently with all this intellectual property," he goes on. "Had patents from the university and all that. But he had no idea about product, about commercialization. He tried to show us all how smart he was, but in a startup environment you don't really care about smarts. You care about action. You're in a startup, right? You get this, eh?" Justin pauses for breath.

"Yeah, I totally get that."

He continues, "I was a first-timer myself, so I didn't know much then. But I've been in startups since then, and now I know that there is no place for assholes like Stronghold. Well, except for VCs – they're all assholes." I start laughing. "What's funny?" he asks.

"Nothing. Just someone I knew said that about VCs."

"Yeah, well it's true."

"I agree. Why did the company keep him on?" I ask, trying to forget.

"I have no fucking idea," Justin replies. "They had a strange relationship," he continues. "At the top. Those guys at CodeGenetics were always meeting in the conference room, and they never seemed to call Stronghold out on anything. It was like, I don't know, like he had something on them, some sort of trump card."

"Any idea what that card was?"

"No idea. I think the core patents were his, and he had his fingers in a lot of the technical pies at the company. I doubt they could have gotten rid of him without him making a big stink. He had a terrible temper, and a lot of people went through the company. Meaning they didn't stay long, either because of their choice or his. I don't know because I didn't work for him, but you could hear him yell a lot. One woman sued, I think, saying that he threatened her or something. I don't know the outcome of that…" He pauses and then continues. "I know a guy who stayed at the company after I left and saw it through a couple of the mergers. Made a little bit of money and ended up out in Silicon Valley at his own startup. He may know more if you want to talk to him. Stewart Cohen is his name, a nice guy. Goes by Stu. I don't stay in touch much with him, but I think I can get ahold of him if you like."

"Yes, please," I answer.

After the call, Jim and I sit for a moment. His brow is furrowed, and I can tell he is struggling with all of this. "Jim?" I ask. "This may be a stretch, but clearly this guy is difficult. It's awfully coincidental that Errol's advisor dies in a car crash and then Stronghold alone gets a license."

Jim clears his throat and replies, "Brie, it sounds like this guy is a complete asshole." I can't help myself. I laugh.

"What's funny?" Jim asks.

"Nothing. Just a lot of people say that about other people."

"Well, Stronghold sounds like an asshole, but I don't know that he is the kind of guy who murders to get what he wants." Jim finishes.

He was right; it probably didn't add up that an executive at a public company would murder not just once but twice. And even if he did, why Errol? Why now? It's been years since the UMass incident. What could trigger any issues now?

Jim leaves to go about Quixotic business. I muse for a while in my office, make a few notes, and get on with other things. I still have a job to do.

. . . .

That night, sitting on my terrace mourning my grandmother's pearls as I sip chardonnay from one of her cut crystal glasses, I think about where this is taking me. I sip my wine, admiring the many facets of the crystal. Arwen is playing with a new cat toy that Neal had brought her. My cellphone rings; it's Amy.

"Brie, I'm sorry I hung up the last time we talked. I just couldn't handle it, you know."

"Don't worry about it, Amy. I understand."

"Look, I didn't mention this before, but you asked about Stronghold. I know that Errol always believed that Martin Stronghold was involved in the car accident, that it wasn't actually an accident." There is a long silence.

"Amy, do you know why he thought that? Did he have any proof, any evidence, was it just a hunch?"

I hear her snort, a kind of derisive dismissal. I used to hear her make the same sound at company picnics and social functions. But it was a happier sound then. "It was way more than a hunch. We didn't discuss this more than once or twice. The first time was before we were married. We had gone on vacation to San Francisco. We had chartered a sailboat for the day, and you should have seen Errol at the tiller. It was a great day of heeling and salt spray. I asked him how he was. 'Soaking wet and perfectly happy,' was his reply. I was freezing when we got back and we jumped into the first bar we found. It was in North Beach, I remember. We started drinking even though it was still afternoon. We were doing malt scotch with beer chasers. I got really drunk, and Errol thought it was hilarious. You know how he was. He accused me of being a lightweight, and I started harassing him about his past in deep, dark liberal Amherst. I mentioned something about his having to have a female advisor/principal investigator because the men were all gay. I wasn't serious; God knows I am a feminist for heaven's sake, and I was just inventing everything for fun, but something that I said about Sall, his PI, really set him off. He started on about how it wasn't an accident and that Stronghold had been threatening her. I asked him how he knew, and he said that Sall told him that Stronghold was following her, sending her threatening letters, or maybe it was emails. He got a call from her shortly before the accident. Errol was convinced that it wasn't an accident."

"Did he go to the police with his accusations?" I ask.

"Yes, of course, he did, but you know how it's a really small town, and their guy was the Dean's brother, something like that. Errol knew everyone, you know Amherst. I guess the cop's dad was a policeman too, and his uncle was Mayor, all that kind of stuff. The allegations didn't go anywhere. Errol had to move on. But he never forgot."

There is a pause as I take all this in. I'm scribbling notes and my glass is empty. "Was there another time that he talked about Stronghold and his conviction that Sall's accident wasn't an accident?" I pour myself a refill. I should save some for Neal. *He'll accuse me of being a lush...*

"Yes, one other time. It was recent. I guess it had to do with the deal with Quixotic. Errol was aware that Stronghold was at NGX. In fact, he was the lead on the deal, Errol told me. At first, Errol was against the deal; knowing Errol, you probably witnessed some resistance at the office?"

I nod, and then realize that she can't see me. "Yeah, I remember, all right," I slurred, remembering his outbursts.

"Well, something happened that turned him around. He said something about getting one over on Stronghold. Something about him not getting what he wanted. I didn't think much of it at the time, but now I wonder if it had something to do with, you know..." she trails off unwilling to say the word.

I don't blame her. Her pain is still visceral. It is the same for all of us, and I can only imagine her lonely nights and mornings. Errol was a giant in so many ways. How do you fill a hole that big?

"Brie?" she interrupts my thoughts, "Do you think that Errol really did piss Stronghold off so much that he would, that he would kill him?"

"I don't know, Amy. I really don't know." I pause as Arwen scampers inside. I follow her, slowly closing my sliding glass door. My apartment is deathly quiet. "But I intend to find out."

"You won't do this alone will you?" she says anxiously. "Like New York. I don't want anything to happen to you..."

"Don't worry, Amy. We'll tackle this as a group. I am going to talk to Jim tomorrow. And I promise to meet with the detective too. He's new at this, but he's good. He'll be essential in figuring this out."

"OK," Amy sighs. She sounds exhausted. I hear a door slam in the background and a passel of high-pitched hallos. "Oh, the kids are just home; my goodness, it's 10 p.m. I have to go."

I drain my glass thinking that Amy has a lot to deal with. "I'll keep you informed. Don't worry."

"Thanks, Brie. You're a gem. You know that, don't you? He thought so too."

"I hope so," I reply. But she has already put down the phone. I realize that I didn't get a chance to tell her that the university has no record of any conferences or events that would take Errol to Saudi Arabia in January or March. Where's his passport, I wonder? I make a note to ask Amy for his passport. One more thing. Would it reveal anything else that I don't know?

Chapter 32
March 31

I sleep fitfully and wake up at 4 a.m. I make myself coffee. Plain Peet's coffee, not Italian Cappuccino. Sitting in my kitchen I start writing on the white board and giving my liver a rest by drinking tea. Neal laughs at me for having a white board in my kitchen, but it's great for scheduling, for reminders, for figuring out thorny problems – like solving a murder.

Errol thought that Stronghold murdered his PI but could never prove it. Of course, that meant a life-long, life-sized grudge. When it came time to doing a deal with NGX, Errol was against it because he didn't want to do anything that would benefit Stronghold or his company. But Errol came around, which means that he must have figured something out. Some stunt that he could pull that would screw Stronghold in the long run. What exactly was it? Did it have to do with how Stan structured the deal? I remember Errol's Cheshire cat grin when the deal was sealed.

. . . .

Errol looked like he had just won at squash.

"What NGX doesn't get," Matt explained at our weekly on-the-same-page meeting "is everything outside of HD66, including the other earlier stage drugs in our pipeline. They don't realize how much we have, how far along those programs are."

Stan added quietly, "They'll figure it out eventually." He glanced at Errol.

Errol put on a Buster Keaton deadpan face.

"We got them," Gigi said, laughing, her dark eyes glinting. "We got them sooo good. I just wish I could be there and see their faces when they realize…" She smiled brightly at Errol who beamed.

Ah, this is how you spell revenge.

....

I call Straler before I leave for the office. No answer. I am done with playing it safe. At 9 a.m. Matt, Jim, Gigi, and I convene in the conference room with the door closed. "You'll need some strong coffee," I announce. They looked surprised. Jim chuckles and immediately goes out. A few minutes pass and he comes back with a tray and cups of coffee. All done exactly how we like it. I smile at him and he smiles back. Complicity.

As they sip their coffee, I drop the bomb, "We know that there was someone else on the boat that night." The bomb explodes.

"There was?" gasps Gigi. She drops her cup.

"Yes, we do. I visited Captain Bob at the lock. He's sure that he saw a second person. Stra… Detective Henrik validated this too." There is a pregnant pause. "That's why we're done suspecting; I know that this is a murder case." Matt's brow furrows. "And I intend to solve it."

There is stunned silence. "To be clear, **N, A, S** and **U** are gone." I add in a low voice. "It's **H**. Whoever did this will go to jail." I let this sink in. I tell them of my conversation with Amy, and my findings from my research about Stronghold. I don't leave anything out. I can tell that they're uncomfortable with what I am insinuating. I finish. They look at me.

"Stronghold has motive."

"Shit!" Matt exclaims. "That's brilliant!" He starts laughing. We all sit there, a bit shocked. Obviously, Matt agrees. "You're right. Stronghold hated Errol. He wanted to take HD66 and what Errol was developing for Parkinson's. It was about retribution for him. We had no way of knowing that Errol was outsmarting him. Do you remember how Errol fought to have only HD66 in the deal and how carefully we worded the exclusions in the contract? It was so slick they didn't even notice. I mean we thought we got one over on NGX."

"We did," Gigi chimes in. "We certainly did, but it wasn't worth it," she says sadly.

"Errol was a better scientist than Stronghold, and I'll bet that our Parkinson's program shows more promise. If he got that in the deal he could bury it to keep his own program alive."

"Or claim it as his own," I interject.

"Brie, you think like a criminal," Matt says approvingly and smiles. "You fucking do."

"So, if I get this right," Jim says, "you think that Errol kept our Parkinson's program out of the NGX deal so that, when it became successful, it would put Stronghold's program to shame? Hamper the company. Maybe even jeopardize his job?"

We all pause. There is dead silence in the room.

"Is that enough for murder?" Gigi asks.

"I don't know," I answer truthfully. "But it's enough to go to Detective Henrik with."

"It's something, not nothing," Matt declares. "Go for it, Brie," Matt commands. *Ever the CEO.*

. . . .

Back in my office I have an email from Justin with a contact number and email for Stu. I email Stu, pithily explaining who I am, that I'm doing research for my company on CodeGenetics, and that it would be very helpful if I could ask him a few questions. We agree to Skype that afternoon.

In the meantime I call Straler and we agree to meet for lunch. "Anyplace but Ritter's," I beg.

"OK," he replies. "Their burgers are really good, though."

I give in, "Ritter's is fine, actually. I don't have much time," I say lamely. I hear his chuckle as we sign off.

Straler is waiting for me when I enter the diner. He gives me a big smile as I slide into the opposite side of the booth. I can feel the heat rise to my face, and I immediately bury my face in the menu. "You don't know it by heart?" he asks, goading me.

I look up. Straler is staring at me, his intense blue eyes boring into mine.

"OK, Brie, shoot. I know you've got something – for me," he teases.

I'm sure that I blush again, but I don't care. He tilts his head like Luna. "OK, I have some thoughts…" He's is still gazing at me. "OK more than thoughts," I admit. "A hunch, a suspicion." I see his blue eyes sparkle.

Ethyl, who has the brightest red hair on the planet, clears her throat. Clearly, she has been waiting. "Yinz know what ya wanna eat?" she asks, her gum popping and a big smile showing many crowned teeth with a wide dark line at the top where they meet her gums.

"I'll take the corned beef sandwich and fries," Straler says. "And for you, Brie? What would you like, dear?" he asks, mockingly.

"Oh, I'll take the vegetable soup and a roll."

Ethyl smiles, "Yinz wan anything to drink?"

I start, "coffee and water, which I see I already have," I add as Straler points to our coffees and water already on the table.

As Ethyl wanders off, I tell Straler the whole story, starting with Amy's call, the enmity between Errol and Stronghold, his suspicion that Dr. Mutase was murdered, the conflict at the university, the license, the startup, and his focus on Parkinson's Disease. Our food comes around the time I am mentioning the license with the university. Straler looks thoughtful as he munches, making a few notes in his book, looking intensely at me while he listens. I finish by telling him about my conversation at Quixotic.

"I wanted to include you, but I thought it would be best to do that in person," I explained.

"You mean after you already decided to take matters into your own hands?" *Is he accusing me?*

"No, I, well, I owed it to them to tell them right away. Anyway, you didn't answer your phone. I tried."

"Shit. Sorry." He's contrite. But he's angry. He doesn't like being left out. I guess that's why he's an up-and-coming detective.

He finishes the last of his fries and sandwich. I haven't touched my soup. He looks at the bowl, "Your turn," he announces.

I start to sip my soup and break my bread into little bits as he lays out a plan of action. It includes both of us. "We have to talk to Stronghold. And we have to do that in person. Can't do that over the phone. Too easy to lie or for us not to catch what he means." He pauses, then asks, "Fancy a trip to Boston?"

"I'd love to," I reply, mopping the last of my soup with a crust of bread.

"I'll take a few days afterwards and head to Amherst to visit my folks. My dad is sick, and I like to get there whenever I can." I add as an afterthought.

"Yeah, I remember," Straler says, reminding me of my trip to New York and the ruse about going up north.

"This time you'll know where I am," I say glibly.

"Yep, very true," he quips.

I don't tell him about the upcoming call with Stu. I figure he'd want to be there, and how would I explain about a cop listening in? Better to do this on my own. Safer, I thought. He's far away in California. *Did Boris ever make it there? He never called back.*

. . . .

I get a bit of background after we wave at each other from our computers as we start our Skype call. Stu had stayed at CodeGenetics through two mergers. He left with a generous severance package when they merged with Neuro Pharmaceuticals. He took six months off, surfing and diving in Hawaii. Then he relocated to the Bay Area and co-founded a startup based on technology that could help detect melanoma faster and cheaper than current methods. I told him that I wanted to talk about his time at CodeGenetics because I was doing research about people who had discovered and developed technologies for Parkinson's Disease. It was not quite true, but it would get to the heart of talking about Stronghold. I told Stu that I had found Stronghold through his scientific publications (this was somewhat true as I had read them as part of my research). I made it sound like we were maybe going to spin something off around Parkinson's and that we were looking for potential co-founders, advisors and board members. "Part of the due diligence is focused on who these people are and whether they would be good chemistry for our effort," I end my introduction.

"Oh sure," Stu says. "I can tell ya lots about Martin Stronghold. "He's been there a long time, you know. He's a good-bad guy. Some people don't like him; he's got one of those strong personalities, pun unintended, where you either are for him or against him, if you know what I mean. Oh, he can be difficult, don't get me wrong. He hired and fired indiscriminately, and there were people who that didn't sit well with. But I think that his science was basically sound, and the company was based on his technology.

They'd been pursuing different things before he came on board. I wasn't there from the beginning. I came on after Martin, but I knew the history. Martin was a master at fundraising. The guy could talk circles around anyone, and he's hard to resist. Particularly when he wants something. I had a good ending there, Martin made sure of that," Stu chuckles.

"I heard he can be prone to temper, that there have been some issues?" I query.

"Oh sure, Martin can be a train wreck when it comes to people. He gets angry, and he can hold a grudge. Not against me, mind you. I'm one of the good guys. But, yes, there have been some issues. Like with anyone with a big ego. You must see them there, in Picksburgh."

Did he just deliberately mispronounce my city? I see him smiling on the other end. "Anyway, like I said, people either like him and get along with him, play with him, or..." he trails off.

"Or what?" I ask innocently. I am sure that I look the part of the stupid strawberry blond...

"Or they don't," he ends abruptly. "Look is there a reason that you want to know? Martin is my friend. He's done a lot for me. I wouldn't be where I am without him. I'm not going to trash him. I really can't afford to get on his bad side..."

"Oh no," I answer quickly. "I'm sorry if you got that impression. I'm just trying to make sure that we get people on board who are able to get along and row in the same direction. I'm sure that you understand how important that is for a startup."

"Yeah, I gotcha there. Martin isn't really a startup guy, you know. He's been with a big company for a while, and he's pretty settled in his ways. He's got plans. I don't think that he'd change those for anyone, and he'd give anyone who tried to derail him hell. Know what I mean?" Stu pauses and then adds, "Look if I can help in any way, don't hesitate, but I gotta go. I'm gonna tell Martin that we talked."

Oh no! "Actually, it would be better for us," I say as sweetly as I can, "If you just keep this between us. I don't want him to get the wrong idea. And we haven't really decided... on the advisors and all that. I'd like us to ask him first, if it makes sense."

"OK," Stu replies. "Well, good luck with your project," and he signs off.

This might have been a mistake, I realize.

Buzz! I get a text message from Straler about going to Boston the next day. Quixotic would have to pay for my ticket, but he gave me the flight information so that I could book on the same flight. The text says that he has arranged to meet with Stronghold at 11 a.m. at his office. *I have work to do!*

Chapter 33
April 1

I am generally not included in board meetings. *What does a board do, really?* Jim is board chair. He runs the meetings like a dinner party, greeting the members individually, asking about their families, then bringing them all to order and proceeding through the very full agenda. There is always dessert – something sweet. He ends on a high note.

In the past, I prepared materials, and once I gave a short presentation. But they asked me to join the meeting today because it is about Errol. I dress carefully, knowing it will be a long and important day. I brief Matt, Jim, Gigi, and Stan about my conversation with Stu and my plan to go to Boston with Straler. No one has volunteered to go with me. Fine, I think. I'll solve this on my own. They all seem preoccupied with other priorities. *What could be more important than solving this murder? Of course, they don't know that I have another reason to find Errol's killer.*

It's 9 a.m. as I enter the conference room. Matt and Jim are the only official members of the board. Gigi and Stan attend the board meetings but don't have a vote. Errol was the same. He is noticeably absent. This is the first board meeting since his death.

Josh is there from Bigfoot. So is Jeb from Sanguine. I didn't pick either of them up from the airport. Glad of that. Errol was right about VCs. Plus they're all middle-aged white men. With names like Josh and Jeb. Bet they golf too. At the table is also Carleen, who runs the GreenBush local angel fund. NGX has no representation. They didn't want a seat, I'd been told at the time by a smug Errol.

I take my seat and glance around. There is a stony silence in the room.

Jim calls the meeting to order. "We are here to discuss some difficult decisions. This is a very challenging time in our company's history. Our drug has failed the final clinical trial. We have lost the deal with NGX. We are in a legal situation with them now about what rights we have to our drug, the data from the trial, and what they owe us. Our legal bills are mounting up. We have confidence that the situation with NGX will be resolved, but we cannot predict when or the final cost. We have lost our chief inventor and scientist. We have learned that his death was not an accident or a suicide. We know in fact that he was murdered." There is a hush in the room. "There is a detective working the case, and he has made some progress, but we have not yet learned the identity of the murderer. We are here today to discuss our future." He turns to Matt. "Anything to add, CEO?"

"Just that we need your support during these trying times."

Josh starts the conversation off. "First of all, I want to say how sorry I am that all of this is happening. I had such great hopes…"

Jeb from Sanguine interrupts, "Damn, Matt. Really? What the hell? We've got a company in the toilet, a lawsuit against a multi-billion dollar company, and, to top it off, a murder investigation that could drag on and on. This casts a shadow on future operations and funding. The stakes are high."

Carleen adds, "We have to face reality. We may need to make some changes."

"I can explain," Matt starts.

"Face reality!" Jeb yells. "You. Have. To. Face. Reality!"

Matt looks flustered. I've never seen him like this. Gigi melts into the wall behind her. Jim is silent but looks grave.

"There's no future here," Jeb continues. "This company is going down the tubes. We can't fund it. It's unfundable."

"Jeb, let's not be hasty," Matt cautions.

"I am not being hasty. To survive, this company will need to change. As Carleen says. We'll need new management and…"

"New management?" Matt thunders. "Are you firing me?"

Jeb answers, "Yes, Matt, that's exactly what we are doing."

"How long do I have?"

The board meeting has erupted into chaos. People are talking over each other, and I can't make sense of what is happening. All I know is that I heard that our CEO is being forced out. We will be leaderless and rudderless without both Matt and Errol. I will likely be out of a job, as will others. I see Jim's hands shake as he tries to bring order to the room. I realize I have nothing to add and slip out unnoticed.

Chapter 34
April 2

We are flying Southwest Airlines from Pittsburgh to Boston. I'm not sure the detective has been on a Southwest flight before. Like most Southwest newbies, he is confused about the open seating and how you line up. When I explain, and he gets in line with the other Bs, he starts joking with the folks in front of him and behind. A big toothy smile and they look like they are best friends. "Guess this makes for a lot more efficiency," I hear him say. I am in the Cs so am not in line with him. Straler looks over and smiles at me, gesturing that he'll see me on board as he moves up in line. Good thing he doesn't have to wear a uniform. A policeman might not be so popular.

"I hope that you know Boston," Straler asks me when I meet him in the gate area as I emerge from the plane. He doesn't have any luggage, and I have just a small carry on. He offers to carry it for me but I shrug him off. He takes it off me after I trip over it, and he laughs as he strides down the hallway towards the exit. I run to catch up.

I arranged to rent a car because I'll drive to Amherst after our meeting with Stronghold. "I'm pretty familiar with the city; we'll be fine. I know how to drive to our location in Cambridge. I can drop you off at a T station or the airport depending on what time we're finished. Unless you have to stay and, like, make an arrest."

He looks at me eagerly. "That's great. I've always wanted to go to Boston. Now here I am. With you," he says and he gives me that certain smile. *Quivers in my stomach.* Oh, Neal, I think.

NGX is on the main drag of Cambridge a few blocks away from MIT. There are several parking garages nearby, and we pull into one a few blocks away. We try to be casual as we walk the two blocks to NGX's headquarters. But Straler's strides are long and purposeful. I can barely keep up. Once inside, the usual young and attractive woman is behind the counter. Why is it never a man?

Straler introduces us. "I'm Detective Henrik. This is Ms. Prince. We're here to meet with Dr. Martin Stronghold," he says with a smile, which is returned in a big way. She says that she will be back shortly. Her hips sway as she moves down the hall.

A few minutes later she reappears with another woman, this one older and smartly dressed, clearly Stronghold's assistant. "I am so sorry, Detective. I apologize for this, but Dr. Stronghold was called away on important business early this morning. I tried calling the Quixotic main number, but there was no answer. It was before business hours and you had probably already left Pittsburgh. I really am so sorry." She does not sound sincere. After a short pause she adds, "Is there anything that I can help you with? Or, would you like to make another appointment?"

"We'll be in touch," Straler replies curtly.

The woman graces him with a tight smile. "Yes, I'm sure that you will." She turns and we hear her heels clicking down the hallway. We go outside into the Boston sun, the receptionist looking longingly as the door swings shut behind us. Straler is fuming.

"I don't buy it; getting called away at the last minute. What a snake," he says. "We'll try by phone. I'll arrange a call as soon as I'm back. We won't let him go. He HAS to talk to us," Straler assures me. "You go on to your folks."

"If you don't mind, I'll drop you at the T station." Straler glances at his watch. I realize that there's quite a bit of time before he has to catch his plane back to Pittsburgh.

"I have a better idea. Let's grab a cup of coffee. I can point out some fun places for you to walk. And, if you're hungry, Legal Seafoods is around the corner. And yes it is da best clam chowdah in de world," I say in a deliberate Boston accent.

He smiles. In the coffee shop I pull up a map of the T on my phone and show him where we are and how to get back to the airport. I give him some pointers on sites that he might enjoy in Cambridge and leave him to walk in the direction of the parking garage. I hear him whistling as I walk away. He's a happy, off-duty detective, out for a few hours in a fun place that he hasn't been before. Arresting a suspect will have to wait.

. . . .

I turn on the radio as I drive off. When I hit the Mass Pike it's only 11:30 a.m. Great. I'll be home by 1 p.m. My folks aren't expecting me until later, so I should call them and warn them. I look at the speedometer and realize I should slow down. I see a red car, maybe a Mustang, on my tail. Geez, he's close. I take a long breath and settle into my drive. Digging into my purse for my phone, I see that the red car is still behind me, really close. Too close. *Shoot. Back off, buddy.*

I swerve into the left lane and pass a couple of cars. Then I squeeze back into the right lane right behind a truck. The red car does the same. I slow down, and a bunch of cars behind the red car pull out into the left lane and pass. One guy flips me the bird as he zooms by. The red car, definitely a Mustang, is on my tail. Dangerously close. I move into the middle lane. The red car follows, cutting off another car.

In my rearview mirror I see something else. A white van is close behind the red car. I change lanes again. They both do the same. They are definitely following me, toooooo close. As I swerve out again into the left lane I see another car a few cars back swerving in and out of the lanes. It's a tan Camry, what my father had always dismissed as "the most generic of cars." Are they following me as well?

I have to call for help. I have Straler's cellphone number programmed into my favorites. I have the phone in my hand and see that I have a couple of missed calls. Then I hear a loud thump, some clattering in the rear, and then more big thumps. I press the call button. Shysta – I am bumped again! The phone is ringing. I hear Straler's voice, "Brie, are you there? Brie?"

I try to steer, but the car is turning sideways. "Oh, Straler..." I yank the wheel, but I have no control over the car. There are cars in both lanes next to me as I start to merge into the left lane. The red car in back is almost inside my car. "Oh no," is the last thought I have. I see green, white, then red, really loud red.

. . . .

I'm on a movie set, and the actors pretend they know me. They call me by my name, ask me questions, and talk to me. They're sweet and I wonder why actors get such bad raps about their egos. Not here. Not in my world. I must be dreaming because I hear my mom's voice. Someone is holding my hand. "Brie, dear?" I hear from far away. It's my mom. I'm home and am never going to grow up. I'm in my room at home. I turn my head to look out my window, at the trees growing by the creek behind our house. But the house is black. It must be night. I don't think I'm in my room anymore. I'm somewhere else. Somewhere where I cannot move. I can move my head but I can't see. I'm blind. I start to scream and I hear all kinds of noise, but through it all my mother's voice. What is she saying? Why am I here? Where's my father? Someone is crying. I sink down into the black eternity. I am sad that I did not get a chance to say goodbye.

Chapter 35
April 4

I hear my mother. I turn my head to the sound of her voice. "Look, she's waking up again," I hear her say.

"Mom?" I try to say. But my voice is thick and soft; my mouth feels full of cotton wool. I move my hand to take the fuzz out of my mouth and my hand hits something not in my mouth but on my face. I feel my face. There is something across my eyes and forehead. I bring my other hand up, but I can't feel with it. My right hand is in a glove. *What the heck?* I probe with my free hand and realize that there is a covering over my upper face that goes around the back of my head. My right hand is in a glove, my fingers stuck together. And one leg, the one I broke skiing, is in some sort of fixture; I can't move it.

"Honey," I hear my mother say. "Nod your head that you can hear me." She is louder than she need be, I think. But I nod. "Brie, you are in the hospital. You had an accident." She pauses, and my body jerks awake. An accident? I remember the car sliding sideways. "You were in a car accident, on the way to see us." Her voice breaks. "Brie, I am so sorry, but you're OK. You had some cuts near your eyes so they bandaged you, but the glass didn't get in your eyes, they're pretty sure. The bandages are a precaution. You have some deep gashes on your hand, your right hand. So it's bandaged too. And your leg, the left one, the one you broke skiing last year, that got kind of mashed, so they had to put in more pins." She pauses and takes a deep breath. "But it's fine; it's not that serious, and you are going to be fine. They wanted to put you out so that you could rest and let your body start the healing."

It takes me a couple of times, but I finally manage to mumble, "How did you know?"

I hear a voice. "I was there, Brie." Not my mother's voice. *Who is there?*

"I am so sorry, Brie. I was too late, just too late."

"Straler? I manage to ask. "Are you here?"

"I'm here, Brie. Right here." He sounds awful. Like he's choking to death or something.

My mom interjects, "Honey, this young man is the one who brought you here. He called 911. Rode in with you. You've been here for two days."

I hear Straler again. "Brie, I called Quixotic. They needed to know."

My mom again, "Brie, it's Saturday. I have someone watching Dad. You're going to be here another day or two they tell me. Neal will be here any second. Your detective friend, Straler, has been here the whole time. He told us about you two traveling together to Boston. I don't understand, Brie. Is there something going on? He won't tell me. Said I had to wait until you could tell me yourself." She pauses and blows her nose. I can't hear, but I know that she is crying. *Don't cry, mom.* She has my hand, my good hand, and squeezes it gently. "Anyway, you're safe now. You can tell me when you feel better."

"Mrs. Prince, I can explain if you like…"

"No need, detective. Like you said. It's best if I hear it from her. We are very indebted to you for doing what you did. That you brought her here, that she is safe now, that's all I care about." She sniffles again.

I hear someone else blowing a nose. And a hoarse cough. "Of course." Is that Straler? Is he saying something? I am slipping in and out of a fog that I cannot shake.

I hear my mother's voice again. "Brie, I'll stay here a while, and then I am going to go home. I'll come back tomorrow." A pause. She is crying again. In all of my years with my mother, I have never heard her cry. She is always the strong one. Not this time. "Brie, we're so lucky that you are OK."

I think I am crying too, but I can't tell because of the bandages. I try to grasp at them. "They will take off the bandages very soon, honey," she says. "The nurse is right here."

I hear a low voice. It's a male nurse with somewhat of a lisp, "Of course we can take those off, honey. Let me just check with Dr. Levine to be sure. I'll be right back, sweetie." I want to laugh, but I can't; my face hurts when I try to smile.

"He's a dear," my mother tells me. "Jack is his name. Jack Grace, can you imagine?" She chuckles and strokes my hand.

Sometime later Jack the nurse comes back and changes the bandages on my face. "Those cuts will heal just fine," he tells me. "You're so pretty, and the doctor made super tiny stitches to minimize the scarring. Most of it is above your bangs anyway, darlin'. We're leaving them on your eyes for another little bit. You OK, sweetheart?" Nurse Jack asks. "Don't worry. You'll be able to see fine very soon. You're in good hands here."

"The best," I say, but I'm not sure the words make it past my lips.

The door bursts open. I can tell that it's Neal. I hear his sound. His voice. "Brie, oh my God, Brie. Brie, my God. You're alright. They told me. I came as soon as I could. What happened?" He is stroking my hair, my arm. I feel drops on my free hand. He lifts it gently. "I got a call from Jim last night, and I couldn't get a flight out until today. I drove. It took me about the same amount of time, but I just couldn't sit there and wait. Are you alright? I talked to your mom last night, and she said that you were out of it, but fine. No real damage, she said. Are you OK? Talk to me, Brie."

I hear the scraping of chairs. "Oh, Mrs. Prince, I'm Neal. I'm so sorry. I should have been here…" I can't hear what is happening, but I hear sobs and clothes brushing. Are they hugging – my mom and my boyfriend? This is the first time they have met. I guess they've hit it off. *I couldn't plan it better than this.*

I hear Neal jabbering at me like he can't stop. He finally shuts up, and I try to smile but it hurts, and so I just say, "I'm glad you're here. I have a lot to tell you." I am not sure that I actually speak or just think the words. I reach out with my good hand. I feel his hand in mine. It is lovely and cool. He strokes my hand with his other hand. I really do love him, I think. He's the sweetest man I have ever known. I feel wet drops again. "Is it raining in here?" I ask. I hear Neal laugh and choke at the same time. "Am I on drugs?" I ask to whoever is there, waving my head from side to side.

Jack the nurse giggles as he answers, "Of course, darling; enjoy 'em while they last!"

I hear another voice. "Hello Neal. I'm Detective Straler Henrik. I've been working with Brie, here, on the Errol Pryovolakis case."

"Oh, hello, pleased to meet you," Neal says. They are probably shaking hands. Neal sounds so polite, like he is at a holiday party. I want to laugh, but I can't. I hear them talking although I have no idea what they are saying. I must have fallen asleep. When I wake, it's quiet. I reach out and startle someone. It's Neal. He was asleep in a chair next to my bed.

Then I hear another voice, a lilting voice that sounds like a bird. "Brie, I am here. Can you see me?" It's Shala, wonderful, sweet Shala.

"Hello," I say. "Shala? You are here? I can't see you, but I will be able to soon. You came here for me?"

"Yes, Brie, I came when I hear what happened. Are you OK? I am so very glad to be here and knowing you will be fine." I hear a change in her tone. "Oh, you must be the very nice Neal that Brie has told me about. I am Shala. I work in university. I am Dr. Errol's post doc. I am knowing Brie for some time."

I hear shuffling. Neal must be standing up. "Oh, yeah, hi Shala. Thanks for coming. I know that Brie is glad to see you. We're thankful that you've come. Very thoughtful. Hey, I need some coffee. While I get that, Shala, you can sit right here and visit with Brie."

"Oh that would be so much wonderful. Thank you very much." She declines his offer of coffee, but she says yes to tea. I hear her sit down. She smells like vanilla.

Jack the nurse putters around me a bit. Then he says something about changing shifts and that he will see me later. He tells me that he will take my bandages off my eyes when he comes in tomorrow. He says something to Shala about sleeping a lot, and then Shala is talking to me in her lilting singsong voice.

I hear Neal come back in the door. "Tea for you, Shala. Coffee for me. And donuts for both of us," he laughs gently as I hear him set the tray down somewhere close. Don't eat too many of those, I want to say, but I am sleepy.

I hear Shala ask me if I would like her to read to me.

"Oh yes, I would love that."

"What do you like me to read, Brie?"

"A good mystery," I say. "A good startup mystery." I don't hear the response.

. . . .

I wake and hear that my mother is back. I am feeling better, more awake. Nurse Jack comes in. I can hear the swish of his entrance. "Hello dahlings," he says. "I'm here to check on my favorite patient! I feel a pinch and hear a few high-pitched beeps. "Here we go sweetheart." Then he unwraps my bandages. I can see. Sort of. I blink. The room is fuzzy. "Give yourself some time to get adjusted, sweetheart," he says. "You won't see right away, but you will soon. And when you do, what a sight." He must be leaning in because I hear him whisper, "You have the cutest men who love you. This one, he's tops." I can see vaguely that he is gesturing toward Neal who is holding my hand. He has little rivulets of tears running down his dark handsome face. *Who says men don't cry? I love him for his tears.*

A doctor comes in. She probes and pushes, and I hear more beeps. Nurse Jack is there the whole time. The doctor tells me that I can go home tomorrow. I will be on crutches for a few weeks, she tells me, but my face and hand are healing well. My mother tells me I should come home to Amherst to recover, but I want to go back to Pittsburgh. I tell her that I can work from home, and that Neal and the Quixotic team will take care of me. I know that she has her hands full with my dad, and I will just be one more invalid. It will be easier this way, although I don't tell her that. We make arrangements for another visit when I am better, about six weeks away. It will be well into fall by then, and I tell her that I will come for a long weekend.

"The colors will be beautiful then," she admits. "I know you love the autumn leaves."

It will be beautiful then. I will bring Neal with me. That will be the right time to tell him, to show him. Neal is holding my hand. I squeeze his. He returns my squeeze gently. His dark eyes are glistening again. We don't talk. We don't need words.

Sunday night, I get a call from Jim. He wants to come up. "Don't," I plead with him. "I'm getting out of here tomorrow and coming straight home, to Pittsburgh. Really, Jim, Neal is here; my mom is here; Shala came, and Straler only just left. I'll need help in Pittsburgh. I can guilt you into lots of help then, OK?" I really don't want any more action in the hospital. I just want out at this point.

"Well, alright," Jim says reluctantly.

"How is Quixotic?" I hardly dare ask, but I can't help myself.

"Not good," Jim admits.

"Matt?" There is a long pause. He clears his throat. I can tell that Jim is thinking of how to tell me. "Is Matt still there?"

"We had a second board meeting. While you were gone. Matt presented a plan, what I thought was a good plan, but…"

"And? I need to know, Jim."

"Matt is gone, Brie. I'm sorry. Particularly sorry to tell you this way."

Jim sounds calm, but I know that it must be turmoil there. I can only imagine the chaos, the pain. I wince as I try and move my leg. "Jim, who is CEO now? It's you, isn't it?"

"They have asked me, yes. I agreed to be interim CEO only. I also requested some other changes. I want to promote you, Brie. I want you as my right hand. We need to decide on a clear plan for the future."

I am wanted. I am the luckiest young woman alive. I laugh out loud at my thoughts. Here I am in the hospital after a terrible accident where I was almost blinded, and I may never walk again without limping – and I think that I am lucky! Neal and my mother are looking at me like I am crazy. Nurse Jack has a big smile and mouths "Drugs" to them, including me.

"Jim, I am happy, of course, and honored. We can get into details later. But what about Gigi? Didn't she want to be CEO?"

Jim chuckles softly. "You are smart, Brie. That's why you are so valuable. We'll talk about Gigi when you get back."

They decide to discharge me on Tuesday instead of Monday. They want me to do physical therapy on my hand as well, and they give me some instructions about my broken foot. Shala calls my cellphone, and I listen to her voicemail. "Oh Brie, we are so happy that soon you will be out of hospital. I know that you won't be meeting for coffee, but I would like to serve you some special tea from my country. It is very good tea you see. You will like it, and I will be so very happy to see you again."

On Monday afternoon I get a visit from Straler. He had gone home for a couple of days. He has someone with him. Straler looks at me. "Brie, this is my boss."

"Detective Small, Jennifer Small," she introduces herself. Everyone is introduced. I see Neal shake Straler's hand after his look of surprise. Straler smiles a big smile. Neal looks at me with a worried expression.

"Wow, they spring for you both to come up here?" I ask. They look at each other. "Did something happen? Is it Stronghold?" The accident rushes back to me. "Did he, was he, the red car, did he try to kill me?"

My mother takes a short intake of breath. Neal chokes. "What is going on?" my mother asks sharply. "Is there somebody trying to kill Brie?"

"Someone wants to kill her?" Neal asks, incredulously.

Detective Small immediately takes control. "Listen, I am sorry about all of this, but, no, no one is trying to kill your daughter, Mrs. Prince. And no, Brie, Stronghold was not in any of the cars in the accident." She pauses. "Detective Henrik checked and Stronghold wasn't involved." She looks around the room.

The fog is completely gone and all I can feel is pain in my hand, my arm, my face. I know that I am crying, but I don't care. "I don't understand. Who would want to…"

"Brie, everyone," Detective Small continues. "For some of you who don't know, we are investigating a murder, or a potential murder. We don't know what happened to Dr. Errol Pryovolakis. We know that someone else was with him on the boat when he died. That's what brought Brie and Detective Henrik up here, when she, when you," she nods towards me, "had the accident. They were here to question a guy at a company called NGX, name of Stronghold, who had some dealings years ago with Dr. Pryovolakis. We came back up here this morning to meet with Stronghold. No ducking out this time. We made it clear that this was a very serious matter, that lives were at stake. So we brought Stronghold in for questioning. At the station, here in Boston. We spent an hour with him earlier today." She pauses and looks around, her glance resting on her subordinate.

Straler takes over. "He didn't do it, Brie," he says simply, pausing after he spoke. "I thought that Stronghold was behind your accident. I was pretty insistent." He looks at Detective Small who rolls her eyes.

"Detective Henrik is a very convincing young detective." She smiles, just a hint of upturned lips.

I look at Straler. He smiles at me. "Actually, it was kind of funny, Brie, because after I landed in Pittsburgh, I almost had to turn right around to come back. I'm starting to get to know Boston. I like the city."

"We gave Henrik only enough time to go home and pack a bag with a change of clothes," Detective Small adds. "We pulled Stronghold in with the help of our Boston colleagues."

She pauses and Straler chimes in, "Brie, there is no way that he did it, any of it."

Detective Small assumes control again. "Stronghold has a rock solid alibi for when he left town. We checked. It panned out. So the rental car accident? He just couldn't have had anything to do with it."

"Did you ask about Errol, about the past?" I query.

"Of course," Detective Small starts. "We got the whole story. There was a lot of resentment about some technology from a long time ago. We gather that they didn't like each other. Actually, they were rivals. I think they despised each other. But Stronghold didn't kill him."

Straler took over. "He has an alibi for when Errol died too. A pretty good one. A board meeting with all kinds of muckety-mucks in the room. All prepared to swear that he was there all night. He couldn't have gotten down to Pittsburgh in time." He stops and the room is silent. "He's not a nice man, Brie. He's, well, he's an asshole. Sorry, boss," he sends a guilty smile towards Detective Small.

"Agree with you actually, detective."

He picks up the story. "A real asshole, like we knew he was going to be," Straler says decisively. "We had done all this research on him, well Brie did most of it," he states to the room at large. He turns back to me and lowers his voice. "But he's not a criminal."

"What about the threats to Sally, to Errol's PI?"

"PI, what's that?" Detective Small asks sharply.

Before I can answer, Straler fills in, "Principal Investigator. Brie means Errol's academic advisor, thesis advisor, at the university when he was getting his PhD. This woman, the PI, she died suspiciously. Or it could be viewed as suspicious. We think Errol thought so. Stronghold was in Amherst then too. He was a professor. Brie found out from Errol's wife, Amy, and from some other folks, that Errol might have thought Stronghold arranged an accident, a car accident, sort of like Brie's, to get control of a certain technology. That was a long time ago. He said that he didn't kill her. To us. He did admit threatening her because she was holding up the deal. But he didn't kill her, or that's what he swears. He said he felt awful about the accident and realized that Errol blamed him, but he never wanted to kowtow to Errol either so he just dropped it."

"He's clean," Detective Small finishes. "He just didn't do it." She turns to me. "Brie, we don't even know if Errol's death was a murder. We are running out of leads and I am afraid that our department is not going to let this be an open case for much longer."

I don't say anything. There is nothing to say. I remember Shala asking me if I wanted her to read to me. I wish that she was here so that I could bury myself in a good book and forget about all that has happened.

Straler's phone rings and he steps out of the room to answer it. "Really?" I hear him almost shout. A minute later, he comes back into the room. "I have news," he said. We all look at him expectantly. He glances at his boss. "The guy driving the red car? Turns out his name is Boris Zokshin." Straler pauses as we take this in. "He's dead."

Chapter 36
April 7

The day after I am back, Straler comes to my apartment. Neal took the day off of work to stay with me. *Is he jealous? Or just curious?* When I ask, he tells me that he is staying home for my safety. "You get into the worst trouble, dear Brie. And I am going to share it with you from now on." I don't see how he really can do that, but I am happy to have him with me today.

Straler looks super cute and clean when I answer the door, leaning on my crutches. Big grin to me and a greeting to Neal. They're like old friends, with their "Hey, Neal," and "Hey, detective." "Call me Straler." "Yea, bro," and all that. It's like a secret club.

We sit down at my kitchen table and Neal makes coffee. Arwen comes in meowing for a treat and rubs up against Straler's leg. "Arwen, stop, I say," thrumming my fingers on the table to lure her away in case Straler doesn't like cats.

"Arwen?" he asks. "As in Tolkien's Arwen, the beautiful half-elven from Rivendell who chooses love of Aragorn over eternal life?" I look at him in surprise. "I read *Lord of the Rings* twice, and I've seen the movies a dozen times," he says sheepishly with a crooked smile.

"Me too!" I exclaim. "Yes, she is Arwen as in…" Neal looks at me and I shut up.

Straler pulls out a notebook. I see that it is almost full. The case has been going on for a while. He looks at me intently, his blue eyes glistening. "Brie, I've done some research on Boris."

I remember Boris zooming off on his motorcycle. Straler's face is lit up like a flashlight. This guy loves his job, I think. And I am his partner. I feel like I'm letting him down. I don't feel any closer to solving who murdered Errol, or finding what he left for me. I reach for the bottle of capsules on the table. "I'm still on pain killers," I explain. Neal and Straler exchange a look with raised eyebrows.

Then Straler launches into a long explanation of what he had found out about Boris. I am not following the whole conversation, but I sit there with a smile on my face.

"The meds," I hear Neal whisper to Straler.

"Yea, right."

I hear snatches of how Boris was involved in the Russian Mafia. It had some other name, but Straler couldn't remember it. I started laughing and he ended up saying that he would just call it the "Russian Mafia."

"Yea, got it," I say. At least I think that I said it out loud. I am not sure because Straler keeps talking. By this time Neal is taking notes. In my notebook. "Hey that's my…" But I don't think that they hear me as they just kept going, Straler talking, Neal listening and writing. They sound far away. I must have nodded off because I wake up on the couch. I am covered by a blanket. There is a note on the coffee table.

"Honey, I took notes. Read them so that you know what Straler told us. I had to run by the office to get some work done. I'll be back tonight." I check my phone, which is conveniently plugged in on the floor next to the couch. I look out the window, and it is nearly dark. 7 p.m., I guess. It hurts to sit up and even more to stand. Neal had put my crutches within reach. I turn on some lights and go into the kitchen. My notebook is on the table. There is a post it marking the spot to start reading. *How thoughtful.*

What I read makes me sit bolt upright in spite of the pain. Half way through, I make myself a pot of coffee. I remember the part about the Russian Mafia and Boris. It seemed that this happened before he came to the U.S. and certainly before his involvement with Quixotic. Wow, was he working for the Russian bad guys the whole time I knew him, I wonder?

Apparently, as a result of his scientific expertise, he got involved in drug distribution – medical drugs – on the black market. He was some sort of wunderkind at his university in biochemistry, where he got his Russian equivalent of a PhD. He had been tapped while he was still at school to leverage contacts between pharma companies looking to expand into Russia and large distribution firms which landed monopolies to distribute medicines to hospitals and clinics. That didn't sound too bad to me, but then I read that the operation expanded into other types of drugs, including heroin, cocaine, and other illegal substances. Apparently, the ring was enormous with business happening all throughout the country. With Putin as President since 2000, corruption and these sorts of activities were rampant. Officials turned a blind eye. Pockets were lined. As Boris rose in the ranks, so did his illegal activities. That's where his interaction with Popov Brothers started.

Straler specifically identified the Popov firm as being part of the ring of illegal drug distribution. In 2009, the Putin kleptocracy cracked down, probably to international pressures. Boris narrowly escaped being caught and sent to prison. He fled to the U.S. *Where he got a job as a scientist for Quixotic!*

I keep reading. Straler had discovered that Boris was wanted on Interpol's Red Notice list, which is a kind of international wanted poster for fugitives. Straler further discovered that Interpol has long been accused of allowing its Red Notices to be used for political purposes. There were some articles that came out in *The New York Times*. Neal's notes state that Straler would send me the links to the articles. The notes end with "Call Straler when you get this far."

Picking up on the first ring, Straler explains that the reason that Boris likely left Pittsburgh is because he was discovered. Even though he had changed his name, the Russians had found out. "Probably through the Popov connection."

"Yes, exactly. Once he was back in touch with them, things escalated and he had to flee from both Interpol AND the Russians. They likely wanted to kill him because of what he knew. He was no longer valuable to them. They had no loyalty to him."

My mind ponders the obvious. "Why was he in the red car following me? Was he trying to kill me?" I shudder and reach for the pain bottle but then push it aside. I have to stay cogent. And awake.

"I don't think so, Brie. But that's my next investigation. I will find out why he was in the car, and why he was following you."

. . . .

Later that night, with Arwen on my lap and Neal at my side, we talk about what Straler had discovered.

"The connection between Boris and Popov must go way back. But why would they want to kill Errol?"

"Or you?" Neal asks gently.

"You know I have half a mind to…"

"NO WAY," Neal shouts. "You are NOT going to Russia. No earthly way, Brie!"

"I was going to say, call the cellphone number that he left me," I reply. Neal was right, I WAS going to say that I had half a mind to book a flight to Russia, but Neal's reaction makes me change my mind to something more realistic.

"He left you a number?" Neal is shocked. "Why didn't you tell me? Tell Straler when he was here earlier?"

"I forgot." It was lame, I knew but it was all I could think of. "I called it before, but no answer. I'll call it again. With Straler, I promise. Tomorrow. Right now I need help getting to bed."

Neal smiles and helps me up. "Now you're asking me to do something I am actually good at," he chuckles to me as he helps me down the hall and into bed.

Chapter 37
April 8

In the morning, Neal drops me off at the office. I hobble in and Jim rushes to hug me. He feels terrible that he didn't visit me in Massachusetts or at my apartment. "I did call, did Neal tell you?"

"Yes, Jim, no worries. And the flowers are lovely." He had sent three bunches of flowers, roses, a spring bouquet, and a lovely bunch of tulips. I didn't have vases and they had looked pretty sad sitting on the counter as Neal searched through my cabinets finding only half-finished bottles of booze and a few of my grandmother's glasses.

"How do you live?" he sputtered as he stormed out to buy a vase. When he returned, he primped the flowers back to life and acted miffed for hours until I melted him with a request to help me set up my apartment better once I was back on my two feet.

"For us," I said, and Neal beamed.

Jim jolts me back to reality. "Brie, I know that you are still on crutches – again – but I have to talk to you right away." In his office, he offers me the job he mentioned before. "A new job: Director of Strategic Relationships," he says with a warm smile in spite of looking so frail a wind could knock him over. "We need you more than ever, Brie. The board and I have some clean-up to do. We have to calm them down. To save the company. You will accept won't you?"

Of course I will. I'd have to be insane to not accept this elevation at my age and level of experience. That I don't deserve it, don't have the experience for it, is irrelevant to Jim. The company is desperate, he says, to "gain normal footing on rocky ground." He seals the deal with an assurance that he will be there with me every step of the way. He also mentions that I will be working directly for him, not for Gigi. I think about her deep, dark eyes. They will be angry.

As I hobble from his office to mine, I pass her. She is looking like the old Gigi in a black suit and high heels. As she clicks her heels towards me, I expect a hug and a smile. I get neither.

"Brie, so sorry for your troubles," and she breezes on by with an icy look. She hates me, I realize. I nearly fall off my crutches. I've been promoted. Jim is CEO, not her. She is no longer my boss. And she is certainly not my friend.

. . . .

I am light years behind in my email. Between my eyes being bandaged at the hospital, and my vision being blurry for a while, not to mention the painkillers and a bottle of Dalwhinnie malt scotch that Neal got me, I had let the email pile up. Now that I'm back at Quixotic, I need to catch up. I close the door to my office and sit down at my computer. I am immediately overwhelmed. All I want is to do is find Errol's killer, find what he left for me, and get back to normal at Quixotic. Most of the email is not important, and I file everything that can wait in a "To-Do" folder. One email catches my eye, however. I don't recognize the sender but the subject startles me: "STOP your investigation." They have my attention whoever it is. I read the email:

> Brie Prince, we know what you are doing. We are watching. Stop your investigation into the death of Dr. Errol Pyrovolakis. No good will come of this investigation. If you persist, you will find things that you do not

want to know and they will be harmful to you and to those around you. I urge you to stop now!

Am I being threatened? Who sent this? I must be getting close. Making them nervous. Good, I want you to be nervous. You won't get away with murder…

My phone buzzes and I jerk it out of my purse. It's them, I am sure. "Hello? Who is this and what do you want?"

"Brie, it's Maya Pendyala," says a surprised voice. "I am returning your call." I breathe a sigh of relief. Maya is Errol's colleague from Centre, who was collaborating with him on Parkinson's.

"Oh, sorry about that. I thought you were somebody else. Thank you for returning my call." I had followed up when I learned that she'd been with Errol in Russia. What I gathered as she talked is that no one is talking to her about Errol. She feels terrible about what happened. But, yes, she had gone on the trip to Russia.

"It was in January, I think. Maybe February, I don't remember exactly. Two years ago. It was after some animal experiments, and we had preliminary data to present at a big neurodegenerative disease conference. I remember being annoyed with Errol because he was so proper about not including any real information. He wanted to keep that a secret because, if it worked, he wanted it to be part of the company and 'you do things differently in a company than in academia,' he kept telling me. Ah, I miss him terribly." Maya sighs. "Anyway, about Russia, it was a short trip. Two days in Moscow and two days of travel, you know how it is."

"Did anything happen while you were over there? Did he meet with anybody or talk about licensing the technology or something like that? I ask.

"I wouldn't know, really. I had caught a cold, so I was in bed early and mainly saw the inside of my hotel room." She pauses. "I do recall that he met someone, might have been part of a group, cousins that all worked together, or something like that. They came up to him after the talk, and I remember they were really interested in the Parkinson's work. They said something about marketing it in Russia. I didn't pay much attention. Commercialization, marketing, and all that was Errol's bailiwick, not mine."

"Was it a good conversation, do you think? Errol didn't get upset or anything?" I knew that I was fishing, loading the bait, but I had to get her to think about this in a way that was not normal for her. Faculty researchers don't get involved in commercialization, but they really don't get involved in murder cases!

"No, not at that time, I don't think. But he arranged to meet with them later that night. I was tired; probably went to bed. I didn't think much of it, but, now that you ask, I remember that the next morning he was absolutely furious about something. Something to do with a meeting that he had had the night before. I didn't connect the dots, but it's very possible it was a conversation with those guys. They were all related. And they had a funny name that was like a drink.

"Popov?" I ask.

"Yes, exactly, like the vodka. I remember thinking that is a pretty hilarious name, given the Russians' reputation for alcohol consumption."

"But you don't know why Errol was angry, what was said? If they wanted something?"

Maya sounds crestfallen, "I'm sorry, Brie. I would tell you if I knew. I really would. But I never did find out. Now, we'll never know."

Oh, we might. "Thanks, Maya. You've been a great help. Really."

. . . .

There is a soft knock on my door. It's Straler. He comes in and closes the door behind him. "What's up with Gigi? I just passed her in the hallway, and I thought she might sting me."

Ugh, bees. "Pay no attention to her. There are internal politics going on. She wanted to be CEO. But she didn't get the job. She's not right to lead this company, anyway."

"Aren't you getting sophisticated and cynical!" Straler says with an admiring glance.

I dismiss him with a wave. We don't have time to discuss things unrelated to Errol's murder. I tell him about my call with Maya. He sits across from my desk, and I put my phone in between us. I tell him about Boris leaving me his cellphone number. "I want you to be on the call in case we find anything out that is important."

"Brie, Boris is dead. We don't know if anyone has that phone or what it might mean. The car didn't belong to him. It belonged to a woman named Vivian Christophe. We are investigating if she has any link to Boris."

"It's worth a try. He told me that no one else would have this number." I unfold the scrap of paper that Boris had left me and dial the number. A woman's voice answers the phone. She sounds surprised, maybe confused.

"Hello? Who is it?"

I explain that I knew Boris at Quixotic and that he gave me this number to call him.

"He gave you this number?"

"Yes, he did. He, um, trusted me." We hear a sob on the other end of the line. "Do you know Boris? Do you know what happened?"

"I am Vivian Christophe, Boris' sister."

Straler and I look at each other. He smiles. He loves this.

Vivian continues, "I live in Boston. Boris left me his phone few days ago. He was all in a rush. He needed to borrow my car right away he said. I was very confused because I had only just dropped him off at the airport. I thought he was leaving, but then he showed up on my doorstep and said that he would be in touch later. I don't think that he meant to leave me the phone. But it was too late. He was out of the door and the driveway a minute later. Then I get the call from the police. He was in a car accident. My car is totaled. Boris is dead."

"Vivian, I am so sorry about your loss. We were very fond of your brother at our company where he worked. I hate to ask you this, but I am with a detective in Pittsburgh, and we would like to ask you a few questions. I know that this is painful, but it's important. It might lead to understanding what happened to Boris." Straler looks at me appreciatively.

"Vivian," Straler steps in. "My name is Detective Straler Henrik, here in the City of Pittsburgh. I am investigating a potential murder of a man that Boris worked for. I was at your brother's accident site."

"You were?" I ask incredulously and Straler quickly punches the mute button on my phone.

"Tell you later," he says. "Let's do this first." He punches the mute button again. "Vivian, I don't know all of the details of the accident but am determined to find out. I believe that there is a link between your brother being in that car and Brie Prince here being in another car."

"What?" I mouth to him. He nods to me and holds up his finger to wait.

"Vivian, I need to ask you some very difficult questions..."

What we learn, in between the tears of his sister, is that Boris had just visited his sister in Boston. He had told her that he was in trouble and was going to disappear again for a while. She took him to the airport to fly back to California. She didn't know much about why Boris was in trouble. Or, at least she didn't tell us. But we already knew some of it from Straler's research.

"So what happened at the airport?" I ask when we hung up with Vivian.

"Guess who he saw?" Straler answers with a glint in his eye?

"You mean me? He saw me? He saw us at the airport?"

"Yep, at least that's what I think. Brie, I think that he saw you and wanted to tell you something."

"What about?"

Straler sighs, "We'll never know for sure, but I'd hazard a guess that he had something to tell you about the Popov Brothers, or about Errol. He knew that you were investigating."

"So you think that he followed me. That he knew that I was in the car. That he was driving close behind because he wanted to..."

"Not to kill you, Brie. He wanted to talk to you. Remember that he left his cellphone with his sister? When he realized that he had no phone, my guess is that he was trying to get close to you so that you would see him and stop your car."

I pause and think through the implications. "So, if Boris hadn't left his cellphone at his sister's, he might have been able to call me and the accident might never have happened?" I remember the missed calls.

"Yes, that's a possibility."

"But he hit me with that red car. Why did he do that? He just wanted to talk to me, right?"

"Brie, there was another car behind him." I remember the white van. Swerving as I swerved. I hadn't understood, but it becomes clear with a chilling realization. "The guys in the van were trying to kill him."

"Oh my gosh, Straler, it was the white van!"

"Yes it was."

"And you were there?"

"Yes, Brie. I had second thoughts of you driving alone to your parents, and so I decided to follow you. I rented a tan Toyota Camry."

I look at him and I know that my face registers shock.

"Brie, it's not that I don't trust you, get it? But I was concerned for you, after New York and all..." Straler looks down at his hands.

"That was you? I saw that car. In fact, I saw that car as I was trying to call you!"

"Brie, I got the call. I was there. I only wish I could have stopped what happened. I feel terrible about you. That's why I was there at the hospital. I couldn't leave until... well, until we knew you were alright."

"What about the white van?"

"The white van got away. I got the license number and we've traced it through a bunch of levels to find out that it's owned by a firm that has Russian connections. To Popov Brothers."

I walk Straler to the elevator with difficulty on my crutches. He smells like fresh cut grass, I think, as I try to regain my balance after he hugs me goodbye. Some men just have an earthy smell.

Chapter 38
That same day

A few hours later, as I recount this to Jim, in preparation for a call to Popov Brothers, I wonder again about my idea of going to Russia. How could we find out anything on the phone? I also remember what Boris said about one of the partners. "You know Jim, Boris mentioned the third partner, the one that we don't know at all, Peter, I think is his name."

"P-y-o-t-r, I think is how you spell it. Let's ask. When we talk. He glanced at the clock on the wall. "Time to call," he announces. "Is the detective joining us?"

"No, he told me to email him a summary after the call. Said he had other things that were urgent that he had to do. I guess this is not his only case?"

Alexei answers the phone himself this time. He sounds anxious as he cuts short the usual pleasantries. He tells us that Grigorii is on the call also.

Jim leads off, "Thank you both for taking our call. As you know, we are investigating what happened with Errol, and a couple of questions have arisen that we want to discuss. That OK with you?"

There is a kind of stunned silence and then Alexei says, "Of course, we help you any way we can."

"We want to start with some questions about Errol. But we want also to ask you about Boris Zokshin. You know him, right?"

"Of course," Alexei says, dismissively. "And good riddance to him."

I am stunned, although Jim maintains a poker face. He mouths the words "Errol first." I nod.

"We'll get to Boris. Let's start with Errol. When did you and Errol actually meet? Was it around the time of our financing, at the introduction of Boris, or did you meet him before that?"

Another long pause. I hear a few low words in Russian. I don't know what they mean, but if I had to place my bets I'd say they were Russian swear words. "Yes," Alexei says. "We meet Errol before that. In Moscow. At conference. He present with woman about data for Parkinson's. That why we so interested in Quixotic. We want very much market drug for Parkinson's in Russia. We have big problem with this. In whole of country, but also in family."

"I see," Jim says. "Please don't misunderstand me; I am not making any accusations, but why didn't you mention this before? And while you are at it, can you tell us why Errol would object to your becoming investors in Quixotic? Because he did, you know. And I want to know about Boris Zokshin too. Brie told me that he had disappeared. That he seemed afraid of you." Jim pauses and then continues. "You see, Alexei, we have a lot of unanswered questions."

I hear more Russian swear words. I try to write them down phonetically to look them up later. Alexei clears his throat, utters a few more words, and then begins. "OK, Brianna and Jim. I tell you whole story. You have time?" I'd like to set the record straight, that it's Brie like the cheese, but, once again, the time is not right.

Jim and I sit in stunned silence when the call is finished. It was quite a story. As we knew, there are indeed three brothers. Alexei is the oldest. Grigorii is the middle one, and Pyotr is the youngest. While Parkinson's is only hereditary in 15% of cases, the Popov family is riddled with it: a sibling, their mother, sister, grandparents on both sides. Pyotr was paranoid about the disease. He had always been unstable, maybe overshadowed by his older siblings?

It was Pyotr's twin sister that had developed Parkinson's at an early age. Without revealing details, they told us a story about the Russia Mafia and how Pyotr became involved over time. They mentioned gambling, drugs, even the sex trade. It was shocking. It seemed that the other brothers, Alexei and Grigorii were not involved and that they tried to get their brother out of the mob.

Another brother; I think of Yahya. This one will also end badly, I fear.

Alexei switched back to their fear of Parkinson's for their families. Apparently, Alexei had heard the talk by Errol and Maya and talked to him afterwards. He was so thrilled by the possibility of a Parkinson's cure that he arranged to meet Errol later, and he invited his two brothers to join him, telling them about the positive preliminary data."

Alexei told us that he hoped Errol would license the technology to a firm that they would establish in Russia. What he wanted were the Russian rights only. He didn't care about the other international rights, and it seemed that this satisfied Errol because he knew that Quixotic would want to keep its rights to the promising drug in the U.S. and other countries. But he was pretty sure that the company would be alright with letting the Russian rights go to Popov. Apparently they agreed in principle about how this would work. But never got that far because of what happened.

Alexei described the plan to establish an entity which would hold the license. Alexei said that Errol started to ask them lots of questions about how the company would work, who would run it, who would be in control, and what would the relationship be with Quixotic. Pyotr apparently started to talk at this point. He laid out his plan before his brothers could shut him up. He wanted to put some kind of puppet in place, a pseudo-entrepreneur, who would ostensibly run the company, but, really, Errol would run it from afar. He basically offered Errol a deal where he would, outside of Quixotic, own shares in the Russian company and be the one in control. Apparently Errol was offended. He got angry. Things escalated, and Pyotr told him how he had a young entrepreneur killed who didn't do what he said.

Errol threatened to go to the police. Pyotr pulled out a gun; it became a big mess. They were thrown out of the bar. Which happened to be the hotel bar. Errol apparently had a hard time getting back in the building to go up to his room.

It would be funny, except that it wasn't.

"So this why Errol no like us. Alexei had admitted. "This our fault. We no control Pyotr and he say terrible things."

"What about Boris? Jim had asked. "What role did he play in all this?"

Alexei groaned then. "Boris, he work for the company that Pyotr control."

"You mean Boris worked for a company where the entrepreneur was murdered because he didn't do what Pyotr said?"

"Please," Alexei said quickly. "Not true like that. Entrepreneur not killed. He had, well, he had accident."

"Ah, I see," I replied. "Why did Boris have to leave Quixotic and Pittsburgh?" I ask.

"Because," Alexei answered me, "Boris, he afraid. He think Pyotr kill Errol. But I assure you. Pyotr not in U.S. when Errol die. And he not have anyone kill Errol."

"How do we know that?" Jim asked harshly.

"Because Pyotr, he dead."

Pyotr had died six months before Errol was killed. It was an organized crime thing of some sort. They also added that Pyotr had exhibited early signs of Parkinson's.

We ended the call. Jim and I spend a minute processing what we just heard.

"Does this explain what happened to Boris?" I ask.

"I don't know," Jim responds quietly. He looks shaken.

"We didn't tell them about my accident, about Boris, that he was in the accident, that he is dead."

"That's right. They don't need to know everything. All of this may be connected," Jim concludes.

. . . .

Straler isn't answering my texts or calls. I leave him voicemail that I am meeting with Yahya and asks if he wants to come. No answer. OK, I get it. His boss has made it clear. She doesn't think it's murder or she doesn't think we can solve it. Either way, Straler is probably off the case. It will remain a **U**, undetermined.

I have arranged to meet Yahya for coffee at the Starbucks in the Whole Foods parking lot. I know it will be an ordeal with my crutches so I'm happy when I find a parking spot close to the entrance. Yahya rides his bike everywhere, and the weather has been lovely; I hope that it holds for this meeting. I don't want to feel any more guilt about him.

I arrive early, but he's already there. I see his bike parked outside, and he sees me hobble the few steps from where I park. He rushes out to meet me. "I hear from Shala about you. I so sorry, am so sorry." We get settled and he orders coffee for the two of us and insists on paying. We sit in silence for a moment. His dark eyes do not intimidate me now. He smiles, revealing those perfect white teeth.

"Yahya," I begin.

He shushes me, "Brie, it not your fault. I understand. In your shoes, I think same thing." He smiles again. His face tightens. It must be hard, I realize. I know that I had nothing to do with the terrorist cell bust; that was just coincidental. But I feel his pain.

"Yahya, I would never do anything to get you in trouble. I didn't really suspect you; I just needed to follow a hunch. You understand what I mean? It's just that the whole situation with Errol is so important. I found out that he was not alone on the boat. Someone murdered him. It's likely that it was someone that he knew. How else would they be on his boat? So, everyone is a suspect. That included you, others, and, I suppose, me. But I'm trying to solve the murder because..." I bite my lip. Should I tell him? Since New York I feel that I can trust Yahya. His pain is as great as mine, perhaps more. He has nothing to hide from me and I cannot hide anything from him. "I have to solve this murder, Yahya, because Errol left something for me. My dad has Huntington's and I couldn't get him into any of the clinical trials. It doesn't matter anyway because, as you probably know, NGX cancelled the Phase III trial for HD66."

Yahya looks surprised. He reaches out and puts his hand on mine on the table. I know how hard that is for him. "My father is doomed, as good as dead. But, before he died, Errol sent me a message about having something for me. I'm sure that it's a cure. I think that he intended to give me something that might help my father. I hope that you understand. That's why I am working with Detective Henrik to solve this murder. I believe that I will find what Errol intended for me along the way." I pause. My coffee is cold but I don't care. I gulp it down noisily trying to hide my emotions.

He lifts his hand from mine. His eyes bore into mine. "Brie, I think you have right idea suspecting me."

"What?" I ask. "But..."

He interrupts me, "Not me, because I not kill Errol, but someone did, and nerve agent is good reason."

He pauses, and we look at each other. "Then who?"

"Who you think?" He lays the question out like an invitation.

"Patrick?" I ask.

"I not know for sure, but Patrick very dark. Has past with IRA. You know this organization in Ireland? It violent. Like what you suspect me of. Like my brother. Patrick has uncle who was killed in what he call, troubles. Nerve agent very valuable to freedom fighters anywhere. Why not in the north of Ireland?"

I don't know what to think. His reasoning is sound, but I have been down this path a couple of times now. False paths so far. I know that I am running out of leads. But I don't want to jump because of that. I want to be sure.

"Can you find out?" I ask.

"Yes, I think, maybe, I try," Yahya answers. "In lab. I try last few days. He seem very dark, angry, he yell at me once. He tell me yesterday I don't understand what is going on. He say a lot of things. Hmph," Yahya snorts. "I live with this violence too. I understand Protestant, Catholic, England occupying, long fight, many years, much pain. I know this." He looks out the window at the parking lot. Cars entering, cars exiting.

"I think I need to get the detective in on this," I say. "I really can't do this alone, particularly now, with this," I say pointing to my leg.

"Yes, agree," he says simply.

"And there's something else."

"Yes?" he asks, his dark brows raised like arches in a cathedral.

"There's been another death."

There is a sharp intake of breath. "What? Who?"

"A scientist. He was with Errol's lab at Quixotic. A Russian named Boris."

"Yes, I met him. He interested in Parkinson's. He no listen when Errol tell him we not have working for Parkinson's."

"Yes, he was very interested in that. Maybe he thought you were close to a solution?"

"Not sure. I be in touch," Yahya announces as he stands up to leave. He gives me a cellphone number for him. "You can text me. I am going to list you in my phone as Mary Stuart."

I chuckle, "Yahya, how historic!"

He is off on his bike before I am two steps out the door. My car seems impossibly far away as I hobble onto the parking lot.

. . . .

My phone buzzes insistently as I make my way towards my car. It's difficult for me to stop on the crutches, and I fumble with my bag, trying to extricate my phone. I lift the phone out triumphantly only to realize that it stopped buzzing a second before – the call is lost. Hmm, no number that I recognize. I put the phone back into the abyss of my bag and continue towards my car. Buzz, buzz again. Having practiced, this time I am quicker and I manage to get the phone out and to my ear before the buzzing stops. "Hello?" I inquire.

"Brie, it's Straler."

"Oh wow, sorry, I didn't recognize the number. You missed the meeting with Yahya, and for that matter you haven't responded to my email about our phone call with Popov. What's up?"

"I'm in Russia, Brie."

I bump into my car and drop my phone. Struggling to pick it up, I drop my crutches. "Straler, don't hang up," I shout hoping that he can hear me as my purse flies open and its contents scatter. I gather what I can and bumble into my seat. I wait, catching my breath.

Straler takes my silence as disapproving. "Brie, I couldn't tell you. First of all, it could be dangerous. Secondly, you're in no condition to traipse around a foreign country. But there was work to be done here. I've found a few things out."

"Like what?" I know that I sound sullen, but I can't help it. He doesn't need me, didn't want me, and he's having the adventure and excitement.

"OK, listen. Are you somewhere where you can take notes?" I slam shut my car door and get out my dog-eared notebook. Searching for a pen I switch him to speaker phone.

"Yes, I'm in my car. Alone. I have a notebook and pen at the ready."

"Great, Brie, here's what's going down. Boris was not just involved in the Russia equivalent of the Mafia, Brie. He was involved in all kinds of activity. As I did some digging with Interpol, I uncovered that Boris was actually an agent for the Foreign Intelligence Service of the Russian Federation."

"He was a spy?"

"Not exactly, but pretty close. Boris started with internal affairs handling domestic issues. He graduated to become an undercover agent in the Russian Mafia, which is actually called the Bratva, or Brotherhood – fitting don't you think? Anyway, he had access to information and activities because of this. Apparently, his science background was part of the cover up, particularly for drugs – both legal and illegal. Of course there were other areas where he had a hand, but he focused largely on the drug trade. He seemed to be profiting on both sides. I didn't get the full story. What I did get however, is that he was turned."

"You mean for us? Like he was a double agent?"

"Exactly. Brie, you were playing with fire having him around Quixotic. Of course, none of you knew. At least that's the assumption, right? But we know that Boris was in thick with Popov Brothers, who are of course part of the Bratva. He was really in the U.S. working ostensibly for the American side, but he still had ties to the activities in Russia. I couldn't tell, but he might have been trying to be a triple agent. If so, it didn't work. Once he surfaced, the Bratva knew where he was. That's why he needed to disappear."

My mind is humming. "Do you think that they killed Errol?"

"Very possibly, I don't know. What I do know is that they killed Boris."

"Do you know why?"

"WE," he replies, emphasizing the word, "will probably never know the full story. But I can guess. Before I tell you my thoughts, what do you think?" *Is he being patronizing?*

"Well, at the risk of sounding like a television show, I think that he probably just knew too much, that they didn't trust him, and that he was a potential threat to them. They had to eliminate him."

"Exactly, Detective Prince." Straler chuckles at the other end of the line.

I giggle with relief. "Yes, sir!"

"Let's talk about Popov Brothers. What did you find out on your call? I am going to make a surprise visit to their office after I talk with you."

I relay the essence of the conversation about Pyotr, how he is dead, and how the other brothers didn't 'fess up to knowing anything about their brother's criminal activities. I tell him that they didn't like Boris and that they told us they had no contact with him. I add that they told us that Boris was afraid of Pyotr, that he thought that Pyotr might have killed Errol. But it can't have been Pyotr, so they said, because Pyotr had died before the murder happened.

"That's great information. I'll find out more when I visit them. That's why I came here. We have to have boots on the ground to get our questions answered. I'll let you know." And he signs off just like that. *Some guys have all the fun.*

Chapter 39
April 10

My leg hurts, and it takes me a long time to get to the office. As soon as I get off the elevator, I see Gigi walking towards me. She is waving, no, she is gesturing, commanding. "Come here," she mouths at me.

But Jim strides past her determinedly and takes my arm. In a whisper he says, "Brie, come with me. It's important." He ushers me down the hall. I look back at Gigi. I don't mean to ignore her, but I have no choice. She glowers at me, her eyes piercing darts.

As we make our way slowly to Jim's office, I start to tell him about Straler. He shakes his head at me and puts his finger to his lips. The hallway seems impossibly long but we end up in Jim's corner office. Funny I never registered that Jim and Matt have the two corner offices on this side of the building. Gigi's is much smaller and in the middle. As we enter Jim's office, I see a man in a gray suit standing and looking out of the window. There is something familiar about him but I don't recall that we have met. Until he opens his mouth. "And this must be our dear Miss Brianna."

I lean on my crutches and peer at the man. I know the voice. "Mr. Popov?" It's Alexei from Popov Brothers. I have to put a hand to my mouth to hide the laughter that is welling up. *Oh my gosh, Straler is in Russia, and the Russian is in Pittsburgh!* Alexei seems to think that I am shocked, and he immediately moves towards me.

"Brianna, please do not be alarmed. Come in and sit. I have much to discuss with you and Quixotic." They help me ease into a chair, and they join me at the small round table in front of Jim's desk.

I know that I need to listen to Alexei as he talks, but I am wondering where Straler is at this moment. What time is it in Russia? When will he actually be popping in to Alexei's office? *Popping in to the Popovs? Oh, it's too much.* I try hard to hide my laugh. Alexei looks at me quizzically. Jim frowns. I stifle my laugh as Alexei continues. But my mind is with Straler in Russia. *Should I tell Alexei that Straler is coming? Will Grigorii be there, and will Straler be able to talk to him? Will we get the truth from either of them?* There is a buzzing in my ears, in my head. I wince. Jim looks at me with concern.

"I'm OK. Just a bit surprised. And I'm still having some trouble, physically, I mean."

"We very sorry to hear of your accident," Alexei says. "But that why I am here. I not want to say over phone. I need to say in person."

Jim pours coffee that has somehow magically appeared. I take a sip. Alexei puts three giant spoons of sugar into his and stirs it, studying me. "Continue, Mr. Popov." Jim says softly.

"Call me Alexei, please. And yes, I continue. Boris Zokshin we know for many years. We thought he no have contact with us anymore. He come to U.S. Finished, we thought. But he was not finished. Not with Pyotr. Boris, he work here with Errol. He know that we want Parkinson's drug. Pyotr want this very much to control distribution in Russia and other areas. He no get along with Errol, but he has Boris. We invest for right reason – we want to help commercialize this drug. We want to help family who have Parkinson's. And we want to help others. But Pyotr he have other ideas. He threaten Boris to reveal him to Bratva. That why Boris have to leave."

I stay silent. I don't want him to know what I already know. At the same time, the man has clearly traveled half way around the world to tell us something important. I clear my throat and look at my hands for a minute. Alexei drinks his coffee in noisy gulps. Jim sits absolutely still looking at each of us in turn.

"I know this." Looking at Jim I continue, "Detective Henrik has done some digging into Boris and told me about the Bratva. That's the Russian equivalent of the Mafia. It means Brotherhood."

Alexei looks at me in surprise. "Brianna, you very smart. Do you also know that Boris find that Errol discover something else? Something in his lab? Something terrible and deadly?"

Both Jim and I are shocked. I know about DeathX, but I haven't discussed it, even with Jim. How does Alexei know?

"There was a new discovery?" Jim asks.

"Yes, something very powerful. Boris, when he find out, he decide to use this to barter – is this right word – with Bratva."

I look at Jim. He is perfectly still, his face a mask. The bones of his face are showing more and more. "Jim, I know a little bit about this. I can tell you what I know later." Jim looks at me. "I didn't tell you because, well, because the detective asked me to keep all information between us. He insisted." I couldn't admit that I trusted no one, not even Jim. I see that Jim's hands are trembling. His head is twitching some as well. "Are you alright, Jim?" I ask.

"No, Brie, I am not alright. This is all a bit much: Errol, Boris, Matt being gone, Gigi is pissed off, you seem to know more than anyone, and, oh by the way, I have Parkinson's." Both Alexei and I stare at Jim. "It's been somewhat under control recently, but it flares up under stress. I'm sorry, sorry to have to tell you like this."

"Jim, oh Jim. I am so sorry. No wonder you have sympathy for me and HD."

Alexei had turned white, and he looks with shock at the two of us. "My got, Brianna, I did not know you. Or about you, Jim. I am so sorry…"

Jim pays no attention and looks at me with soft eyes. "Yes, Brie. I suspected for quite some time before you told us that there was something behind your curiosity about how to get someone in a clinical trial. I figured it out. But I didn't want to tell you that I knew. First of all, I might have been wrong. Secondly, I wanted you to tell me when you were ready. I had to earn your trust, Brie. I thought I had…"

I know that I am crying. "Jim, I do trust you. I always have."

Alexei drains his cup. Jim somewhat shakily pours him more. Three more spoons of sugar. He stirs and drinks. "We know that Boris try to double cross. That why Bratva kill him. Car accident. We know because before Pyotr was killed he tell us whole story. Pyotr was killed by Bratva. This before Errol is killed. Boris is killed by Bratva."

Jim reaches out to hold my hand on the table. I inhale deeply, wondering if life will ever be normal again. I ask the obvious, "Did Bratva kill Errol, Alexei?"

"I not know, Brianna. But I want to tell you all this. I go back to Russia, and Grigorii and I are stopping all business. I am tired and we have lost too much. Before I go I want you to know what I know."

I tell Alexei and Jim that Detective Henrik is in Russia. That he either has or shortly is going to be visiting the Popov Brothers' office. Alexei is amused at first, understanding the irony of him being here and Straler being there. He laughs from his belly and says, "Your young detective friend and you make great pair." Jim cracks a smile although he looks worn and old.

Then Alexei shifts his tone and tells me in a soft but menacing voice, "Get your friend out of Russia now."

. . . .

I am exhausted. I sit in my office not knowing what to do. Straler is not answering his phone. I send a text anyway:

"Popov is here. Says they are closing down.

Says for you to leave immediately. Call."

I receive an email from Yahya. No news. Apparently he can't find Patrick. Or Shala for that matter. I know that I should go to the lab, but I don't have the energy. I call for Neal to come pick me up. I ask him to bring my prescription bottle from my apartment.

. . . .

It's the middle of the night. I hear angry bees. My phone. No, it's knocking. Urgent knocking on my door. Neal has gone to his apartment, and I am alone. "Who is it?" I ask, feeling naïve and scared.

"It's me, Straler." I open the door and there is Straler looking disheveled. He looks like he hasn't slept in a week. Or shaved. "Sorry, Brie. I had to come straight here. First of all to find out if you are OK. And I have a lot to tell you. I don't even know what time it is. I'm sorry if I woke you. Can I come in?"

He drops his bag on the floor, and helps me into the kitchen. He looks around.

"Would you like a drink?" I ask.

His tired face lights up in a grin.

"You'll have to get it, though," I gesture to him where the new bottle of scotch is and the glasses. "Nice glasses," he says, as he pours.

"My grandmother's."

"Where's Neal?"

"He's at his place." Straler smiles and takes a long drink. He wipes his mouth with a dirty sleeve and launches into his tale. When he got to the Popov brothers' office the morning after he called me, the office was closed.

"The door was unlocked, however, and I went inside. The place was trashed. Like it had been ransacked. Either by the Popov brothers leaving or by someone looking for something. Either way it was a dead end. When I left the building, I discovered that the office was being watched. Or, I was being watched. Or both. I had asked the taxi to wait for me but it had disappeared. I saw a black car in its spot. I needed to get back to my contact at the Russian police force. I started walking like I knew where I was going. The black car followed slowly, but there were men in the street as well following me. Fortunately, I ended up in a busy area of the city, a roundabout and was able to flag down a cab. I am not sure that's common in Russia, but I was pretty in his face. I had the taxi drive me to my hotel. I asked him to wait while I ran up and got my bag. The black car was still following me, but I went straight to the police station where I had checked in when I landed. My contact was gone, but she had left me a message. It was bad, Brie."

"What did it say?"

"Basically it said that it was no longer safe for me to be in Russia. That the Bratva knew about my coming. She said that Pyotr Popov had been killed and that they were covering their tracks. She urged me to leave immediately with a police escort and that she would follow up on her end."

"So that's it? You left?"

"Like I had a choice? Yes, I left. But, before I got on the plane, here's what I found out. We know that the

Bratva killed Pyotr. And it had to do with Errol. Pyotr and Popov were unsuccessful at getting Errol's discoveries into their hands. They wanted access. But they couldn't go directly to Errol because someone got to him first."

"What about DeathX? Did they know?"

"Yes, they wanted it."

"Meaning what exactly?"

"That someone else killed Errol."

"Not them? How do we know?"

"Because they were as surprised as we were that he was dead. They didn't want him dead. They wanted him alive."

Chapter 40
April 11

I reach my desk and collapse into my chair. It took me two hours to get here. That's a mile an hour. I am sweating, and I know that I look disheveled. I look forward to getting my walking cast on in two days. It will make life so much easier. There's a sharp rap on my door and then it immediately opens. It's Gigi. She looks pale; I'm not the only one stressed these days. She once again has no makeup, and her outfit is simple and severe. All black and a lovely silver necklace. High heels again, though.

She closes the door. "Brie, you wanted to talk?" She looks uncomfortable standing there. I'm usually the one standing in front of her. I hate myself for what I am about to do. But Jim convinced me that it was the only way.

"Gigi, thanks for coming. You know that I admire you, that I owe you, that..."

"Cut to the chase, Brie," Gigi snaps. "I don't need bullshit or excuses."

"OK." I inhale deeply looking straight into her razor eyes. "As you know we have to regroup, resize. We have to cut costs, Gigi. Really down to rock bottom. Which means..."

"I get it. I'm out, right? Anything else?"

"No, that's really all. Just that it's effective immediately."

She opens the door behind her and grimaces. I feel sorry for her, but I remember that I have other business. "Before you go," I raise my voice and look levelly at her.

"What?" she spits.

"Did you kill Errol?" I look at her, prepared to assess her reaction.

"Did I what?" she nearly shouts. She slams the door shut and takes two long strides on her pointy stilettos. "How dare you ask me that," she hisses.

"Gigi, we know that someone did, and, quite frankly, you had as much reason as anybody. Why, with Errol out of the way you might have been able to turn the board against Matt and take over yourself. That's what you wanted, wasn't it? Is that why you did it?"

"Why you little bitch. You have no idea. Yes, I wanted to be CEO of this company. Of course I did. It's what I was born to do, and I thought I could make it happen here. But I wanted to do it with and for Errol. We were the vanguard of Centre University. We made it from a small school, practically a community college, into a huge research engine – together – from the first grant to the first student suicide. He was a physician, and I was a microbiology professor. He was the idea behind Centre; I was cooking up corporate deals while he spun out new technology. We grew it from agriculture and veterinary studies to the powerhouse it is now. It is our child. And now he's gone. I've only ever wanted this – and with him gone I can't have it anyway."

She looks at my shocked face.

"I had no idea," I respond.

"That's right, you had no idea. Why do you think I work so hard? Why I'm so good at my job? You're a woman. You should understand. We're in a man's world. And, we're not wanted. He never made me feel outsourced, or beautiful. You don't have to butter up your best friend."

"I'm sorry..." I feel like a fool. It wasn't personal. Gigi was trying to toughen me up – the only way she knew how.

She leans towards me, her perfectly painted nails looking like daggers on my desk. "But, in answer to your question, no I did not fucking kill Errol. Why would I do that? I needed him. You think I could run this company without him? He was the genius. There was – is – no one else. Surely you know that. I needed Errol and he knew that."

Gigi takes a step back and wobbles on her heels. As she exhales, she seems to deflate. Suddenly she looks old, tiny and tired. I realize how much pain she has been in since Errol's death. I want to make things right.

"Plus, I loved him, Brie. Amy thinks that we were lovers." I see rivulets of tears running down both sides of her face. "But you certainly don't need sex to signal love and affiliation – we were already too close without it."

I get up and stroke her arm. "I'm sorry, Gigi. So sorry, for everything."

"Find him, Brie. Find who did this to Errol." She spins and abruptly exits my office.

I have one less path to follow in a murder case. I'm running out of time. Don't they say the odds of solving a murder go down exponentially the longer the time from death?

. . . .

The next morning I am determined not to let my leg slow me down. I stop for coffee at Tazza D'Oro and read over my notes. As I hobble towards my car, I see a familiar figure. It's Straler. "Hey, detective!" I call out.

He turns and sees me, a broad smile showing up on his face. But he is not alone. He's holding hands with a gorgeous woman with long brown hair to her waist. They walk towards me.

"Brie, great to see you. I want to introduce you to my fiancée, Renee. "

I am dumbfounded. I must look like an idiot, staring with open mouth, leaning on my crutches, scabs still all over my face. I glance at her left hand. Yep, right there, a small, very tasteful, solitaire diamond.

Straler sees my look. "We just got engaged. We're shopping. For a small party we are having for our families."

Renee extends her hand, "Brie, I've heard so much about you. I'm so glad that you are OK. Straler was worried sick after your accident."

I feel like an idiot. All of those butterflies, those smiles. I think that my smile is frozen on my face.

"Hey, I hate to talk shop on a beautiful day, but what's going on?" he asks. "Where do we go next? I don't mean to pressure you, but I am plumb out of ideas. We haven't talked about why Boris, why he would be..."

I take a deep breath. I come out of my trance. "Following me? Yes, we have to talk. There's a lot to say..."

He smiles. I realize that I am relieved. He's awfully cute, but my heart belongs to another. So does his — obviously.

"First let me congratulate you both. He's a wonderful detective," I say to Renee. She blushes. How cute. He looks at her adoringly. "It's great to finally meet you," I add. "Maybe Neal and I — my boyfriend — Straler's met him, maybe we could all get together?"

Straler smiles that broad toothy smile. No butterflies this time. "That would be awesome," he says.

I tell him that I'll call him later. About the next lead.

That afternoon on the phone, I tell him that I am checking something and will let him know as soon as I am sure.

"Great, no heroics, promise?"

"Yep, done with that," I assure him.

"Hey Brie," Straler says tentatively. "I hope that you, well, that you didn't think..."

I interrupt him, "Straler, it's business. I loved meeting Renee today, and you know that I meant it that the four of us should get together."

"Yeah, that would be great. I really like Neal. He's a great guy, Brie." There is an awkward pause. "I don't mean to be overly personal, but he loves you. He really loves you."

I feel a small choke starting to rise in my throat. I cough and then say, "I know, Straler. I know that. I love him too."

"I can tell," Straler says. "The way that you looked at each other in the hospital room. Your mom noticed too."

. . . .

It's after 11 p.m. I am on the couch trying to get comfortable. Arwen had stalked off with a disgusted look on her face a few minutes ago. I guess sleeping on a cast is not that comfortable for her. I desperately want another cup of herbal tea, but I don't want to disturb Neal, who's sleeping soundly in the bedroom. He's gotten very little rest since my accident. My phone buzzes. It's Straler.

"Hey, Brie," he says quietly. "Hope I didn't wake you."

"Hey Straler, what's up? I can't sleep anyway."

"Know how you feel. Me neither." I gather from the semi-whisper that Renee is in the other room just like Neal is here. "Listen, I did some investigating about Boris."

"Some what?" I tease. "Like you're a professional?"

"Hey don't knock it." I hear a light chuckle. "I have access to resources."

"Yea, good for you."

"Hey, we're still partners. I need you."

"Yes of course. I'm just tired, and my leg hurts like heck."

"I'm sorry," he says. He pauses.

I state the obvious, "We're running out of leads."

"I know. Don't stop. We'll get there."

"Hey you sound like a detective." The line goes dead. I'm exhausted and pull the blanket up to my chin. Arwen jumps back on and curls up by my neck. Her purring is like waves on the sea.

Chapter 41
April 13

I cannot go on. The voice inside my head tells me I am finished. I have done a terrible thing. I cannot live. I climb over the rail thinking my last thoughts about him. As the wind rushes past my face, I know that I cannot make the world right. I cannot atone for my actions. I will be a disappointment — forever — to those I loved. The last thing I feel is the cold embrace of the water as it soothes my soul.

Chapter 42
That same day

Buzzing in my ears. Buzzing coming towards me. The swarm is after me. I run away knowing that I will not succeed. They are angry, these bees, and they will get me. I hear a dog barking. I run towards the sound. The barking is louder, insistent. The bees are getting closer. I hear a high-pitched howl. No, it's the unmistakable bah-roo of a beagle. I run towards the sound and see Luna howling at me. With an ear-splitting scream, she jumps at the swarm, mouth open to swallow the bees.

I awake with a start. I call Straler as soon as it's light. "I know who killed him."

"You do? Who?" he asks quickly.

"We have to go to the lab. Bring Detective Small too. She'll want to be there. I'm sure this time."

"It's Patrick isn't it?" Straler concludes.

I tell him that I'll meet them in the lobby of the university lab building at 10 a.m. I know that it'll take me a long time with my leg.

The detectives look tense when they arrive. I've been waiting for them at Tazza D'Oro in Bocci Hall. I had time to get an Italian Cappuccino and take my last sip as they approach. "You ready for this?" Detective Small asks. "Straler says you're sure."

I struggle to my feet. "Yes, I am."

"I found out that he has ties to the IRA. It's bad, Brie."

I'm disappointed. I like Patrick. He's intimidating, but he's Irish. I'm fond of anything and anybody Irish. Even the North. I have a cousin from there on my dad's side and I visited during a summer in high school. The countryside around Belfast was beautiful – egg basket hills the locals called it. The people were fantastically friendly. I remember asking someone in downtown Belfast for directions. "Excuse me, I'm lost…" I had said to an older gentleman in a cap. He gave me a gap-toothed smile and didn't miss a beat, "Glad to meet you, Lost, I'm Jimmy. Now what can I do for you?" It makes me smile to this day.

By now we're are at the lab's door. As we enter, I see Patrick on his cellphone. He seems hysterical about something. Shouting "no, no no no no" into the phone. Yahya's face is ashen. Patrick puts down the phone. "Damn me, damn you, damn us all fer fuck's sake."

"Patrick!" Straler says sharply.

Detective Small steps in. "We'll have none of that, lad. You know probably why we are here and what we want to know is why. Why would you do this?"

"Patrick looks at us, shock registering on his face. "Why would I do this, are you kiddin' me?"

"He didn't do it," I say quietly.

"Brie, what are you saying?" Straler asks, frowning.

"He's not the killer. Where is she?" I demand, looking at Patrick.

"Who are you talking about?" Detective Small asks.

"Brie, what's going on?" Straler asks me, looking at me like I'm crazy.

I look at Yahya. "It's too late," he says dropping his head.

Patrick is near hysteria. "You knew! Yahya knows too. Oh hell, I didn't stop her. I knew, I suspected, and I had a chance to stop her, but I didn't." He gives a tortured gasp.

Yahya breaks in, "She has done something terrible."

I stare at them. "Where's Shala? She's always here."

Patrick explodes, "Are you daft? Didn't you hear what I just said? Shala's gone and done herself in. I tried to fuckin stop her, but it was too late wasn't it? I figured out about her and Errol, but I wasn't sure, and I didn't know how to find out for sure so I did nothin'. And now it's too late."

I'm in a daze. The room slowly starts to move and I lean on the closed door behind me. "Let's get this straight," I hear Straler say. "Shala has killed herself, at least that's what you think, and you think that she killed Errol? Do I have this right? Help me out, man, we're trying to understand. That's what you think, right Brie? Will somebody tell us what is going on?"

Yahya slumps down to the floor.

Patrick sighs and drops his arms, helpless.

"Shala killed Errol. I figured it out, too," I say, looking where she usually stood at the lab bench. "It was Luna. She knew all along. Amy thought Shala was hiding behind you because she was frightened of dogs. She's right. But Luna knew that she killed her master. And Shala knew that she knew." *Dogs know bad people.*

No one says anything for a minute as they absorb this information. Straler looks at me. I can see that he is amazed and something else, maybe jealous?

Patrick says in a slow, pained tone, "She's right. I'm sorry. I was upset. I didn't explain, you must have thought... Brie's right. Shala killed Errol. It took me a long time before I knew. First we thought it was you, Yahya." He glances towards Yahya and lowers his eyes. "But Brie here solved that one too, didn't she? I knew it wasn't me. And no one else knew about DeathX but us. I suspected Shala, but she was good. She kept talking about Yahya and how it must be him. Thinking back, she was too obvious, a little too contrived. I'm Irish. We know bullshite when it's served for breakfast. And I should've seen it..."

He's so Irish, I think sadly. Behind those dark eyes and brooding expression is probably a poet dying to get out and express itself.

"We thought it was you, actually." Straler says. "That's why we came here, or so I thought."

"Me! You thought it was me? Arq, for God' sake, detective, I was trying to protect 'em. First Yahya, then Shala. I couldn't have done it. I was too busy trying to get them to stop it. Oh God, I let her go. I had the chance, and I didn't stop her."

"How did she..." I can't finish the question.

"She jumped off the Highland Park Bridge. It was hard to hear her. That's what she said, though. She called me."

The detectives have their phones out. They step out in the hall.

"It's maybe not too late?" I ask.

Yahya responds, "She could never live with such shame."

Straler steps back into the room and says, "We called. The police, ambulance, the rest are on their way. We talked to the guy at the lock – Captain Bob. They'll search. Someone must've seen. You have to climb the fence to do it. But we know what happens when you are in the water," he trails off.

"She used DeathX. On him. And now on herself." I notice a drop of water on the floor by my crutch. I watch the water spread and another joins it. A small pool of sad. Lovely, lilting Shala. How could the world be so wrong?

. . . .

The next morning, April 14

Jim and I crowd into the conference room. Alexei is there. So is Jeb from Sanguine, Josh from Bigfoot, and Carleen from GreenBush. Victor Williams, the medical examiner friend of Amy's and Errol's, is there also. Now that we know that it was the nerve agent, he has questions, and we have some too. Dr. Williams stands as we come in. Amy is here too. She deserves to know – everything.

There is a knock on the door, and Patrick and Yahya step into the room. The pair look stiff in ill-fitting suits. The same suits that they wore at Errol's funeral, I bet. The pair are clearly nervous and uncomfortable.

As usual, Jim puts them at ease, "Patrick, Yahya, good to see you." They shake hands and there are vigorous nods as we all acknowledge their presence. Jim makes introductions. "Thank you so much for coming here. You realize how important this is to Amy here," he says with a wave in her direction. "And you know that it is very important to all of us at Quixotic, including our investors who have put their trust in us." He gestures to Alexei, Jeb, and Josh. He pauses as he looks around the room. "But we also know that it is very important to you, to understand, to be a part of this… unraveling." *What an appropriate word. I am unraveling. I cannot bear to think what will be left.*

"We don't know everything," he continues. "What we do know is that Shala has killed herself. That presumably she did so out of guilt. That she killed Errol. That she did this to get her hands on some kind of powerful discovery that comes from Errol's university lab. Something powerful and dangerous. Deadly. Please explain about the discovery," he says gently.

"Yes," Patrick says in his thick Irish accent, "DeathX, we called it." No one says a word. Patrick looks around the room. "It was an accident, this discovery. We, Errol, that is, we were actually working on something else.

Something to help the brain when it is attacked by these, you know, terrible conditions, like the one your company addresses with its HD66 drug. We were hoping to find a cure to Parkinson's Disease. But we mixed the chemicals wrong, or something, I don't know. These things happen. You're doing these experiments, and sometimes you just think like a cook, you throw a little of this and little of that – in a beaker, you see. I'm oversimplifying here, but you get my point, eh? We accidentally created something that had properties that none of us imagined were possible. I'm from Northern Ireland, from the center of the city of Belfast, Falls Road, some of you may have actually heard of it. That and the Shankill Road, we're both famous for bein' on opposite sides of the fence when it came to The Troubles. It all was kind of before my time, don't you know, but my family was involved, really involved. Anyway, it's of no importance to you, but I grew up around violence – I know the meaning of one human being hurtin' another – and the stories around my kitchen table growin' up were about Uncle Charlie and Aunt Jeannie, and Cousin Seannie. A lot of them died. Some of them ended up in jail and were part of hunger strikes and so on. Anyways, it's just by way of background that I'm tellin' you all this." He pauses and looks at his hands. It's dead silent in the room.

"I knew, when I saw the dead mice. I knew that we'd bumped into something terrible. Something that we would wish we hadn't done. And now look; it's gone and come true. I'm no soothsayer. I had no idea. If I had, I would'a stopped the poor girl. She had a horrible life back home, and I think she was usin' the discovery to gain some kind of leverage or respect for her family. Somethin' like that was going on inside her head. Somethin' terrible had happened to her sister. Did you know that? She's crippled for life as a result. A brutal gang rape. It happens all the time, Shala told me. And she wanted it to stop. She felt that she could make it stop. If only she had…" Patrick shakes his head as if to clear it. "DeathX provided a way. I think it was very personal, for her, for Shala. And I only wish I could a done somethin' for her. Because I suspected, but I didn't really know for sure. Not until it was too late anyway…" He stops talking. We are all moved beyond words.

Yahya has been quiet all this time, looking at Patrick like it's the first time he has seen him. "I so sorry, Patrick," he says. "I not see this and I focus only on my brother and stopping him from what he doing. My brother, he think he do this for our country, but he cannot win this way. We see. We know there is no life in killing because others are being killed. Yes, is unjust – what happen in Syria. I know. But I no want to take part in killing. That just propagate killing. You see history of this from time of mankind beginning. But I regret so very deeply that I not see what is coming in Shala, what you struggle with. I see science of DeathX. I see that bad for people if they use, but I no suspect that Shala or anyone – you, Errol – do anything about it. To me it like separate from my life at home. I see only science. I miss important lesson. Errol be proud that I see this now," and Yahya smiles that white toothed smile that hopefully will earn him a deanship someday. "I see that I miss importance of people. I not make this mistake again. Patrick, I with you. We continue. But we no let out any bad from lab – ever."

My life in a startup. Except I am crying. And this is real. These are the people who will discover the next generation of what Errol has spent his whole life working on. These two represent the next generation of science – inventions that will make their way to a market, passing through innovation to commercialization. I'm going to write my own damn blog post, I determine. Errol's trust in me will be worth something. I will help them.

I am not the only one crying. There are snuffles around the room.

. . . .

Victor has a few questions about the nerve agent. "Could it be ingested like food, in water, in any other way? How quickly did it act? What was the chemical makeup?"

Yahya and Patrick dutifully answer all of the questions.

"Errol's lab notebook, where was that and who had access to it?"

I pull it out of my backpack and hand it over to Dr. Williams.

"Who else at the university knew about DeathX?" he wants to know.

As medical examiner in a **U** situation – Undetermined – Dr. Williams had kept samples. Tissue samples, blood samples. He is going to re-test those samples. For DeathX. We know what the answer will be.

Amy sits there, tears streaming down her face. There is no way that she will ever make sense of all this, I realize. You don't get over this. You may move on, but it's always with you. Some people believe that murder is an act that needs to be resolved. I believe that murder itself is an act of resolution.

. . . .

The next day I get a letter in the mail. I know who it's from because it says Dr. Errol and his lab address. My hands tremble as I open it. I pour the last of the latest bottle of The Balvenie in a glass. And I call Neal. Well, I actually just call to him. He has moved in.

"For your safety," he told me. "It will be better if I am close by." It was funny and sweet and all the things that

I love about him. He comes into the kitchen, sees the drink, pours himself one from a lesser bottle, Johnny Walker, and joins me at the table.

"It's a letter," I say.

"Yes I see that," he says. "Who's it from?" he asks. I don't reply. "Is it Shala?"

April 13

Dear Brie, I know that you will be reading this after you already know about me, and I feel that you must be thinking terrible things about me. They are all true, and I write this letter not to excuse myself. I know I have done something terrible, and I cannot forgive myself. But I want to explain to you because I always admire you so much, how you try to solve crime even though you not professional. You are the person that I would like to be. But I cannot. I am not from here. Even worse, I am from border of two countries, and we are nothing, my family and me. You do not know because you are not from there. In my country women are not prized. Not valued. We are nothing. You have read about the rapes? This happens not just now but all the time. Men in my country feel it is their right, there are no rules there to stop. To them, we are objects to be spit upon. My sister was raped and beaten. Nobody brought to justice. My parents try hard to send me school far away so that I would not suffer same. My family very poor. Poorer than anyone in your country. We no have food, shoes, clothes. No school. My parents send me to big city, to cousins for education. I work hard because I know their sacrifice. It is hard. I must leave home so that I live.

I try hard. I very good student. I pleased to be with Dr. Errol's lab. It is big honor. Dr. Errol, he tease me but he not like men at home. He say things with smile and he not do anything to make me afraid.

When we discover this terrible thing, DeathX, I see something I never have courage to see before. I see my family – clean and in the United States. I see men having respect for me. I see helping women all over my country to stop men beating. I can do this because nerve agent have much value. I know people will pay. I think, what matter if some are dying if others are living?

But Dr. Errol he no agree. He say no to contact buyers in my country. I very angry with him. I see so much good coming even if some bad too, and I tell him about my family. I show him pictures from when I went home last year. He seem very sad and he say he will help me, but he not help me. I try hard in convincing him.

I did not mean hurt Dr. Errol. He is my hero. He wonderful man, husband, father, scientist, and entrepreneur. He so perfect and my family in such dirt and lacking in freedom to choose. I get letter from my mother that my sister kill herself because she so shamed. She killed herself with kitchen knife. She wear sign on breast saying 'I am free.'

I with Dr. Errol that night on boat. I meet him from my boat I am rowing. I unpeel a stamp of DeathX. I know it will not be detected. I thinking that if Dr. Errol not here then I take nerve agent to my country and sell to terrorists. I know people who will help me. I am very angry so angry inside, and I know that I can do this terrible thing so that I can be free. I thinking I will go now to my country and no one will know.

But it is not like I was thinking in planning. I see how sad everyone is because of Dr. Errol. I feel guilty, and I think that maybe I not do what I planning. I see you and know that you solve murder. I help you. I thinking that Yahya is terrorist, and I thinking that in New York he is planning terrible things so not think badly to tell you my thoughts because I thinking that this is good to stop him. Then I think Patrick can be blame. But this is also not true. I cannot live with this now. I am the one of blame, Brie. I am guilty. No one else.

I much mistaken. You are smart and you not stop. You will keep going until you find me. I cannot bear this, on my people, on my country. It is terrible I have done. It is terrible thing I do now. But it is more terrible if I do my plan. I have to stop these terrible things. I am stopping.

I am sorry. I think that if I were friends with you long time maybe I not thinking these things. But it too late for me. I so sorry to be telling you all things in this letter but I must. I do all this my own. No one else part of plan. I not want hurt anyone anymore. I know you understand.

Your friend who is now free,
Shala

. . . .

I am drowning. That there could be such pain in the world. I never want to wake up.

Chapter 43
May 1, one year later

It wasn't straightforward, but we finally got our data and the samples from the NGX clinical trial. I know that statistically a failed trial in Phase III is not uncommon. Heck, let's face it, there are a lot of drugs that make it to market and then get pulled – for adverse reactions, previously unnoticed side effects, one or more of these. But we got stopped. Mid-stream and without warning. "Is this normal?" we asked ourselves. Answer: "Well, it happens." In the world of startups, you are at risk. You do all you can to de-risk: you get the best people, you solve a real problem, you have great technology, strong intellectual property, and financing.

It doesn't make any sense that large companies lack an appetite for risk. They can't have begun there. And if they end there, they end. You can't take the risk out of innovation. You have to build it in. And your people – your team, your shareholders, your board members – they all have to accept that you are trying to do something greater than is even possible. You face the cliffs of Normandy because you don't know what is impossible – my dad told me that. If you knew it was impossible, you would never attempt to get past the status quo.

"Mankind is hard-wired for innovation," Jim has often reminded me. Does someone beat that out of us I wonder? When a company gets big, do they just forget how to manage risk?

Matt is back. Jim convinced the board to give him another try, and he jumped back in with a few four letter words but no hesitation.

Jim has been working with me to take over his NewVenturist blog. We both write posts about entrepreneurship, but he does less and less, and I do more and more. I am honored at this passing of the torch. I won't let him down.

. . . .

It took us a year, but we have a new HD program. When we examined the data from the trial, we found some unexpected things. One was that the drug had no side effects. NGX didn't stop the trial because something happened. The drug simply didn't work for the end point that we had established. Six months into it the principal investigator at NGX decided to pull the plug. But he wasn't very thorough about his analysis, and we were right. If he had kept on going, if he had really looked hard at the data, he would have seen a glimmer of hope.

Turns out the drug doesn't work for all HD patients. That would have been our dream come true, and Matt and the others might be basking in the Bahamas right now if that had been the case. But some patients did improve. Unfortunately, it was only a small sub-group of the trial's population that seemed to improve. Had the PI at NGX looked deeply into this, he might have noticed something unique about those patients. They were all at different states of the disease's progression; that's what made it difficult to see at first glance. But they all had heightened blood counts of a certain protein. While there were a million possible proteins of interest, Matt had found something in Errol's notes. Something that popped out at him. And, as he looked at the data, he noticed that particular protein. As we re-tested HD66 on the retrospective samples, we noticed a remarkable pattern. It was something new. Something no one noticed before. What we think we have discovered may actually be a new form of HD. As in cancer, not all Huntington's is the same. We could actually test this theory in new trials.

We are now conducting a new Phase II trial – more refined perhaps than previously. Certainly, much wiser. I didn't know the details as it's ongoing – blinded, and all that. Matt had insisted that we recruit my father's physician as part of the trial so that my father could be included in the patient population. Apparently my father fit the blood type of the sub-group.

One of life's little ironies is that I found out about the effects of the drug on the sub-group before anyone else. After the whole thing with Shala was over, I went to see Amy. She hugged me and offered me a glass of retsina. "I remember that you liked it. He would love that you are drinking it now," she said sadly.

As I sipped my drink I wandered into their home office. Right there on the white board were a bunch of marks. Funny that he should have a white board at home, I thought. Like mine in my kitchen. But then it hit me. These were not random scratchings. These were formulas. Of the HD66 drug. But they tracked to different blood types and some other things that I couldn't place initially. I remembered the email. "I will leave it for safe keeping..." Of course, what could be safer than his home. His refuge.

Amy came in behind me. "I didn't have the heart to erase it," she said quietly. "I leave it there to remind me of him."

"Amy," I said turning to her and looking at her, knowing that tears flowed from my eyes like the river. "It's not nothing. This is important. You didn't erase it. You didn't erase him. For a reason. This means something. It's a cure."

Amy looked at me, and I walked up to her and hugged her long and hard. "It's for me, Amy. You couldn't have known that. My dad has HD. Errol has found a cure, specifically for him." She looked at me in wonder. "He was a great man, Amy. He has saved my father because of this. And me. It's hereditary," I explain.

. . . .

I called Neal on the way home. I had told him almost a year ago about my dad's HD and what that meant for me. We had gone up to Amherst for the weekend. I wanted him to see it first-hand. He was great about it.

"Brie, you should get tested," he told me in my childhood room.

"But you know what this means, what this might mean, for us?" I had responded.

"Yes of course, but I don't want to marry anyone else." And he had popped a lovely little diamond and sapphire ring out of his pocket. "This was my grandmother's. My mother gave it to me thinking that we might…"

I started to cry, and Neal held me close. I realized I have never felt safer with anyone. And I'm an idiot that I didn't tell him sooner and told him so.

"No Brie, not an idiot. You're my startup entrepreneurial sleuth. You did what no one else could do. I love you now and forever. For who you are, Brie."

. . . .

The next morning, Neal talked to both of my parents.

"He actually asked for our permission to ask you to marry him," my mother told as she emerged from the dining room. "Your father and I cried. We're so happy for you, Brie, my dear."

I finger the lovely set of pearls Neal had bought for me to replace my grandmother's set. I don't know if I'll ever take them off.

. . . .

I get tested two weeks later. Negative. I call Neal when I got the call from the doctor's office.

"I knew it. I knew nothing would stop you or us." He sighs. "Let's get married, Brie. Let's have babies."

I laugh, "First a wedding. Then we'll see."

I call my mother the next day. I tell her about my dilemma, about how afraid I was to have the test done. About what it would mean. And I laugh the fears away.

"Oh Brie," she says, gasping. "I'm so sorry."

"But Mom, it's good news."

"Yes, of course. But… can I tell you something?" she asks gently.

The story. Her story. It was a long time ago, of course. My mother had a flame at Reed College that had never died away. He showed up in Berkeley, and they had an affair. He was my father. Genetically that is. She felt guilty about the whole thing and broke it off when she realized she was pregnant. She never told my father. She didn't have the heart. And she loved him; she told me that she hoped that I realized that. She didn't mean to hurt anyone. Just that she was young and reckless. But she knew when I was born with those green eyes, that they were his.

I look out over my terrace on Howe Street and feel numb.

"Are you alright?" she asks. "Do you want to know anything about him, his name or anything? I'm stupid to have kept this in for so long. I almost told you so many times, but I never wanted to upset your world. I never wanted to slow you down. That's my only excuse."

I'm not going to cry. I'm done with tears. "It's OK, Mom," I tell her. "I don't think it's important anymore. And no, I don't want to know about him. I have a father."

About a week later I go to visit. My mother picks me up from the Hartford airport. She gives me a long firm hug. When I open the front door, my dad comes walking towards me. I don't know whether he is taking the drug or the placebo. All I know is that he walks with a very slow but steady gait and holds out his arms to me. I stare at his fingers. They are not shaking.

. . . .

What happens in a startup when you have lost your scientist forever, when your investors abandon you, when your lead product fails, and you have no idea what to do?

Answer: you start up… again.

#######

Acknowledgements

I want to thank those who have helped me on this journey:

Dottie who was my first source of inspiration

My beta readers, Carol, David, Elin, Felicity, Kerry, Len, and Natalie

Sisters in Crime Pittsburgh Chapter whose members are my heroes

Karol, who graciously edited

Mary who edited some more and fixed a plot line disaster

Gwen who helped me with publishing and marketing

Zane who helped me follow instructions

Tom and FJ, who gave me advice when I needed it

Guilherme, who has helped all along with NewVenturist

My daughter's cat, Arwen, for being a furry friend

My beloved beagle, Luna, who is sorely missed

My kids, Justine and Straker, for their unflagging encouragement, including Justine's fabulous cover art

And mostly my husband, Tim, who read more drafts than I thought possible and who quoted Churchill to "never ever ever ever ever give up!"

About the author

Babs Carryer is a serial technology entrepreneur. Having spent the bulk of her life creating and advising startups, she has now turned to writing. Babs's New Venturist blog has attracted thousands of readers interested in startups and entrepreneurs. Currently, Babs is director of education and outreach for the University of Pittsburgh's Innovation Institute where she encourages and supports innovation and entrepreneurship across campus to all students, faculty, researchers and clinicians. Previously, Babs helped develop the entrepreneurial ecosystem at Carnegie Mellon University where she taught entrepreneurship, was embedded entrepreneur, and innovation advisor. Babs was director of training and faculty development at VentureWell, (formerly the National Collegiate Inventors and Innovators Alliance). Babs is President of Carryer Consulting, and has worked with hundreds of companies and startups to grow their businesses. Babs co-founded LaunchCyte, which today has a portfolio of five companies which have commercialized university technologies into marketplace products. Babs co-founded the Pittsburgh chapter of Women In Bio. Babs has a Masters in Public Management (MPM) from Heinz College at Carnegie Mellon and a BA from Mills College. She lives in Pittsburgh, PA with her husband, Tim, and travels often to the Chesapeake where they have a cottage and two boats.

Note from the author

Thanks for reading *HD66: search for a cure or a killer?* I hope that you've enjoyed it! This is my first venture into fiction and I hope that you stay in touch for future startup mystery novels and non-fiction books about entrepreneurship.

I'd be grateful if you could post however many stars you believe the novel deserves on its Amazon page.

Please write a review if you are so inclined.

Also, please feel free to follow/message me on social media:

Email   babs@carryer.com
Facebook babscarryer
LinkedIn   babscarryer
Twitter   @babscarryer

You can find other publications and more about me on my website:
http://babscarryer.com

*A portion of the proceeds from sales of this book are donated to organizations addressing the challenges of two causes introduced in the story:
        Huntington's Disease
        Violence against women.